Praise for

THE TASTE OF BLUE LIGHT

'An achingly moving read. Lux is vivid, feisty, vulnerable, brave, darkly humorous, as she fights a battle she doesn't understand. Ruffles' writing is mesmerising and beautiful. I was immersed in Lux's world from the first page'
Debbie Howells, author of *The Bones of You*

'Vivid, overwhelming, powerful, this is a visceral novel exploring first love, obsession and the curse and wonder of synaesthesia'
Fiona Cummins, author of *Rattle*

'It's very brave, and fierce, and electric'
Sara Barnard, author of *Beautiful Broken Things*

'This is a beautiful book, both inside and out ... I devoured every page'
Alice Feeney, author of *Sometimes I Lie*

'Startling and mesmeric. Lux is a refreshingly complex heroine'
Daisy Buchanan, author of *How to Be a Grown-Up*

'Beautiful. Visceral. Gripping. If Sylvia Plath wrote a novel for young adults, *The Taste of Blue Light* would be it'
Louise O'Neill, author of *Asking for It*

'Brimming to full with tenderness and caustic wit. Immaculately written, the journey inside the damaged mind of Lux Langley will leave you feeling overwhelmed and amazed'
Richard Skinner, author of *The Mirror*

THE TASTE OF BLUE LIGHT

LYDIA RUFFLES

First published in Great Britain in 2017 by Hodder and Stoughton

3 5 7 9 10 8 6 4 2

A CIP catalogue record for this book
is available from the British Library.

ISBN 978 1 444 93674 2

Printed and bound in Great Britain by Clays Ltd, St Ives plc

The paper and board used in this book
are made from wood from responsible sources.

Hodder Children's Books
An imprint of
Hachette Children's Group
Part of Hodder and Stoughton
Carmelite House
50 Victoria Embankment
London EC4Y 0DZ

An Hachette UK Company
www.hachette.co.uk

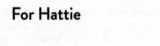

For Hattie

Colours are light's suffering and joy.
Johann Wolfgang von Goethe

PART ONE

ONE

I will find the old Lux and when I do I will climb back inside her and sew myself into her skin so I never get lost again.

The last time I saw her, me, properly was at the Leavers' Ball. I was wearing the shortest, reddest dress I could find. This was before colours meant what they do now. And before I got lost.

I remember every detail and I can't say that about many times since.

I felt eyes on me all night. The gaze of those girls who feel pretty when they're hungry. And the guys – a host of blandly handsome XY chromosomes, winking at me in the semi-dark. Winking at every girl who walked by probably but, in the presence of wit and the black-tie promise of a beautiful life, I'll forgive anything.

It was the start of the summer; an elaborate ball to send off the Upper Sixth. The annual goodbye to another tranche of maladjusted Artists set free to paint or pretend their way through life. I'd just finished Lower Sixth but our year was invited too; I don't know why as there has always been plenty enough people in each year to make a decent party.

In fact, despite the head director's best efforts, Richdeane Arts School is famous for parties. A few years ago, five Artists were caught doing ketamine and having sex on the golf course. After that particular incident, we had to stop calling the staff by their first names – like that would affect whether or not we wanted to interfere with each other by the ninth hole. There was even talk of a curfew for a while, as if Richdeane were a normal school, but the governors voted against it in favour of 'preserving Richdeane's liberal ethos'. Anyway, the 'orgy' was all over the papers and the Golf Course Five were expelled. I put a lot of thought into determining how I would deal with that kind of attention. Nonchalantly but as publicly as possible, I decided.

At the leavers' after-party, we all sucked on shots and toasted summer and goodbyes, showing the required amount of disrespect for the host's property.

I was in charge of the party favours, as always, producing pills and powders from inside my tiny dress like a pharmaceutical magician. Soundtracked by nineties' trip-hop, kids who had never spoken before shared muses and made each other promises they believed they would keep, while the many bedrooms and dark corners were claimed by temporary collaborators.

In the basement, a select crowd sketched, scratched, painted or inked our names at the edges of one of the long white walls while two girls worked soundlessly around each other to spray phosphorescent snowdrops, flags and faces in the middle. As more of us added our names and messages, the wall began to belong to us, not to someone's parents. It took my breath away. Flanked by the friends I knew I would keep close for as long as I lived, I wished those journalists who were so ready to trash Richdeane could see what we could create together, without even really trying.

It was so, so hot down there and the spray paint fumes made me sway but I wanted to stay forever, watching our shared mural creep across the walls like neon vines.

When we couldn't take the basement heat any longer, we staggered up to the kitchen to do more shots of spiked bubble tea, which Mei said tasted like baby gravy, chasing them with Dirty Coconuts, a cocktail of vodka and coconut water.

I lost my virginity to a sculptor named Henry that night – seventeen was late to lose it; I was the last of my friends to give it up. My experience lagged behind my reputation, if only in that department. Henry was lean and hyper-focused. I chose him because it seemed the ideal collaboration – he was good with his hands and I could play the scene as required.

Plus, he'd been selling me drugs all year and it took zero effort to get him to follow me upstairs into a guest room.

I pulled him inside and told him to lock the door.

'There's no key. Should we find somewhere else?'

I didn't want to lose my nerve. 'No, come here. Be quick.'

'Romantic,' he said. He picked up an armful of coats from the bed and rolled them together in front of the door to block it.

'Come here,' I said again. I pulled off my shoes and lay on the bed, looking over my body down to my feet. Angry welts marked them where I'd done the straps up too tight. I thought of Olivia and her dancer's feet and how she'd told me dancers aren't supposed to show pain or effort, they must silently turn agony into art. That's the Richdeane pledge: *We pledge ourselves to the will of the muses, and to the words of the greats. We give it to art and we let go.*

Music pulsed through the floor and up the stairs. It was a girl growling tunefully about being a black man in a cell and calling the government suckers.

I didn't take my dress off – it was so short I just pulled it up around my thighs and held my breath as Henry climbed on top of me.

'Is this OK?' he asked.

'Yes.'

He was a good kisser. A sweet guy really.

The lights were on and I could see powder collecting in the corners of his nostrils as his neck strained above me and he grunted towards the headboard. We were safe; I'd told him, 'No balloon, no party.' Henry concluded before the song did. He tasted how the word summer tastes to me now: a mix of tequila and ash.

In the bedroom mirror afterwards, I looked the same as I did before. I felt mostly the same too – lucky, happy, high – although I wanted my friends.

I mussed up my hair so there could be no doubt to anyone who saw us emerge about what had happened behind the closed door.

I had done it.

'You OK?' Henry asked.

'Yep.' I hadn't told him it hurt but he'd been gentle anyway.

I waited until I heard the zip of his fly going up, then I turned round. He pulled a little bag of white powder from his tux pocket. 'Want some?'

I dipped my finger and rubbed the powder into my gums, then double-dipped for luck, not caring how many greedy fingers had already been stuck in the bag.

He tried to curl his hand round mine as we went downstairs. His fingers were cooler than they'd felt in the bedroom. Mine twitched away. I think I was nervous.

'You don't need to do that,' I said.

Maybe he was relieved, maybe he was hurt. I don't know; I didn't look at his face.

'Fireworks!' came a voice from the garden.

'That's Davy,' said Henry. 'He and the guys have been planning this for weeks.'

'I'm going to find my friends,' I said. 'See you later.'

A crowd tumbled out of the back door into the warm night and gathered by the side of a small pool. It was more for show or maybe for cooling off than for swimming, I think.

Mei and Olivia were already outside. I snuck up behind them and clamped a hand on each of their shoulders.

'Guess who?' I whispered just as a rocket burst above us, showering the sky with fiery teardrops.

I remember the thrill of it echoing across the sky; that's how I know the old Lux was normal.

'Only you would make an entrance to fireworks,' said Olivia.

'Where've you been?' asked Mei.

'With Henry.'

'Called it, didn't I?'

'You did,' Olivia replied.

'Only took you a year to get it together.'

'Oh, please,' I said.

Colours exploded below the stars. Dense bursts of purple and green streaked the sky, their long smoke trails reaching down to us like willow branches. We faux-jumped with each bang, and oohed and aahed with sarcasm at first and then with real wonder.

Then came the fizz and scatter of white light as Davy set off more close to the ground. We took a collective step back, clutching arms and holding our breath.

It was our show. The neighbours could watch if they wanted but it was ours. We were the actors, the directors and the audience. Part of our script came from films we'd seen, parties we'd been to before. The rest we made up as we went along and it was perfect.

Whistles and crackles sounded above us, shooting out swarms of fireflies that faded before they reached us.

We were magic and fearless.

'I want to light one,' I heard myself say. I ran down to the end of the garden. 'Davy, let me light one.'

'Are you drunk?' he asked.

'Not drunk enough.'

'Have you done this before?'

'Tonight is a night of firsts.'

I took my lighter from my dress pocket and rolled my thumb over the top to make sure it would work first time. The flint caught and sparked a tiny flame.

'Don't be ridiculous – you can't light fireworks with a lighter.'

Davy was pleased to have the opportunity to instruct me. I let him tell me what to do in exchange for lighting the last ones.

'Use this.' He picked up a little blowtorch like the one my father used to burn the tops of crèmes brûlées.

Henry appeared, saying, 'Give her your gloves, Davy. And the goggles.'

'Thanks.'

I put them on and waved to Mei and Olivia.

'Go, Luxy,' they yelled.

Davy led me over to where he and his friends had planted the last row of rockets ready for the finale. 'Light one at the bottom and then get back quickly, even if it looks like it hasn't caught properly.'

'Careful,' called Olivia.

'She has no idea what she's doing,' I heard Mei say.

I leant down. My heart was banging but I couldn't change my mind. At least fifty pairs of bright eyes were fixed on me. I fumbled with the torch a few times until the flame glowed steady. I lit each fuse and jerked my hand away as if they'd explode instantly.

I had this idea that I wanted to light them all in one go. The lit tails sizzled.

'Get back,' said Davy.

I shook my head and waved the flame under the tails of the three remaining unlit ones. As the last one caught, I scrabbled to my feet and Henry pulled me to the side. A second later, the first one shrieked into the night sky, followed by the next, then the next, then the next, throwing their booming light across the garden and beyond. The crowd stamped their feet and cheered as my glittering comets rained down on us.

Thinking about all that colour and sound now makes my skull tighten and my brain shriek but at the time it just made me certain of who I was and who I was going to be.

'Good job,' said Davy. I hugged him and Henry, and skipped back to Mei and Olivia.

With the show over, some people drifted back inside. Maybe fighting melancholy, one of the leavers turned the music back up.

I had full-body goosebumps as the music shot through my skin. Its invisible wires were inside me, moving me like a puppet.

I thought I saw Davy kissing our friend Isabella out of the corner of my eye, but something inside me wouldn't let me stop twirling so I'm not sure. Henry watched us for a bit and then he was gone.

Mei, Olivia and I flung ourselves around the garden to the beat until our hair stuck to our necks and our hearts raced in unison. For a minute, I forgot to dance like people were watching.

Song after song, we shook our limbs and swung each other round and round until, sweaty and brimming, we fell on the ground.

'The sky is spinning,' said Olivia.

'Close your eyes for a minute,' I told her, 'you're just drunk, it'll wear off.'

'I am absolutely car-parked, door-knobbed and gelatoed,' shouted Mei.

'Let's swim,' I suggested.

'Easy tiger – I don't think it's heated.'

'I'm going to dip my toes in.'

I pulled off my shoes for the second time that evening and plunged my feet into the cool water. Distorted beneath the rippling surface, my toes bulged like plasticine sausages.

'So, where's Henry?' one of them asked.

With my back to them, I slipped a hand between my legs then trailed it across the surface of the pool. A shock of red billowed from my fingertips, turned candy pink in the chlorinated water before dissolving like soluble ink.

Henry.

I had finally done it.

I was everything I'd said I was. I'd finally caught up with myself but I couldn't make a big deal about it because I'd told Mei and Olivia I'd done it with an American I'd met a couple of summers before.

'Lux?'

I turned to see them lying on their backs on the lawn, making star shapes with their moonlit limbs.

'Grass angels,' sang Olivia.

I jumped up to join them.

The sky hung pregnant over us. I wanted to travel the world with my friends, to see whether the sky looked the same in Africa, Thailand, China, everywhere.

'One more year,' Mei breathed. The words sang out like fairy dust, sprinkling our tangled hair and flushed cheeks with wishes for the future.

We were quiet for a minute while the stars shone just for us.

'Do you think they're scared?' asked Olivia.

'The stars?' I said.

'The leavers.'

'What's to be scared of?'

'No more Richdeane,' said Mei.

'Doubt it,' I said. 'Sad, maybe; not scared.' I used to know all the emotions and understand which was which.

'Let's have the best last year ever,' said Olivia. I tilted my head to look at her. Tears slipped out of the corner of her eyes, through her hair and into the grass. She smiled and I realised I was crying too. So was Mei. Not the noisy kind of crying, just happiness leaking out.

Love rushed through me. It wasn't just the drugs; I was so lucky. So plugged in. I knew nobody had ever felt how we did. If they had, they would never have grown up. They'd have kept painting, writing, flying like Peter Pan, scared to land in case touching their feet to the ground ruptured the magic, making them old and scared and slow.

We hatched plans and whispered secrets until, too tired and overwhelmed to move, we fell asleep in the itchy grass.

I dreamed I was flying.

At first light, Olivia stirred next to me. She smiled and I knew we'd all been having a version of the same dream. My mouth was claggy but we hadn't been asleep long enough to come down.

'Morning, glories.'

I tipped my head back towards the voice to see Mei step out of the back door and tread over to us, a bottle in each hand and one under her armpit. She handed us each a beer. 'Thought we might need a soft landing.'

The pool glowed golden under the rising sun.

We clinked bottles in the quiet dawn and whispered our pledge: *To art and let go.*

It was a perfect night and the last one like it that I remember. If I close my eyes and keep very still I can see us, laughing and dancing until the moon went down. The picture develops in the darkroom in my mind and I feel it all again. I forget the stone in my stomach and the confusion in my blood. I was alive and brave and potent. I was found.

I will find my way back to that Lux.

TWO

People read a lot into it if you blackout and wake up in a hospital. They really think it means something, especially if you haven't exactly been on the straight and narrow up to that point. Maybe they won't let you go back to school when summer ends. Maybe you'll come back two weeks late and never completely catch up on the time, or the you, that you lost.

And you're definitely in for a lot of conversations with professionals with a perverse obsession with you remembering the exact circumstances of how you got there. Maybe you'd tell them if you knew. Maybe you'd wish you hadn't lost your phone, and you'd google yourself, and check Instagram and everywhere else for clues but find no trail.

You might feel lost; you might feel nothing. You might feel trapped inside and locked outside yourself at the same time.

I wonder what the professionals would make of my little dalliance with Henry the sculptor.

My parents pay people, professionals, to ask me questions that hurt; mostly they're questions about my experience this summer, not things that came before it. That's what my mother calls it – my 'experience' – the pivot point that took me from rebellious to sick. I haven't given it a name yet.

But the professionals aren't that interested in Henry or the Leavers' Ball. They're interested in the party I went to a month later at the end of my gallery internship, the one I don't remember, the one I went to before I woke up in hospital and couldn't remember how I got there.

When I woke up on the ward, I had trouble staying in my body. I floated away from myself with the tequila fumes that lifted from my skin. I was a million miles from everything. A faraway sun. In and out of sleep. Each time I woke up I inched a little closer but didn't quite make it all the way back.

I was vaguely aware of my mother fussing while nurses rushed with subtle urgency. My father pretended to do crosswords while visitors came to the beds around me bearing grapes that they ate themselves. The subtitled TV in the corner described tales of terror while the hospital radio hosts played track after cheerful track. Eighties' classics provided an incongruous soundtrack to muted war and scandal as orderlies served jelly and things in gravy.

The only other thing I remember is the still-drunk girl tethered to an IV drip in the bed next to me. She had marks on her wrists and arms where the sadness running through her wine-stream could no longer be contained, where something had willed her hands to cut through the skin to drain the sorrow out.

Looking down at myself from the ceiling, I noticed a matching cannula with a drip-line running off it in the back of my left hand. The fabric tape holding it in place covered the small snowdrop tattoo on the underside of my wrist. The Richdeane crest is stained into my skin forever. I watched myself fiddle with the tube. A nurse swatted my hand away. Her touch brought me back into my body. 'Just fluids,' she said. 'Salts, water.' Because I'm competitive, I tried to suck in the saline faster than the drunk girl. But our dehydrated flesh pinked up in tandem because the drips were metered. It's not like donating blood; you can't pump your fist to hasten the process.

On my other arm, a wound itched. It was there when I woke up, swaddled in a dressing, a grotesque present to be unwrapped later. Its diagonal line, shaped like a feather or dagger, points from the outside of my elbow down towards my wrist. It's fifteen centimetres long; I measured it. It will scar because I can't resist raking my fingernails through the healing skin whenever it's just about to seal itself shut. What if going through that cut is the only way to get back inside myself?

I watched as the drip sobered the other girl up, as she realised she felt worse sober than she had drunk. She was definitely in her body. Her hair hung in her eyes as her face twitched and crumpled, and I wanted to tell her not to cry, not to spill out those useless buckets of soul. Now I can see the benefit; she could weep to reset herself.

I divide the professionals into two groups: the body doctors and the mind probers. The body doctors do diagnostic tests and take bits of me away for examination (blood, saliva, pictures of my insides). The mind probers are interested in taking invisible things, information mostly.

Dr Purves was mainly a body doctor.

I had to go back to the hospital to see her after I'd been released. It was before I came back to school and before my mother went back to Singapore. My father had flown ahead, sick of the fights probably.

My mother came with me to the appointment. We'd fought the night before; I'd caught her in a lie I think, but she came anyway. Besides, my parents had been keeping me hostage ever since I'd been discharged so there was no chance of me flying solo. 'For your own good, try to understand,' they told me.

Before we met the doctor, I had to have a brain scan. A leaflet explained they'd use a machine with magnetic fields and radio waves to make images of the inside of my head.

My mother waited in reception. I imagined her avoiding the germ-harbouring magazines and dabbing hand sanitiser round her nostrils while I took off my jewellery and got changed into a stiff hospital gown.

The scanner was a doughnut-shaped block with a table jutting out from the tunnel running through the middle. The whole thing was encased in white plastic with a purple CerebroVista logo emblazoned at the base. There were three silver steps pushed up against the side of the table, like a Borrowers' version of aeroplane steps.

'Just some quick questions before we get started,' said the man who had introduced himself as the senior radiographer. He had fluffy hair on his chin, which made him look not very senior at all. I hoped he knew what he was doing.

He asked whether I suffered from various medical conditions, and if I'd ever had shrapnel in my eyes or a metal stent placed in my body. The wound on my arm poked out of the end of the gown sleeve but he didn't ask about that. I could see the questions had already been answered on his sheet and that my mother had signed it. Did he think I'd been to war and forgotten to mention it to her, or that she'd lied?

Next he rolled a paper cover on to the table and asked me to lie down. I climbed on to the giant napkin and lay there like an oversized piece of sushi.

I tried to roll my eyes back to see the size of the tunnel I'd apparently be going into head first. I wanted to run but the radiographer was already strapping my head to the table.

Seeing my anxiety, he said, 'Too late for a sedative, I'm afraid. And you'll need to be alert for the other tests.'

He gave me some foam earplugs. 'Put these in.'

What are they going to do to me?

'Here's the panic button; try to stay inside though – we'll only have to get you back in again to finish if you come out. Just close your eyes and breathe,' he advised. 'You'll be in there about twenty-five minutes. I'll be watching you on the monitor from the other room.'

I heard the door shut behind him. I was alone and tethered to the scanner.

I gripped the cord to the panic button and kept my eyes squeezed shut while the table started moving backwards. Then the machine began making a horrible noise like someone was banging on its inside walls, trying to escape or send me a message.

A disembodied voice came over the tannoy: 'Keep as still as you can.'

Why didn't anyone tell me it would be this loud?

I jumped again as the table lurched further into the tunnel. A different noise started up – louder and more of a click than a bang.

I'm being buried alive in slow motion.

I tried to work out how long I'd been in there. About two minutes, at most. Twenty-three to go. I was rigid and my shoulders hurt from clenching, so I forced them to drop and started to count my breaths.

One in, one out. Two in, two out. Three in, three out. I'd get to ten and start again. The banging sounded a little further away.

Fear had me paralysed or I would have wriggled again just to hear the tannoy voice telling me not to.

One in, one out. Two in, two out. Three in, three out.

I counted forever and finally the radiographer got me out to meet Dr Purves. I was so tired, as if the counting and the machine's magnets had hypnotised me.

Dr Purves had boring brown hair cut into a boring bob and asked a lot of boring questions. Maybe the questions weren't boring, maybe they just hurt to think about. Maybe they made my mind burn in technicolour.

'I see from your file that you've not been feeling yourself for some weeks now, Lux. That you've been experiencing some nasty headaches together with some anxiety and nightmares since you blacked out. Is that right?'

She made it sound so simple.

'And you don't remember what you were doing when you lost consciousness?' she asked.

'No.'

'What's the last thing you remember?'

'I was at a party.'

'With school friends?'

'No, I was doing an internship. It was with some people I didn't really know. That was the Thursday night.'

'Did you leave the party alone or with someone?'

'I don't remember. The next thing I remember is being in hospital, but I think that was the Friday.'

My mother nodded to confirm.

'I already told the other doctors I don't remember.' *They all have the same script with the same questions on it.*

'You told me that too,' she says. 'We met on the ward the day after you woke up. Do you remember?'

'Yes,' I lie, because it's rude to forget people but I must not be a very good liar because she asks:

'Really? It's important that we know whether you remember or you just think you remember.'

I knew she was trying to help me and I should let her but something was rising in my chest so I closed my eyes and went to find Mei and Olivia and the leavers' party in the darkroom in my mind. The questions continued even though I had my eyes closed. Shutting off one sense does not dull the rest, unfortunately. A thick elastic band formed around my head and the pressure started to build.

Then my eyes were open. Dr Purves and my mother were staring at me like they wanted me to say something but I wasn't sure what, like I couldn't remember my lines or didn't understand the parameters of the improvisation. I took a sip from the mug in front of me and immediately wished I'd asked for a Coke and not coffee. Although it was worth it to see my mother's eyebrows do their special dance, silently asking, 'Oh, you drink coffee now, do you?'

Looking down at my hands, my second wish was that I hadn't drawn eyes on my palms and fingertips. We used to do it all the time at prep school and then hold our hands up in front of our actual eyes, wiggling our fingers like tentacles. Just because. But you really had to be there for it to seem funny and I didn't know how to explain it to Dr Purves, or my mother and her eyebrows, so I just took a few more sips from the mug and waited for the caffeine bump.

My mother prefers things clean and perfect, and without eyes drawn on them. She's one of those people who sleeps with a watch on and makes the bed while you're still in it. Singapore is a good fit for her.

The caffeine tickled my brain and I started flicking through my darkroom again, blinking to change the image. The professionals call my darkroom an avoidance mechanism. Anything to stop the headaches or the colours descending.

Dr Purves redirected her questions to my mother to answer on my behalf. Even though she was technically a body doctor, she had questions about other things too. It made sense since my mind lives in my body. She asked about my mental health – any history of hearing voices, drug use, mood swings, extreme behaviour, imaginary friends, etc. – 'Just to rule things out,' she explained.

When I was little, I used to bite my hands until I'd punctured the skin and say my brother or sister had done it. I am an only child. But even then I understood that visible wounds got sympathy; more sympathy than loneliness. I would wake up sobbing, convinced that I'd sent my little siblings away and hadn't tasted the regret until it was too late to call them back. My father interpreted this behaviour as early evidence of my flair for the dramatic. 'My little Roberta De Niro,' he called me, depositing me in a creative prep school, chosen because it was a 'feeder' school for Richdeane. I was hard to discipline even as a child and they felt I would flourish in such an artistic, liberal place.

My mother didn't tell Dr Purves about the biting or the fictitious siblings. Maybe she'd forgotten; I'd only just remembered myself. Memories are strange; how does all that stuff fit in our heads? How do we know where to find things without Googlebots or web spiders to index and dredge them up? Not for the first time since I'd blacked out, I wished I were a robot or a machine that could be rebooted or upgraded.

'I know this is difficult, Lux. Perhaps you could just tell me the main things that are bothering you, just so I can make sure I have it all noted down correctly,' the doctor said.

So I told her what I'd eventually told my mother after weeks of saying it was just the headaches while thinking I was losing my mind. That since I blacked out I feel like my head is not connected to my body, that I panic about weird things and that my senses get confused sometimes. And, if I get really strung out, colours get brighter and more intense, and it's almost as if words and sounds have colour.

I didn't tell her that I sometimes see words in the air, sometimes even punctuation, which makes it hard to follow what people are saying.

'I feel like I'm in a video game or a play,' I said.

'A play?' asked Dr Purves.

'She goes to Richdeane,' my mother said, as if that explained everything.

'Richdeane?'

'It's a school for creative children who perhaps aren't suited to traditional education environments. There's a lot of support for them. No television, that sort of thing.'

She was wrong, we do have TV, but Richdeane is one of those schools that claims things on the website such as 'nurturing spirited, creative children to make autonomous and artistic choices'. That's a euphemism for 'your broken offspring can do what the fuck they please as long as you pay the fees'.

'Ah, yes, that makes sense,' said the doctor, checking her papers. 'Lux, you were saying you feel like you're in a video game?'

'Yeah.' My tongue was having a hard time pushing through the seal on my mouth but I forced it harder. 'It makes it hard to know what's real and what's not. Sometimes I feel like something is watching me, as if I'm not safe or I'm being controlled by someone that's not me.'

I didn't tell them that I've convinced myself I took acid but that I don't remember doing it and that's why I blacked out and now my brain is permanently broken.

'You have an unusual constellation of symptoms, Lux. Your circumstances are very interesting.' The doctor again. A sabre of sunlight holding levitating skin particles streamed from the top of the window and disappeared into the back of her skull. I wished she'd stop saying my name like that – although I had to give her props for making my weirdness sound romantic and astronomical. 'I don't imagine that's much of a consolation.'

Nope.

'I'll give you a different medication for the head pain. There's also something called synaesthesia that I'd like to test you for,' she continued. 'It's not an illness but it causes people's senses to overlap, which could explain why you sometimes become so overwhelmed, and might account for some of your recurring thoughts. People are usually born with it but there's handful of cases where it has developed later in life. Usually as a result of a trauma. Anyway, the tests are really just to rule it out.'

Dr Purves read a list of numbers. She asked me to write down each one and the corresponding colour, taste or smell I associated with it. It was the same as one of the tests that her assistant had done to me on the phone the week before, except the numbers were in a different order. I guess they wanted to compare the results.

Next, a nurse stuck circular stickers on my chest and hooked me up to a machine to check my heart. I watched my little life on the monitor. 'Don't look so worried,' the nurse said, nodding at the green blips on the screen. 'If there were no ups and downs, you'd be dead.'

Then she needed some of my blood. I hate needles; I could never be a heroin addict. My veins were shy so she gave me some warm water to drink to coax them to the surface. She changed the dressing on my arm then tried again, sticking the inside of both my elbows, before giving up and trying a wrist instead. She got what she wanted in the end, leaving a mark on my wrist that started as a small pink dot and turned into a magnificent bruise which spread down into the base of my thumb. In the week that followed, it went black then green then mottled pink and then faded away. I'd lost my phone when I blacked out so I couldn't take photos of it and I missed it when it went. It was one less thing to point at and say, 'This hurts.' I had to work extra hard to keep the feather-shaped cut on my arm alive after that.

When the rest of the tests were done, my mother asked Dr Purves how long it would take for me to go back to normal. The doctor had a smear of greasy tangerine lipstick on her upper lip, half a citrus moustache, which I knew would be driving my mother to distraction.

'Well, we'll wait for the test results to come back and we'll do something called watchful waiting. It might not sound like much but it can be very helpful. You might hear it being called "wait and watch" or WAW if you like,' said Dr Purves.

I didn't like. WAW sounds just like war.

Dr Purves told my mother, told us, 'Trauma reveals us sometimes, heightens our senses. Lux just needs more time.'

I made a mental note to refer to all hangovers or anyone blacking out as trauma going forward. Mei would like that.

My mother asked me to wait in the hall while she spoke to the doctor alone. When she came out a few minutes later, I asked her what they'd discussed. Since there was nothing physically wrong with me, Dr Purves had suggested I talk to a different kind of professional. The mind-prober kind.

We went back to the flat in Waterloo where I'd been staying while I completed my internship at the gallery. Or rather almost-completed; the Friday that would have been my final one was the day I woke up in hospital.

My parents bought the flat so they have somewhere to stay when they're in town. It's in the kind of block that feels like a hotel – all corridors with wall lights like portholes and Yale-lock doors that open into identikit apartments. Bet they weren't counting on staying there for weeks after collecting their wayward offspring from hospital.

We sat in the kitchen, looking out of the triple-glazed window on to the back of the Royal Festival Hall and the dirty Thames. My mother made us milky tea. We clinked cups and pretended that drinking tea was something we always did together.

I felt like I was on the other side of the thick-glass window looking in at us. I was outside an imaginary house with half-lifted blinds, staring at the laps and torsos of people frozen in the ritual of taking tea.

I think my mother was trying to reach through, but her voice was fading in and out like someone whispering then shouting underwater. I clamped the sides of the porcelain cup with both hands until the burning sensation pulled me back into the room.

We didn't fight that night. I excused myself to take a bath. Slipping under the hot water, letting it fill my ears and nostrils, I pretended it was amniotic fluid and that my mother could protect me.

THREE

I was caged and disconnected in my parents' flat for over five weeks. My mother said they weren't angry when they brought me home from hospital and they didn't shout at first. But they took away my TV and laptop, and wouldn't let me go anywhere by myself. I tried to say sorry but my mother just shushed me and said it wasn't my fault, that they shouldn't have left me alone for the summer. The tighter she hugged me, the guiltier I felt.

Then the fights started. My parents' words bounced off me, refracting back to them, until we were stuck in a continuous loop of damage.

'Listen to us, Lux. Try to hear what we're saying.'

'Stop pretending you care. Just let me go back to school; I want to go home.'

'Richdeane isn't home. This is your home.'

It was the same argument over and over. The professionals are interested in that too. I can't remember all the words to the fights now because they hurt and they tell me that the human body is built to forget some types of pain.

But I do remember the final one, a particularly savage row that sent us all to bed early.

They took it in turns to plead with me, 'It's for your own good. We're trying to help you.'

'I can't live like this. If you don't let me go back to school, I promise you, one day you'll wake up and I'll be gone. I mean it,' I'd screamed.

They had hushed debates behind their bedroom door late into the night while they thought I was sleeping.

In the morning, my mother booked an emergency appointment with the professionals. We saw the doctors separately and then together. They finally agreed I would benefit from the relative normality of Richdeane and that a break could be good for all of us.

Then I told my parents I didn't want to see them for a while. I could see the heartbreak on their faces but they agreed to respect my wishes. They said they didn't want to hurt me any more. I'll still have to see the professionals though, for the headaches and the things that don't make sense.

The professionals say I need to work on naming my feelings. There's a chart on the wall in one of the shrinks' waiting rooms titled 'Teddy-Bear Feelings'. Fifteen square teddy-bear faces staring out of the poster, expressing themselves for all to see, their little jumpers helpfully labelled with the feeling that corresponds to their facial expression. There are only three aspirational teddy-bear feelings: loved, joyful and safe. The rest are bleak: lonely, scared, jealous and so on. Anyway, the professionals say just to focus on working out whether I'm sad, mad or glad and go from there.

The first therapist was the worst; she obviously wanted me to fall apart more visibly so she could Sellotape me back together and give me back to my parents all fixed. She asked me the same questions over and over again, waiting for a different answer.

'What happened at the party?

'How did you get to the hospital?

'What happened when you woke up?'

I don't remember; I don't remember; I don't remember.

My mind is lost.

I thought if I could squeeze out some tears perhaps we could call it a day. Could she hear the rasps of my tear ducts dry-retching as I willed them to vomit up some salty water? She bleated about connecting with my body so I tried to notice my cells die and collide and copulate, or whatever the hell cells do. But all I could feel was the coating on my tongue as it played dead in my mouth, rusty with silence.

The last shrink I saw before my parents let me come back to Richdeane was obsessed with my red dreams. He made me record them in a special notebook so we could interpret them together. Dreams are made concrete by writing them down or talking about them. Otherwise the wisp disappears not long after you've opened your eyes. Yet this is not generally true of nightmares; in my experience, the latter tend to linger long after your screams have woken you up.

I actually started to dream about the shrink. In one, I was lying on one of those psychiatrist couches when an invisible hand that I knew was his reached up my jumper, crawling to find some side boob. Awkward. I didn't keep any more of my appointments with him.

The facilities at Richdeane were conceived to ensure we have everything we need to keep our pledge, so the campus is littered with anything an Artist or the untalented child of one could want. Among the kilns and canvases are a legion of 3D printers, hipster typewriters, deep freezers full of ingredients, and hauls of metal ore and other finite resources. We bring our own imaginations, which, we are told, are infinite.

Richdeane's is that most inconsistent and permissive of parents, willing to bend to accommodate the whims and needs of any Artist, if they are talented enough, yet totally intractable on the subject of art. My own transgressions, for example, are forgiven because I've won prizes for writing stories.

'Bespoke therapeutic interventions' are part of the curriculum so there are special rooms for talking here too – all carefully styled with feng shui pot plants and tactically placed tissues. We have classrooms as well. A few. But we spend most of our time in the studios or the dorms.

I've been back in my and Mei's dorm room among her mood boards, notebooks and other general clutter at Dylan House for six days. For someone who runs her life with military precision, she is a slob of the highest order. We've shared this room since we started here. I realised a long time ago that Mei will do anything for her inner circle. I used to think you had to tell her specifically what you needed, that she wouldn't get there on her own because she assumes everyone is as resilient as she is, but she has a better idea of what I need right now than I do.

She's barely left my side since I got back but when she's in the shower I search the internet for sad videos and sneak to the mirror to make beautiful, fake-sobbing faces. I squirt eye drops down my cheeks and imagine I'm a TV talent show judge crying diamond tears at some contestant's sob story.

I haven't told anyone that I think my tear ducts are broken; people are already whispering about me (I'm 'Blackout Girl' behind my back, I expect). Two days ago, Mei, Olivia and I watched a sad, old film called *My Girl* where this kid dies after getting stung by bees. Mei and Olivia were both wrecks. I tweeted along with them about drowning in my own tears and needing a rehydration sachet to replenish my fluids but, really, I couldn't muster a drop. Not even the clips of soldiers coming home from war and the rest of the emotional porn on YouTube can touch me now.

In those seven weeks since I woke up in hospital, Mei and Olivia have accelerated. I only missed two weeks of school but in that time they've taken a quantum leap together. Meanwhile, I learned how to be alone; how to forget the horrible fights with my parents. While my mind is lost, theirs are on the future; on what they are becoming and where they will go.

I thought that once I got back to school, things would go back to normal. I thought the headaches and the red nightmares would stop. I'm still waiting.

The thing about this place is that people come, go and come back with semi-regularity, so my absence for the two weeks after summer shouldn't have caused much of a ripple. I'm far from the first Richdeaner to find herself in a hospital bed. But I can feel people looking at me, and not in the way I used to want them to. Acting like I don't care is exhausting; I'm ready to lie low this weekend.

But, first, poetry. Just two hours of Word Arts are all that stand between me and the end of my first week back. Director Harrins is a big fan of the Harkness method. It's used by our counterparts in America, he says. I like the idea that we all have a long-lost soul twin or doppelgänger somewhere. Maybe mine feels as dislocated as I do, or maybe she's rebooted herself and feels better.

Maybe the girl in the hospital was my counterpart, my soul twin, and I missed the chance to speak with her because I fell asleep and, when I woke up, she was gone and a fresh bag of tear juice hung over my bed feeding my veins.

I wonder where she is now and whether she's back at school trying to figure out what happened to her too. Does she feel as guilty thinking about me as I do about her?

This type of class means we, the Artists, do all the work. Director Harrins tees up a topic and then sits back while we debate it. So we're all sitting round an oval table like we're at the G8 Art Summit or something.

I usually sit with Isabella for Word Arts but she's by the window today so I'm next to Georgia Temple instead. She's folding something out of paper in her lap. We're friendly but not friends so I don't ask her what she's making. We've never collaborated; her collective comprises only the most achingly committed Artists.

She is also part of Richdeane legacy. Her older brother was rumoured to be the founder of the short-lived Richdeane 27 club, a semi-secret group of Artists supposedly dedicated to burning short and bright like their heroes Kurt, Amy, Heath and the rest.

Richdeane 27 was disbanded the year I started here when the press got hold of details of the club's more dangerous activities. The directors seemed to court the attention for a while. After all, what's better for the Richdeane brand than a group of demonstrably passionate young Artists giving everything to their craft? As it turns out, rumours of performance art culminating in a joint suicide pact is where the line is.

Georgia is dating one of the Fifth Form girls called Millie. When her friends first found out last year, they gave her grief for a week. They called her a cradle snatcher and a paedophile, saying she was a pervert for not getting a girlfriend her own age. The Artists she hangs around with are poisonous, especially Millie. A school of jellyfish, they would sting each other to death if they had any extra flesh to wound. Jellyfish pulse like hearts to push themselves upwards. Tentacles swaying and tangling, they seem immune to each other's stings. Not like humans; we tend to take each other out when we're thrashing about.

My thoughts are starting to get mean; I remind myself that villains are just victims whose stories haven't yet been told. A professional told me that, like he was conveying something super meaningful and all I could think was how much Lux sounded like a villain's name.

Director Harrins stares at me. 'Concentrate,' his eyes say.

The poem is long. It's about three guys my age who go to

war. They talk about pink mist. When some of the boys get home from war, part of them wants to go back because their bodies are home but their minds are not.

Director Harrins explains the poem is about psychological hunger and something called soldier's heart or shellshock.

He says something like, 'All the humours are represented in this poem. From the sanguine to the melancholic. One cannot rely on the brittle mechanism of objective judgement, so feel it, let it move you. We give it to art and we let go.'

He's won a lot of poetry prizes so we do as we're told and are duly moved until an alarm starts to sound. Nobody moves. I hold my breath and count, then my ears pop so the alarm rings far away like my head's inside an astronaut helmet.

The professionals are also interested in my astronaut suit.

Its material is thick so it's difficult to feel things through it but alarms can penetrate it and they definitely make me feel something. I run through teddy-bear-feelings faces in my mind. Am I sad, mad or glad? Alarms definitely don't make me glad. Alarms make me feel nervous and scared and guilty and as if I can't breathe. As if I have soldier's heart but I only have a teenager's one. Director Harrins's lips are moving and nobody is evacuating. He must be saying the alarm is just a drill.

If they organised us, they could assign each of us a piece of the school's art collection to save in the event of a real emergency. I guess it's all insured but the originals would be lost forever if there was a robbery or an earthquake. We have on-campus bunkers; the height of high-society paranoia. I like to imagine the head director has a lair down there where he sits in a swivel chair with a cat on his lap.

The shelters were built after the Twin Towers were toppled, when I was still in nappies and Richdeane was just a regular boarding school. When London was hit on 7/7, I wasn't even in double digits but I remember the news showed a mosque with a makeshift sign outside that read 'All faiths welcome'. I thought about running away and going to live there. Or maybe I didn't; I was only eight so I probably just saw it in a documentary later.

It's been like this my whole life – terror in the spaces and places we tell ourselves are safe – but lately it seems as if I'm the only one who feels like we're under attack. I count my breaths and the alarm fades.

We get back to the poem for a while and then, finally, it's the weekend. Georgia is whisked away by her collective before I can say goodbye, leaving a tiny origami flower behind on her seat. It could be a snowdrop – the Richdeane crest. I'm not sure what it means or even if it's meant for me but I pick it up and tuck it into my sleeve for safekeeping.

I want to catch Isabella before she leaves; I haven't seen her since the summer.

'Isabella,' I call. She looks like she might run but she recovers herself.

'Hey, Lux, welcome back.'

'Thanks. How was your summer?'

'Good,' she says, her eyes like cold marbles. 'How are you?'

I tell her I'm OK. We're not that close. We talk about school and Mei and Olivia for a bit and then she says she has to go.

'OK, see you.'

'Sure,' she says so frostily I wonder if she heard about me

and Henry and she's in love with him or something. We were always quite competitive.

The shrill beep of the alarm set something off in my body and I spend Friday night with a migraine. Fridays are not good days any more. Since I blacked out, the slightest thing seems to aggravate my brain and fill it with fire.

Mei helps me into bed back in our room at Dylan House. This is the third attack in the week I've been back. She and Olivia have been amazing; they haven't asked me any questions. No 'What happened? What's wrong with you? Why can't you remember?' But already Isabella and the rest are falling away like they're scared of me.

'How can I help?' Mei pleads. 'I'm going to go and get someone.'

'Thnurnuhnuh.' My tongue won't say the words my brain is telling it to.

'Should I get someone?' she asks.

'No, don't. Please.'

'I think we should call your mum. Where's your phone?'

'Don't. Promise me you won't.' Month-old arguments with my parents echo inside me; the sound of my own voice screaming at them reverberates through the swollen tissue in my brain.

'OK, I won't. I promise.'

Mei gets my pills and some water. I have to take them half a tablet at a time and swallow hard to stop them coming back up. I try to tell her she doesn't have to stay with me. I can't pretend I'm not lost if she sees me like this.

'I'm not leaving you and that's that.'

She turns off the light and sits in the corridor with our door ajar, snipping out pictures from magazines and prospectuses for her mood boards. Sticking them down and conjuring her future.

I try to mind-over-matter the pain by summoning a mental image of the leavers' party, but the lights are off in the darkroom in my mind so I can't see the pictures. Even in the dark, I know everything in there is splintered and spoiled.

A minute later, nausea takes over and the red pain swallows me whole.

FOUR

My dreams are hot and shrieking. I see everything in red. Luckily, the pain has subsided when I wake up on Saturday morning. The sheets are damp and, for a second, I think I've wet the bed – but it's just sweat.

My blood seems to have been replaced with some slow-moving substance in the night, poisoned treacle maybe. But I'll take exhaustion over pain.

'I didn't know whether to wake you up. You had a rough night.' Mei is already dressed and putting on her shoes. 'Assembly in ten if you can handle it?'

'I can handle it,' I say, wrenching myself from my pit.

Two hundred and fifty Artists dressed in our requisite black clothes congregate in the Churchill Theatre (named after the playwright not the late prime minister) to recite the pledge and listen to what we call the shares. It's optional but only in the way that having another tequila is optional.

The black clothing was the head director's idea. No logos, no labels, to keep our bodies neutral until such time as they are transformed by costume. Or maybe it's like the professionals say, we all need to build our own identities and we don't need some famous guy's name on our underwear to do that.

Every day, one or two Artists tell their story while the head director and his cast of tutors look on. I was up there at least once a week last year, racking up points to trade off against my bad behaviour. It's like a perverse stock exchange: the more times you share, the more your Richdeane stock goes up. Today it reminds me of a large-scale version of one of those AA meetings on TV where addicts drink from disposable coffee cups and sob about their lost childhoods. Although, of course, there's no actual caffeine on our campus. Caffeine takes us out of our experience, they say.

From his secular pulpit, there is something off about the way the head director spouts his context-less truisms today. People don't know whether to watch his address or stare at me, the newly returned Blackout Girl. I fiddle with the hair at the nape of my neck, coiling it round my finger, yanking almost to breaking point then releasing it.

After he leads us in our pledge, everything he says rings false: 'Most things happen gradually. Change usually creeps up on you and you don't realise it's happened until someone points it out. But sometimes change comes in an instant. Deft and seismic. When it does we are, at least, united in this. So in moments of lassitude, I encourage you to remember time is precious. Time not spent creating is time wasted. Draw strength from the pledge: *We give it to art and we let go.* Change can happen in an instant.'

Or it can come in the time it takes to do one shot too many and pass out. My head starts to fuzz again. This is the world's longest hangover and I barely remember the party.

He continues his sermon, telling us the art market can withstand anything. One second I'm listening and the next my body is pushing past the Artists in my row to get to the door.

'I need to get out.' Heads are turning to look at me again. 'Please, let me out.'

Outside, I sink on to a low windowsill and Olivia appears. She plops down on to the ground and sits cross-legged in front of me. She puts a hand on my juddering knee to steady it. It burns so I shake it off.

'Sorry,' she says, clouds of hurt drifting across her eyes.

'Sorry,' I echo. I can't explain that I'm burning from the inside out. My brain clenches and pulses. 'I don't know what happened. I just had to get out of there.'

'It's OK. You're OK.'

'Am I?'

'Maybe it was too soon for you to come back. Do you want me to call your mum?'

'No.' The panic erupts again. 'I don't want them.'

She peers up at me. 'Are you sure?'

I nod.

'OK. I'll take you back to Dylan.'

'I think I'll go for a walk.'

'I'll come with you.'

'Don't take this the wrong way, but I'd rather be by myself.'

'OK.'

'I'll find you soon, Livvy.' It's an old nickname that we left behind years ago, before we'd even met Mei.

The hurt clouds cross her eyes again but she nods. She stands up, takes my hands in hers and pulls me up too. I hug her. The touch doesn't burn this time; it's like nothing at all.

After assembly, we are free to do what we want anyway. Most Artists go to the studios or the theatres to work, spreading out to productive corners of our colony. I find a spot on the field that's far enough away that people won't be able to tell who I am but still close enough to feel part of things.

Richdeane looks jumbled from a distance; the old, original cottage where the head director lives makes the newer studios and boarding houses look even more futuristic with their solar panels and glass balconies. We're hemmed in by woods and private fields so the inconsistent architecture can only be seen by us and the birds.

The grass is full of things I never used to notice – tiny bugs, flowers and different coloured blades. The last of the summer bees buzz and dive face first in and out of petals, off their furry little faces on Richdeane's high-grade pollen.

I see the shadow on the ground before I see the head director's assistant's face, her husky body changing the air currents around me.

'Could you come with me, please?' She looks down at me through mirrored sunglasses.

'Am I in trouble?' I ask, staring at my own face as I seek out her eyes behind her beetle lenses.

Is this about my behaviour over the summer or running out of assembly? I've tested Richdeane's liberal principles sufficiently to have been called to the head director's cottage before. I've always believed in the pledge but have a natural inclination to experiment with limits. My father is the same; we are genetically predisposed to do the exact opposite of what is required in a given situation.

When we get inside the cottage, the assistant disappears. I hover outside the head director's study, wondering if I should go in, when the door opens and the head director steps out with a tall man I recognise but can't place.

'Ah, Lux,' he says, 'perfect timing. This is Dr Baystone. He joined us at the start of term.'

'Hi, Lux,' the man says. He bares his Hollywood teeth.

'Hello,' I say.

'Come in, Lux,' says the head director. 'Thanks, Paul. We'll talk later.'

He closes the door behind us and gestures for me to sit down.

'Is this about assembly? Because I'm sorry about that.'

'No. Well, yes, in a way. I wanted to make sure you're feeling better.'

'I'm fine.'

'Pleased to hear it. Really, I just wanted to see how your first week back went,' he says, 'but I'm glad you got to meet Dr Baystone. He has a very interesting background. I'd like you to meet with him properly next week.'

'Why?' slips out before I can stop it.

'I understand you've missed a few classes since you returned.'

'Artists miss classes all the time. I wasn't feeling well; I get headaches.'

Headaches: what a euphemism.

'I know. I understand you're waiting for some test results from your doctors.'

'I just need to get on the right medication, then I'll be back to normal.'

'In the meantime, your parents and I would like you to meet with Dr Baystone. Just to make sure you have everything you need while you settle back in.'

'But I only missed two weeks,' I say. It comes out like a whiny protest. I clear my throat and try again with something I think a grown-up might say. 'I just need to get back into the swing of things.'

'That's part of why I called you here actually. I know there's a trip to the Tate Modern next week. We think it would be best if you waited a little while before leaving campus.'

'I don't need your permission.'

It's true, in theory – we're free to come and go as we please. The website calls this 'a pioneering, open residential school model'. They want us to learn to regulate our own behaviour because Art knows there'll be no one to do it for us when we leave here. Actually, apart from official trips, we rarely leave for longer than an evening. Henry kept my party favours stocked last year so I didn't even have to go off-site for those.

'I'm afraid you do,' he says. 'Your parents have signed some additional paperwork.'

Of course they have. I was their prisoner for weeks and now I'm a prisoner here. Not that I'm inclined to go far; I don't want to get more lost.

'But Mei and Olivia are going,' I say.

'I know, but I've promised your parents we'll look after you.'

'But I really feel like I need to go.'

'I'm sorry,' he says. 'It's not appropriate.'

Not appropriate. What kind of non-reason is that?

And suddenly, it's true, I know I need to go there. 'I've got to go – I can't explain why, but I've got to.'

'Lux,' he says in a calm-down-little-girl voice. 'Why is it so important for you to go?'

'I just told you, I can't explain. Can't you just listen to me?' Anger surfaces and I have to say it loudly to make myself heard over the sound of my heart roaring.

I'm out of my chair. Something is filling me with fury.

'Lux. You need to calm down. Take a seat, please.'

I sit and squeeze my thumbs inside my fists. What would happen if I hit him?

'Thank you,' he says. 'Take a second to calm yourself down.'

'I'm calm,' I say, trying to expel the anger with my breath.

'OK.'

'Please don't stop me going. I need to go.'

'My concern is that it will be too much for you. You've been very ill.'

I try playing the pledge card: 'But aren't you always telling us we should take strength from Art?'

No dice.

'I feel like there might be some answers for me there.'

This seems to strike the right chord.

'I'll tell you what,' he continues. 'I'll check with your parents and, if they say it's OK, you can go. But you'll have to promise me you'll do exactly as the supervising directors say and meet with Dr Baystone next week. Do we have a deal?'

He smooths his oily black hair behind his ears and leans over to offer his hand for me to shake. I will the pores on my palm to seal over so his hair grease can't soak through my skin into my bloodstream.

'I'll be honest with you, Lux. We don't know if this is the best place for you at the moment.' This stands to reason since I was caught with drugs on campus just before the summer (one of few offences that can get you kicked out of Richdeane, that and violence towards others), so he's probably made his own assumptions about how I ended up in hospital.

I know it will make me feel better if I can get into the city to the gallery, so I shake his hand.

I can avoid Dr Baystone when the time comes.

'One more thing: your parents wanted to tell you this themselves, but I gather you haven't been answering their calls.'

'There were arguments,' I say. 'We're having a rest from each other.'

'Yes. They've asked me to reiterate that they are very keen that you join them.'

I swallow and shake my head.

'Very well. They will respect your wishes but they've decided on a deadline. If you're not feeling better by the end of term, you will have to go to them.'

'That's almost three months away; of course I'll be better by then. And then I can stay?'

'We'll reassess at the end of term. Or prior to that, if need be.'

He continues: 'Do come to me if you find yourself struggling. I've also asked your tutors and Dr Baystone to keep an eye on you.'

I can feel their eyes on me already.

'I'm sorry I shouted at you,' I say as he opens the door.

'Give it to Art, Lux,' he reminds me.

I go to the Contemplation Room. (Built to give Artists a quiet space to meditate on the pledge and named so as not to stifle any kind of religious and spiritual exploration. Some sexual exploration has taken place there too.) It's heaving so I only stay a few minutes then go back to my dorm room.

I google Dr Baystone.

Looks like he's a mind-prober, but he used to be a performer. A celebrated character actor from the Noughties with a psychotherapy doctorate and connections to the celebrity Dadaist scene, to be precise. Naturally, the school will be thrilled to have him.

I start to look up 'soldier's heart + symptoms' but remember I'm not supposed to consult Dr Google. I'm meant to share my concerns with a professional.

And how dare I think I might have soldier's heart when I've never been to war.

FIVE

'You'll never guess who's coming to assembly today,' says Mei. 'Jade Grace!'

'You didn't let me guess, but wow.'

Richdeane's most famous alumna is returning. She graduated three years ago so I didn't really know her but she had a thing with Olivia's brother Lawrence.

Apparently she's just wrapped a superhero movie, a role that will send her further into the celebrity stratosphere – especially if her publicist can get the whispers of an affair with her co-star to stick.

I take three of my tablets so I can make it through her visit without a migraine.

Most of the school gathers in the Churchill Theatre. For most of the productions staged here, the rest of the audience is usually made up of agents, media and local parents. Today it's just Richdeane people and a few representatives from Jade's sponsors, plus her other sponsor who goes by the title of Sober Companion. What a depressing job: the official fun police. If the rumours are true, he has quite a job on his hands.

I feel Mei squeeze my arm while Olivia leans forward next to her. Angry Jack is on my other side. A horseshoe of small, connected tattoos starts at his jawbone, crawls up his face, across his acne-scarred forehead and down the other side. Anywhere else, that ink might as well be a statement saying 'societal dropout', but here, where extremes of expression are rewarded, some see it as brave.

One of Jade's songs plays over the sound system. She sings so slowly that the words imprint on my mind as they unfurl from the speakers, as easy and silky as pulling a ribbon through fingers. The chorus sticks to me:

'And now, that hungry little voice
I know so well
Is on my shoulder,
Whispering dreams and ideas.
And I'm going mouth to mouth,
I'm seeking out
Resuscitation,
Breathing their air,
And then saying
Goodnight.'

It's an open, expansive song that you could climb inside and make a home in.

There is range in it but not so much as to stretch to the limits of her voice, which slides up and down the violet, indigo and blue notes, occasionally dipping into green but no further.

'That was kind of a weird song,' says Angry Jack when it ends. 'Is she some kind of a succubus going round sucking the life out of people?'

'Melodies to wet the bed to. It's so bloody pedestrian,' says the guy next to him.

'A bloody pedestrian would be exciting.'

'You're right – it's just regular pedestrian. A regular pedestrian with all the blood still inside.'

'Shh,' I say.

Finally, Richdeane's prodigal child glides out of the wings on to the stage. The lights are wrong so her face is obscured but we know it's Jade. We bang our hands together and stamp our feet. Her cloud-white trouser suit makes her look so much older than us. She must be wondering why we're all wearing black; we could wear what we wanted when she was here. The audience vibrates with expectation. Jade unites us; the conducting hub that completes our circuit.

As the lights settle, her face comes into focus and her hair gleams a dazzling red. She's dyed it. A bright, familiar taste glitters over my tongue. The bandage around my arm tightens like a blood-pressure cuff as the universe takes one of those leaps where everything new clicks into place and you can't remember life the old way, and in that moment I know her. Maybe we met in a past life but we're definitely connected.

The screens flick on at either side of the stage so we can

see her in zoomed-in high definition. A spotlight fixes on her, lighting her hair like a bleeding halo around her face.

She has the requisite disproportionately large eyes of a screen star. People should study her to find out exactly what the optimal face-to-eye-size ratio is.

In addition to acting and singing, Jade is now a writer and a charity spokesperson. All this compounds to makes her media fodder, so this event, like every other in her life, is being filmed. Richdeane doesn't permit live-streaming so it will air, edited as need be, later.

Our head director takes centre stage and leads us in unison: 'We pledge ourselves to the will of the muses, and to the words of the greats. We give it to art and we let go.'

Presumably, they'll cut this bit for the broadcast. Trade secrets and all that. Jade's lips move but her microphone doesn't seem to be turned on yet so we can't hear her pledge.

'Have you ever noticed they never tell us exactly who the greats are?' whispers Mei. 'Or exactly what it is that these muses want?'

'That's just occurring to you after four years?' I ask.

'I think we're supposed to find out on our own,' says Olivia.

'Do they have to be dead?' Mei asks.

I know instantly that Jade is mine.

The head director starts a heartfelt but somewhat non-linear overview of her career. He looks earnestly into camera one as he rambles fervently about her artistry and numerous projects. The producer nods his approval. This is good stuff. Eventually and seemingly reluctantly, our polysyllabic messiah gives up the lectern so that Jade can read to us.

Although she was born and schooled in the south of

England, her accent oscillates unpredictably between the Home Counties and Los Angeles, finally stabilising somewhere over the mid-Atlantic where her 't's become 'd's but her 'h's remain resolutely British.

She shares three short stories from her collection – *The Cost of Applause* – which she will later claim are personal but not autobiographical.

Each story goes straight into me; Jade's words project on to my inside walls like a galaxy.

The first piece is about an out-of-work actor who gets into the S & M lifestyle while researching for a role as a dominatrix. The actor has to move back in with her parents and, unable to pursue her new sexual obsession under her parents' roof, she decides to take on the role of a submissive and starts playing up so that Mummy and Daddy will punish her.

My cheeks get hot as she reads. I'd like to be like that one day – able to write something so direct without being embarrassed or feeling as if it's a lie. My prize-winning stories seem like child's play in comparison; I write about road trips I haven't taken and boys I haven't loved.

I write about nothing at all since I blacked out.

The second story is about a girl who accompanies a friend to an abortion clinic during a snowstorm. Afterwards, they go for a picnic. They roll down a bank of snow teaming with snowdrops and, at the bottom, find themselves in a new world; a world much like ours but gentler. It's so beautiful, I wish I could cry. Mei and Olivia snivel at my sides.

By the third extract, Jade is almost English again. Just the occasional American twangs, particularly on words containing 'a's, punctuate an obsessive tale of imaginary love and non-imaginary loneliness. Her voice drops half an octave and she occasionally stops to swallow extra oxygen as she concludes the story.

She reads: '*When I am scared, I imagine he is with me. I feel his steady hand on the bottom of my back or steering me by the elbow.*

The first time a man did that, I knew he was more experienced than me. And I liked being temporarily absolved of responsibility for my own path.

Now, when I arrive back for another night in a hotel by myself, I hold the door open for a few extra seconds so his spirit can follow in behind me. We have great conversations, he and I, usually in bed or in the bath. Sometimes we talk about the same things night after night, so as to make them perfect. I invite him to join me inside all my choices and all my mistakes. I possess nothing because we share everything.

When I am sad, I imagine he is sadder and needs me to be brave. My stoic fingers move in small waves and circles as I try to feel his hair while he cries in my lap, an empty hand reaching for a phantom muscle memory.

'I no longer starfish across my king-size. I stay on one side but face hopefully towards the middle and coyly bare one nipple over the duvet lest he materialise by morning.

'I talk to him in my sleep and I mean everything I say. And when I worry I will jump off my hotel balcony into the traffic below in my sleep, it's his voice that reminds me I have never sleepwalked in my life.

'He is my favourite person that I have never met.'

It's like she wrote the story for me. Her words and red hair are clues on a map, guiding me back to myself.

I don't even mind that she used starfish as a verb. I read an article once about a mass starfish plague where they all ripped off their own limbs and rolled away to die – did they mean to kill themselves or were they just desperate to get away from the necrotic parts of themselves? Does Jade know about the plague?

She shuts the book and thanks us. The applause reminds me it's not just the two of us in the room.

An assistant runs on to the stage to move the lectern while another pulls forward two large armchairs. The head director is to chair the Q & A with Jade. They take their seats.

'Your first professional role was as a modern royal in the adaptation of popular tween book *Princess Lola*. Tell us a bit about that project,' he says.

'Well, I wouldn't be where I am now without Princess Lola, but I don't make that type of art any more. I'm truly grateful for the opportunity and what it's led to but there's no nourishment in that stuff; it's just popcorn.'

Given the resources that go into nutritionally optimising our meals, I'm surprised popcorn isn't a trigger word for the head director, but he just says, 'It certainly brought a lot of people joy. Was it a collaborative process?'

'I can try to collaborate, but I'm not in charge of whether a movie turns out well – all Artists are at the mercy of their directors and a hundred other variables. Actually, being on set is a lot like being a toddler – someone tells you what to wear, when to eat, what to say and even how to say it.'

The audience titters with recognition and the head director says: 'Wonderful. Nostalgia is so powerful. Tell us, was it exciting being on location for your latest film?'

'We were on a soundstage most of the time and we spent the rest of the shoot filming in a disused factory. The locations are all dictated by tax breaks so it's not really that glamorous.'

'Fantastic. And if you could have a superpower, what would it be?' he asks, like it's the first time she'll have been asked this despite being halfway through an international press junket for a superhero film.

'I'd like to be able to speed-read or learn a new language in a day.' The producer is visibly disappointed by this answer so she adds, 'And I guess being a mind-reader would be cool.'

'Great, brave choice. Now perhaps you can describe for us in one word how it feels to be so successful at such a young age.'

'One word to describe ...'

'How you feel.'

'I feel ... plundered,' she says.

I'm not sure whether she means this as a good or a bad thing. Laying waste brings the opportunity to start again but she seems full and empty at the same time. Or maybe I'm projecting; the professionals warned me about the perils of projection.

'Tremendous. Very visceral.' The head director nods. 'Now, and I hate to bring this up, but you seemed a little upset during your recent performance at the Watchers' Awards. Why were you weeping?'

'I wasn't weeping, I was hysterical.'

'Yes. Why such an emotional performance?'

'Because all those people were so happy. The audience, I mean.'

'And you were moved by their happiness.'

'I was crying because they were so happy and I couldn't give a shit. Can I say shit here?'

'You can say anything you like,' he says and then clarifies, 'pertaining to yourself and your art, I mean. You'll remember we try to stay in our own experiences here.'

'Cool. Yeah, so, I just thought it was unbearable that all these people cared about me when I wasn't sure if I did.'

'I see. And what about those, shall we say, *unusual* selfies you've been sharing on social media. The naked ones of you in your bedroom. I mean nude. The nude ones. Some people have dismissed them as a publicity stunt for the book. Any comment you'd like to make on that?'

'I basically realised the paparazzi and the hackers were going to have me eventually anyway so I decided I'd just give myself over to it. They can have me but only on my own terms. That's why I made the pictures so gruesome and violent – maybe I'd be so ugly they'd leave me alone. But I guess it didn't work.' She lets out a weak laugh.

'Right. Brave choices. The media has also made much of your other new hobby …'

'I don't read my press any more.'

'I'm talking about the snowdrops.'

'Oh, yeah.' Her face blooms. 'I'm a fully fledged galanthophile these days.'

'That's a collector of snowdrops to us laypeople?' He's done his research.

'Yes. When I was here it seemed like they flowered all year round, although I'm probably remembering it wrong. Anyway, I've met some super chill people on the snowdrop circuit. And I just got some Virescent bulbs on eBay this morning. Well, not full bulbs, obviously, they're bulb chips, but hopefully they'll take off.'

She shimmers under the hot stage lights and my fingers and forehead tingle.

'We're very lucky they bloom here. I know our current Artists enjoy them very much. I always liked snapdragons as a child,' he offers.

'When snapdragons die, they shrivel up and look like skulls.'

'How very *Hamlet*. Maybe we'll get some for the Earth Arts department. So, let's talk about your writing. What's your process?'

'As an actor, I'm a talking meat prop. As a writer, I'm a mouthpiece for stories. They find me and demand that I tell them.'

'That sounds rather passive,' he says. 'A lot of them are about the dark side of art and celebrity. What drew you to those themes?'

Jade closes her eyes and tilts her head back a fraction. 'You're right. My stories are very personal; I wanted to write and I don't know anything about anything else. Sometimes I feel like there's a terrorist in my mind and I've got to write to get it out. You can't be afraid of the truth.'

I sway into Mei.

'You OK?' she whispers.

'Yeah, sorry.' I had been holding my breath.

The head director opens up the Q & A for audience questions, most of which are lame. The sponsors want to know what it was like to kiss Matty James, her co-star in the superhero film, do redheads have more fun, and whether she got to keep the tiara or any of the clothes from *Princess Lola* … Could she look at the camera and repeat the brand names, please.

A guy a few rows in front of us raises his hand. Camera three picks up his face. He looks American. I can imagine him all red, white and blue, with bigger teeth and bigger friends all called Brad and Chad and Tad. An assistant runs the microphone over to him. He asks how Jade stayed faithful to the pledge.

'Who's that?' I whisper.

'New guy,' says Mei.

'Cal,' says Olivia. 'He's in some of my classes.'

'Sounds like he smokes forty a day,' I say.

Angry Jack leans over and whispers, 'Millie told me he got shot in the throat.'

Wow. That's the Richdeane rumour mill for you. Millie's dad is some famous tabloid journalist so people might actually believe it.

'He seems very serious,' I say.

The next Artist's question is about what Jade asks for on her rider (water, whisky, Wispas).

I take a deep breath and raise my hand to ask a question. The microphone weighs heavy in my hand and a voice booms over the sound system; I don't recognise its timbre but the words are mine as I ask what's the best advice she's ever been given.

I don't know if she can see me through the stage lights but I feel an invisible thread uncoil and fix us to each other as she says, 'Nobody told me it, but the best advice I've given myself is expose yourself to what you're afraid of.'

And, with that, the head director thanks Jade for her candidness. There is more applause. He gives her a one-armed hug while she presses her palms together in front of her heart and bobs her head, avoiding his eye contact as she carries out this hollow gesture of gratitude. Then she's escorted away by her Sober Companion.

LYDIA RUFFLES

We get stuck in a bottleneck behind some Fourth Form girls on our way out of the auditorium. They're having an unnecessarily loud conversation about Matty James.

'Jade is so lucky she got to hook up with Matty. I would totally gob-job him,' says one.

'Would you swallow?' asks one of the others.

'No way. I'm vegetarian.'

'But doesn't it have, like, loads of protein in it or something?' another one chips in.

'Yeah, I heard it's basically a superfood, but I still wouldn't,' says the first one, picking at her teeth.

'Stick to blueberries, ladies,' Mei tells them as we shuffle through the double doors. 'Now, off you fuck.' They giggle and scatter.

'Must be weird for Jade being back here,' says Olivia.

'The girl can write but she didn't seem very happy,' says Mei.

'She probably gets asked the same questions fifty times a day.'

I can relate. Except I get: 'What happened at the party? How did you get to the hospital? What happened when you woke up?'

'Do you think your brother would give me her email?' I ask Olivia.

'She dumped him pretty hard the night of their Leavers' Ball so probably best not to bring it up, but his password has been the same since he was twelve so I'll see if it's still in his contacts.'

I tap her arm to say thanks.

That night I dream of tiny foetus snowdrops, lonely starfish and invisible comfort. A black and white dream, for once.

Olivia delivers on getting Jade's email for me and I decide to send her a message. Sometimes it's easier to communicate with people you don't know. I want tell her that her advice made me realise how I can fix myself, but I don't want her to know that I'm sick, especially as there's not a name for what's wrong with me.

Dear Jade,

I don't know if you read messages from fans but I hope this reaches you. I was in the audience when you came back to Richdeane and wanted to ask you some questions I couldn't ask in front of the other Artists.

Here goes:

When you said there was something in your head that you needed to get out, what exactly did you mean?

I understand why you did it, but what did it feel like to cry in front of all those people at the Watchers' Awards?

Why did you dye your hair red? It looks perfect.

Do you still believe in the pledge? Did you ever believe in it?

All an Artist can hope for is an audience and you have that. But you seem lonely and I wanted you to know you have a friend in me, if you want me.

I dreamed about your words last night. I think I know how you feel about the guy in your story, the one you haven't met yet. I haven't met mine yet either. I need to get better first.

Please write back or send me a sign. I think we might be the same.

Lux

PS Come back and see the snowdrops this winter?

A few minutes later, I refresh. Jade hasn't replied but I have another message from my mother. She must have sensed I was online. Her umbilical noose reaches through cyberspace as I open it.

Lux. Your head director told us you're going to a gallery tomorrow. Call us anytime and we'll come and get you. You can come home whenever you want. We love you. Mum and Dad xxxxxxx

Now she's playing nice after they made me ache with pain and held me captive all summer. Besides, Singapore is not home.

Refresh.

No message from Jade.

I have to park that for now. I've got to figure out how I'm going to do what I need to do at the Tate with the directors and my friends watching me.

I double up on my medication to make sure I don't have a migraine for the trip. If I can't get to the gallery, I can't cure myself.

SIX

We go on a lot of trips at this school. It's part of the immersive, healing experience our parents or sponsors pay for to teach us to be viable Artists. They laugh about how, in their day, being an Artist was considered a risky career move. Now we rebel by threatening to become bankers.

But market forces still rule the world; it's basic supply and demand. And Richdeane found a gap in the market, so instead of preparing its pupils to become parliamentarians or captains of industry, it aspires to spit us directly into the waiting mouths of the capital's art schools – despite predictions of a severe correction in the art market. Attending Richdeane guarantees you a seat at the easel. We are the ones to watch.

My class was the last to join the school when there were still lessons dedicated to the study of oxbow lakes and the use of Bunsen burners. We still use labs to grow copper sulphate crystals like our peers at other schools, but ours are supersized and used to create chemical installations.

Most traditional academic pursuits have been consigned to weekly General Education lessons. The hazy memory of Science, Geography and the like will fade with us when we have our Leavers' Ball next summer. Instead, alongside mandatory classes in Media & Discretion Coaching, Art Therapy, Appreciation & Valuation, Critic & Dealer Relations, and Sales & Representation, we take electives from Live Performance, Body, Visual, Multimedia, Urban, Social, Earth, Chemical, Instrumental, Culinary, Movement and Word Arts.

During our frequent and diverse trips, we're instructed to keep our eyes and hearts open to anything that may inspire us or help us to know more. But being open comes more naturally to some of us than others. While behaviourally challenged, most of the school's Artists have exceptional talent. Or their parents do and their offspring have been sent here in the hope that Richdeane's unique form of nurture can draw out what nature suppressed.

Then there are those who join from strange corners of the education system when it didn't work out for them. Their parents hand over big money or heirloom art to get their kids through Richdeane's postmodern doors. Angry Jack with the face tattoos, for example, was discharged from a celebrated defence training academy and had nowhere else to go. We are taught to create art about what we know so he's producing a graphic novel about a sheik-funded, Hogwarts-eqsue military school. Jack is a human grenade with a propensity for pulling out his own pin. Maybe he has soldier's heart.

Forget the pledge – 'Broken but brilliant' should be the school motto.

It's only twenty minutes by train into the city then a short walk to the Tate, but the school insists on transporting us by coach. We crawl through Friday lunchtime traffic for twice as long as the train would have taken.

Olivia and Mei sit in front of me so I have a double seat to myself. Isabella used to join the three of us sometimes but today she pretended not to see when I patted the seat next to me.

'What's up with her?' I ask. 'I have the distinct feeling she's avoiding me.'

'Maybe she is. I don't think she's good with sick people,' says Mei.

'I'm not a sick person. I'm me.'

Olivia says, 'I think maybe she just doesn't know how to be around you.'

'We can swap seats,' they take it in turns to say, swivelling round every two minutes to enquire about my well-being.

Who cares what Isabella thinks? Today could be the day I find the old me again. I take an extra tablet and roll up my sleeve to scratch through the dressing on my arm until dots of blood appear through the fabric.

A raspy laugh drifts down from the back of the coach. It's Cal, the new guy. Ordinarily I'd have made sure I'd got to know all the new Artists and they'd definitely know me from my centre-stage position in assemblies. I've been off my game. But I can already see everything seems to come so easily to him. I think I was like that before I blacked out. I was winning, like him, just a bit messier about it.

Out of the window, people on the streets are costumed for all seasons and seem to be carrying props for any eventuality. While I'm opening my heart as instructed, my eyes meet with a hairy homeless man at some traffic lights. He's looking up with one arm on the top of a bin and the other inside it like a vet birthing a calf, except his hand comes out holding half a Big Mac, not new bovine life.

When we get off the coach, Director Harrins and Director Daniels usher us past a bunch of people standing open-palmed and handing out leaflets at the front of the gallery. Probably a written lesson in 'What does metamodernism really teach?'.

Cal talks earnestly with one of the prettier women, but none of them approach me. Do they sense my belief in art is wavering?

My breathing gets shaky and shallow. I wonder if I should try one of the mindfulness techniques the professionals are always talking at me about, but I can't remember exactly what to do and, besides, my mind is full enough as it is.

Just by the gallery entrance, there's another homeless man. He's made his bedroom among the dirt and stained coffee cups. He wears fingerless gloves and holds a sign that reads: 'The debt and the dogs need feeding.'

A feeling forces itself over the sound of my breathing. The same sense as when we went to visit Grandmother in the care home and I wanted to tell all those bent men and women I would straighten their backs for them if I could. Sometimes, I want to be the kind of person who makes life easier for other people. And sometimes I wish everyone I love would die so I wouldn't have to worry about them hurting any more.

Mei asks why, if the man went to the trouble of finding

cardboard and pens, didn't he put more effort into making the sign less crappy.

I feel something sliming up my throat and starting to choke me. Jealousy? I wish I could hold up a cardboard sign asking for what I need. Maybe it's guilt, like the time my mother spent loads of money on handbags and Whole Foods this summer, and then spent the evening afterwards crying at the news like all the terror in the world was her fault.

I drag my eyes from the man and follow my friends into the gallery.

As I step through the doors, my heart tries to punch its way out of my chest. Since the hospital, it does that sometimes. I ignore it. I have a plan to follow.

'Expose yourself to what you're afraid of.'

There might be a bit of a fuss if people recognise us as Richdeane Artists. I look for security guards and make a mental note of all the exits. We keep our distinguishing markers covered, the tattoos and scars that most of us bear, but we're hardly incognito. Suddenly, even though nobody can see it, I want the snowdrop on the underside of my wrist gone.

With our all-black clothes, and colourful hair and headscarves, we resemble a troupe of clowns in mourning but, inside a gallery, we're among our people. They're too cool to stare, it seems.

Director Harrins and Director Daniels, are supervising us. This usually means they liberate us the minute we're inside.

There are X-ray scanners just inside the door. Even we, the Artists of the future, or maybe the now, are subject to checks. We walk through one at a time and the security guards pass our bags, coats and shoes along the moving belt through the X-ray.

A man behind us grows impatient and, possibly in a display of control, the security guard makes the man put his sandwich through the X-ray machine. I wonder if it will give him special powers when he ingests it.

When we get inside, we huddle by the bookshop.

'We'll be right here,' says Director Daniels, staring at me.

'Why am I being singled out?' I say as we all disperse. 'As if I'm such a liability I'm going to start snorting something in front of a Picasso.'

I have to shake Mei and Olivia because I need to go upstairs alone. They get quite huffy about it so I agree to message them when I'm done.

When I get to the bottom of the escalator that travels up through the bowels of the cavernous building, I see Cal and some of his collective lolloping towards the top. He gives Luca, a guy I've got previous with, a slap on the back and they laugh. The head director probably asked Luca to help Cal acclimatise – a sponsor of sorts.

Luca fawns over him like he's his adopted puppy. Good, sweet Cal. I can tell his type a mile off: biddable and loyal, gifted and golden. I wonder if my reputation as a blackout drunk precedes me and he knows all about me too, though we've never spoken.

When I get to the top of the escalator, they're gone. Not that I was following them or anything.

We read this play in Fifth Form called *Red*, based on the painter Rothko and his assistant. His paintings are part of my plan. I've visited them before but not since the hospital. I like that they are displayed in a darkened room at Rothko's request.

How nice to have some control over how people view something you've created, or at least how it is framed.

The paintings are in a room of their own but it feels too small to hold them today. I pick the largest mural and sit square in front of it on a big bench with my back to the doorway. The lights are dimmed, as always. At first, I can still hear the video installation from next door but soon all I know is the low hum of the red on the paintings. I'm looking at one but I can feel them all. I need to unfocus; let everything open and my eyes go loose.

I breathe in the different shades, from maroon and burgundy to oxblood and cherry. Since I've been dreaming in disturbing technicolour for eight weeks now and the professionals don't have an answer, I'm trying my own breed of overexposure colour therapy, like when you smoke a whole packet of cigarettes to try to put you off ever wanting one again.

Jade Grace is right.

'Expose yourself to what you're afraid of.'

I push the thought that it's Friday today to a dark corner of my mind; Fridays are the worst kind of red. I try to expose myself to the colours and to let go.

As the reds and darks charge through me, the bench starts to sway as the knots and lines on the wooden floor twist and contort. The grey walls behind the murals close in like a storm. My forehead is fuzzy and heavy, pressing down on my eyes and forcing them shut. The red soaks through my eyelids as I push down the panic and focus on the pledge.

We pledge ourselves to the will of the muses, and to the words of the greats. We give it to art and we let go.

'Hey, Lux.'

I hadn't felt anyone sit down next to me but that voice is distinctive. A dark croak that doesn't match the light of its owner.

It's Cal.

Sitting next to me.

Saying my name.

How long has he been there?

He's next to me in this womb-like room, which, for some reason, is embarrassing.

I turn to him. His eyes are silver and gold, moonlight trapped in ancient amber. They're not; they're brown. But they are beautiful.

Suddenly I know deep within myself that he's going to kiss me. That we'll be like two beautiful people biting opposite sides of the same ripe peach.

Except that he doesn't. He just pushes his hair back from his face. We're in the minority of Artists whose hair is still the colour we were born with. Evidently, Cal can express himself without dyeing his hair a colour not found in nature and I'm doing my best to appear average, outwardly at least. Though maybe I'll dye it to be like Jade Grace.

'Hi,' he says again, then adds his name, 'Cal.'

'Hey.'

We sit in silence, almost forever, until he rasps: 'There's a great story to these paintings, you know – they were originally painted for a restaurant.' He looks at the time on his phone. 'Better find Luca. See you downstairs.'

I will that full stop to be a semicolon; I need there to be

more. I flash a prayer to God or Calliope or Simon Cowell for a new chance, a new paragraph. But he's gone.

I'm left absorbing the murals. The darks and reds swim as my head fills with blood. The paintings morph into faceless oblong bodies turning inside out, displaying their crimson hearts and bulging arteries to the world. My blood runs hard through my veins; the red cells are like spiked stars carrying death around my body instead of oxygen, too numerous and violent for my white cells to defeat. I wish they'd given me a transfusion in the hospital, but even if they had, all the clean stranger blood would have been replaced with more of my own by now.

Breathe, I instruct my lungs.

It's not real.

The painting leaks off the edges of the huge canvas in front of me, on to and down the walls, dripping its oily blood on to the floor and down into the metal grates.

Just breathe.

Oxygen floods me and my own blood roars. The spikes thunder against my insides, desperate to shred their way out. The paintings sing their lowest, reddest notes and my pulse thumps in my brain as the bandage on my arm strangles it tight, tight, tighter. My fingers tear through the dressing and surgical tape holding me together. My seams are split and red seeps out of me, chanting through the cut on my arm, over my wrist and down my fingers.

Relief.

I press my hands together as if in prayer, passing the red hum from one to the other.

It feels peaceful to fall apart.

I blink and shake my head until the paintings reconstitute themselves.

I am calmer now but dizzy.

So dizzy.

The floor spins, rises up, catches me roughly.

I drag myself up from the ground onto the bench, pull down my sleeve and lie on my back. Just as I've closed my eyes, a voice says, 'Are you OK, miss? Miss?'

'I have to rest,' I say.

'Miss, I'm sorry but you can't lie down here.'

I force myself up again.

A little girl and her mother are hovering over me with a gallery attendant.

'Come on, Immy,' says the mother but they don't move.

'What's wrong with the lady?' the girl asks.

'She's not feeling well,' her mother answers.

What lady?

Oh, she means me.

The attendant puts a firm hand on my shoulder and I shake it off.

'There's nothing wrong with me.' My voice comes out louder than I mean it to.

'Miss, you need to calm down or I'll have to get security.'

The mother reaches into her nappy bag and pulls something out to give to me. I stare at her outstretched hand. A Wet Wipe hangs from her fingers like a limp white flag.

The girl stares up at me. She's barely as tall as the bench I'm sitting on, but brave. I look up at her mother and the attendant, less brave.

'For your hands,' the lady says.

I look down to my lap where they're wringing each other, smeared with blood. A little goes a long way. It seems important to her that I clean them.

My legs feel light, like the air is too thin, so I use my hands to push myself up off the bench.

I take the Wet Wipe.

I surrender.

'Come on, Immy,' says the lady.

The child's little pink face is level with two faint red handprints on the bench. Mine. Should I wipe it clean?

Her mother lifts her and strides away.

I yell after them: 'There's nothing wrong with me.'

'Miss. I won't tell you again,' warns the attendant, reaching for her radio.

'I'm going, I'm going,' I say.

I turn round to the door where Director Harrins is hovering, about to intervene. I hope he wasn't watching me the whole time.

'I'll take her out,' he says to the attendant. 'She's sorry.'

He leads me away from the paintings, the handprints, the now quiet room.

'Are you OK?' he asks.

I nod. A fine spray still veils my vision like the pink mist from the war poem he read us. He takes the wipe from me, folds it and pushes it into the dark of his pocket like a secret.

We head to the down escalator.

'Jesus, Lux, are you OK?' asks Mei when we reach them.

'I knew we shouldn't have let you go off by yourself,' says Olivia.

'She wasn't by herself, girls,' says Director Harrins. They all look at each other like I'm not there and I realise he was watching me the whole time I was with the paintings.

'I'm fine,' I say.

'You're shaking.' I'm not sure which one of them says this; I'm too busy concentrating on not passing out.

'Let's get her outside,' Director Harrins says. 'I knew this was a mistake.'

Out in the air, everyone tries not to stare while I pull myself together. Someone says something about blood sugar and runs off to buy some chocolate.

'I've seen this on TV,' says Mei. 'We need to put a Mars bar up her bum.'

'That's for diabetics and I don't think it's true.'

'Oh. Can't hurt for her to eat it though.'

Chocolate is contraband on campus but we're not technically there so Director Harrins allows it and my breathing eventually regulates.

'OK?' asks Director Daniels.

I nod. I don't know her very well; she teaches all the Art Commerce classes that I try to avoid.

On the way back to the coach, the directors make us wait at a crossing even though nothing is coming and we'll all be out crossing roads unsupervised and probably drunk this time next year. Although our various body parts are insured and the tragic loss of an Artist is always exciting news, they'd rather avoid the paperwork so we wait for the green man.

Cal is telling whoever will listen that humans shouldn't have invented electronic crossings as now our lives are run by machines that we programmed to talk.

He's right because now they control us. They show us what's inside our heads and tell us when to walk and boss us about when they're supposed to be our faithful servants.

'We must never teach them to paint,' says Cal, and then he and his friends stride ahead to the coach.

I tell Mei and Olivia about my conversation with him. I repeat our words verbatim but leave out the bit about thinking he was going to kiss me and the part where I almost had a nervous breakdown just from looking at paintings.

'What do you think he meant?' whispers Olivia.

'He meant he had to find Luca and he'd see her downstairs,' says Mei.

'I meant do you think he was looking for you?'

'No, but I think Director Harrins might have been stalking me,' I laugh.

'Do you like Cal?' asks Mei with her usual subtlety.

'I could talk to him for you,' says Olivia. 'We have some classes together.'

'Please don't,' I say.

The space between my ears throbs and I realise I'm clenching and unclenching my fists. Lately, rain makes my hands ache. Or maybe I saw that in a film sometime. On cue, it starts to spit. If we were the type of people to carry umbrellas, we'd put them up now in anticipation of a deluge. But, even in this city of umbrellas and filthy rain, we're too young for that.

After supper, I feel the hand ache leading to another headache. My best estimate gives me twenty minutes before it gets too painful to stay awake. I brush my teeth, hard, and spit blood, then go back to our room and pick up a top from my bed.

'You've folded that one already,' Mei says. She's sitting on the floor among her mess, cutting and sticking things on to mood boards.

'How can you tell? They all look the same.' She's right though, I've been folding and refolding the same black jumpers since we got back to our room from dinner. Greens, brown rice and protein, as always. I put chilli on mine and it burned my raw gums. My eyes streamed in a release of sorts.

Folding clothes is one of the things I do when my head fills with colours and words. Sometimes I don't even relise I'm doing it.

'This is a good one of Jade.' She holds the page up for me to see.

'Can I have it?'

'Sure. If you want.' Mei cuts the page from her magazine and hands it to me.

'Do we have any Blu-Tack?'

'On my desk.'

I stick Jade on the wall so she can watch over us.

I get on to my bed and pull out my laptop. She still hasn't replied to my message. Maybe it got lost. I send another.

Please, Jade, I just want to talk to you. Please, please message me back. I feel like I know you.

Lux

PS I'm at Richdeane

I search for new news about her. We're supposed to use our judgement with regards to the internet. I don't know if Richdeane secretly monitors us. I hope not because last term, Mei and I went on YouPorn to see what all the fuss was about. The women in the videos didn't look like us. Most didn't have any body hair; some had a tiny tuft between their legs just to prove they could grow it, I guess. We flicked through a few of the clips, thinking they'd be different, but they were all the same. I found them sort of frightening. I think Mei did too because she laughed and said, 'This is lame,' then closed the site and put on *Spring Breakers*, a film about finding your soulmates.

Anyway, I'm not looking for porn today. It's a consultation I'm after. I always delete my browser history because I read somewhere that our search engines know us better than we know ourselves but, if I didn't, all my listed searches would start with 'Symptoms +'.

The gallery plan failed miserably and I only have until Christmas to find out what's wrong with me and get better. My stomach clenches and spits acids up towards my heart at the thought of feeling like this forever or having to see my parents.

Calm down.

I allow myself to think about Cal for a few seconds. He could be the ultimate pledge; I wonder how he ended up in a place like Richdeane. He must have just come for the art.

I ask Dr Google about 'Symptoms + dizziness + panic + red dreams'. It gives me all the usual results; all the things the professionals say they've ruled out even though they've only asked me the same questions over and over again.

I need to make my search terms more specific, so I add 'art gallery + extreme reaction' to the list in case galleries are secretly made of asbestos or something.

Search. *Click. Click. Click.*

Buried a few clicks deeper is a link that takes me through to Wikipedia.

It reads: 'Stendhal syndrome. A psychosomatic disorder that causes rapid heartbeat, dizziness, fainting, confusion and even hallucinations when an individual is exposed to an experience of great personal significance, particularly when viewing art.'

'You OK?' asks Mei.

'Yeah?'

'You flinched.'

'Getting a headache.'

'*... when an individual is exposed to an experience of great personal experience, particularly when viewing art.*'

Pain tightens along my shoulders and up the back of my head like a coat hanger made of spikes.

I'm so stupid. Of course I don't have Stendhal syndrome. I spent four weeks interning at a gallery feeling absolutely fine, better than fine actually, and the two months since have been the worst of my life and I hadn't been near a gallery until today. This has nothing to do with art.

I snap off my light and wait for the red pain to come.

Mei wakes in the night to find me looking for something to force open my head with to release the pressure. There's an explosion in there and it needs to get out. My eyes aren't working properly and my hands are thick and clumsy. The astronaut suit is back.

'Where's the corkscrew?' I try to say but my saliva glands go into overdrive and my mouth fills with water. I run to the bathroom and vomit up a waterfall of acid and some of the pain.

'Lux, this isn't right,' says Mei. 'Should I wake the duty director?'

I shake my head and the movement sends shockwaves around my brain and eyes. My skin screams.

'Maybe you should go back to the hospital for more tests?' It hurts too much to remind her I'm still waiting for some results.

Once I've finished throwing up, we go back to sleep.

SEVEN

Mei and Olivia follow me around like bodyguards for a few days after the corkscrew incident. Between that and the scene I made at the Tate, I'm pretty sure they think I'm losing it.

Word must be spreading because Isabella and even our wider circle of friends still seem to be keeping their distance as if I'm contagious. They prefer Lux with the party favours to Blackout Girl. So do I.

I manage to avoid Dr Baystone all week and Olivia somehow convinces the head director to let me go to her parents' house for a family gathering at the weekend.

So on Saturday, after assembly, Olivia, Mei and I take the train across county lines to West Sussex.

For some reason, it's deemed OK for us to take trains away from the city, just not into it. I try not to stress about the position of our carriage at the front of the train. I read this morning that the safest place to sit is a middle carriage, facing backwards. In any case, I have to settle for just the sitting backwards part of the advice.

We sit drinking coffees (black for Olivia, the ice-creamy kind with a straw for Mei and me) in caffeinated rebellion. Heading away from Richdeane, my organs start to unclench. It's easier to pretend to be OK when you're not under surveillance.

A small wind farm reflects in Olivia's sunglasses. They're the extra-tall turbines that can access 'better wind' and carry bigger blades. There was a presentation about renewable energy in assembly last term because the head director wants Richdeane to run on sunshine and air like us one day. Their synchronicity is hypnotic; each revolution a wink from the universe. If they started to march, I would follow them anywhere.

'Earth to Lux,' says Mei.

Olivia suggests we play a game.

'How about Shag, Collab or Kill?'

We end up in a full-on debate about who we would shag, collaborate with or kill. We're all too peaceful to kill anyone – though we do debate the relative merits of a certain young male pop star snuff movie – so we just end up with a heavily caveated list of people we want to collaborate with one way or another. I beg them to put Jade Grace at the top.

Lawrence, Olivia's brother, picks us up from the station. He is rounder than last time I saw him. He smiles so hard upon seeing his sister that his eyes all but disappear into his newly chubby face.

'You've certainly got the tortured Artist look down,' he says, surveying our black clothes. I hate that, the idea that creativity and craziness go hand-in-hand, but I don't say anything because these days I'm pretty close to living that stereotype.

Mei calls shotgun, and she and Olivia clamber into the muddy Land Rover while I offer Lawrence a hand with our stuff.

'No need, thanks though.' He takes our bags and slings them into the boot, then peers at me. 'How are you doing anyway?'

'I'm OK. Thanks though.'

Their house is in the kind of village where people have honesty boxes at the end of their driveways to sell garden-grown broccoli and rare-breed duck eggs. It's very, very safe.

Her parents have been renovating since the dawn of time, before our mothers met at childbirth classes when they were pregnant with us. Every time the house is almost finished, Jasmine is overcome with inspiration and changes the theme. It's a beautiful house, big and warm.

The last time we were here, we smoked and sniffed things, and taught ourselves to drive on their fleet of ride-on lawnmowers. Her parents were away, as always. In fact, this is the first time in years they're home when we're visiting.

Jasmine hugs me before she hugs her daughter.

'My darling girl,' she says in a tone that makes me think she might cry. 'I spoke with your mum earlier – she sends her love.'

'Thanks.' My cheeks pulse as I clench my teeth at the thought of my parents.

'It's good to see you looking so well.'

Clearly my mother has filled her in on my blackout.

'Mum,' warns Olivia.

Jasmine flushes. 'Come here, Mei, darling.'

She hugs Mei and finally reaches for Olivia who looks more like Jasmine than I remember. Both are slim and poised with smoke-thin blonde hair. Olivia's has pastel-pink tips, at which Jasmine flinches but says nothing. She gives Olivia a light hug and scrapes her daughter's hair up to mirror the bun style she herself wears, a throwback to her days as a not-quite-prima ballerina. She has nothing to secure the strands with so lets them fall, a delicate disappointment clouding her face.

Caterers have taken over the kitchen and a couple of girls set up under Jasmine's watchful eye. Everyone takes it in turns to fall over Scruffs, the Whetstones' Labrador, until she's dispatched out into the garden for the evening.

We help Olivia's stepfather, Francis, bring up bottles from the cellar. He uncorks the Burgundy to let it breathe. I hear vapours curl through the open lips of the bottles.

'We picked this up on a booze cruise to Calais. Panic-buying for party season,' he explains. 'Social lubricant.'

'Grim,' says Olivia and we go up to her bedroom. It's the same as it was when she left for prep school, a shrine to her eight-year-old dog-loving ballerina self.

We do our hair and change into our evening blacks.

'Can I borrow your brush?' asks Mei. She tugs it through her hair and hands it back to me filled with long strands that are black for the first fifteen centimetres and royal blue for the next twenty.

She clocks me looking at the hair. She grabs the brush back and pulls the hair out of the bristles before returning to me. 'You never used to care about hair contagion.'

When we're ready, we take photos of ourselves making peace fingers to display the matching snowdrops tattoos on our left wrists and post them online. Would they be offended if I got my snowdrop lasered away? I look puffy from the medication and my gums are red from pummelling them with my toothbrush too often.

I won't hold my breath waiting for Cal to like the pictures but part of me hopes he will. We haven't spoken since our two-sentence exchange at the Tate and I need an excuse to talk to him.

'Red carpet ready,' announces Mei and we go downstairs to join the party.

Time to perform.

Apart from Lawrence and the girls doing the rounds with canapés, we are the youngest by at least twenty-five years. Olivia's parents are relaxed about us drinking: 'If you're sure you can, Lux? Make sure you eat something then.' I'm not supposed to drink on my medication but it's not like we're doing shots so we take the opportunity to (de)hydrate with the sweet rosé they bought specially for us.

'I'm not much of a sweet tooth,' says Jasmine. She doesn't eat any of the canapés except for one butternut soup shot served in an espresso cup, so I guess she's not much of a savoury tooth either. Lawrence's chubbiness is starting to look like an act of rebellion.

Olivia grew up at parties like this; she coasts effortlessly on the runoff of spilt cocktails. I wonder if my parents throw parties in Singapore, and try to ape her self-possession and social fluency while I talk to the adults. In two months, legally at least, I will be one myself. I feel younger than I've ever felt.

One of the neighbours is Kathleen Crown, the Minister for Arts. I kiss the air near both her cheeks and look directly into her eyes as I peel my lips back from my teeth into what I hope is a respectful smile, even though my real smile has no teeth. I tell her it's nice to meet her and nod as she talks. That's active listening. We learn soft skills at Richdeane too. She says she's visiting Richdeane soon and she'll look out for me.

Olivia's parents' friends, the West Sussex glitterati, murmur their approval as we answer questions about our art. 'I don't know how you do it, focusing on one thing so young – it's a very mature attitude,' they marvel.

People always think we're older than we are. They don't know that Richdeane promises to teach us what it calls 'maturity of expression' and what normal people call 'using big words and thinking a lot'.

We practise key messages in Media & Discretion Coaching so we give them the rote answer: 'It's how we develop into Artists; we trust our directors.' We leave out our obligation to the pledge; Richdeane is nothing if not discrete regarding its methods. Satisfied that we are not under undue pressure, they say stuff like, 'Our son is off to study horticulture. Smart kid. Hedges over hedge funds these days.' Then they wander off to find more prawn skewers, giddy with their own wit.

Later, when all the champagne has been drunk and they've moved on to brandy, they all become experts on coalition governments, international relations and pretty much anything else they can think of. Our maturity of expression doesn't extend to these topics because we don't watch the news, so we resort to nodding and smiling. The Richdeane factory default setting.

The conversations turn to things like, 'I heard he was paid a huge advance for his next play. Not a word written yet,' and, 'Plugging pension deficits with pictures, whatever next.' Others join in, monologuing about 'casino arts' and 'that's how we got into a mess last time, betting on things that didn't exist'. I haven't been drinking lately so I'm woozy from too much wine, but I think I understand what they mean: art is not safe.

Olivia steers us to a corner once we've done the rounds and, at midnight, we wave off Kathleen Crown and the last of the other guests.

'I'm glad you girls got to meet the minister. Your mother hoped she would come,' says Francis. 'Speaking of, where is your mother, Livvy? Jasmine. Jas, where are you, darling?' he calls into the big house. 'Livvy, see if you can locate your mother, would you? I'm going to let Scruffs in.'

Jasmine might not have much of a sweet tooth but she sure was thirsty. Olivia and I find her in the pantry, shimmying to music only she can hear and slopping her martini on to the floor. She is inordinately excited to see us and starts jumping up and down so the shoestring straps of her dress slip. The dress falls to her waist and reveals her tiny breasts. (We call this a 'nip slip' or a 'wardrobe malfunction' in the trade.) My cheeks burn on her behalf but she doesn't seem to notice. Olivia rearranges her mother's dress and lifts the glass from her hand. Scruffs skids into the pantry to join us and helps by licking up the gin puddles. I'm not sure a drunk dog is what this situation needs, but nobody else seems to be concerned. Francis suggests we all go to bed and let the housekeeper tidy the rest in the morning.

There are plenty of spare rooms, but Mei, Olivia and I

all squash into Olivia's bed with a swiped bottle of Francis's Laphroaig – 'the most punishing of whiskies', according to him. We give the standard toast: 'To art and we let go,' and talk for a long time, but it doesn't feel like we're sharing the same conversation, just that we're waiting for the other two to stop talking so we can talk some more ourselves.

I try to explain the gamble we're all taking, putting all our faith in the pledge, but they just murmur like they don't understand and are too tired to try. I give up and they drop heavily into sleep. I take a few more swigs from the bottle, enough to hold back the technicolour dreams, I hope.

Sunday. A milky yellow day with letters that are raised and bubbly like fridge magnets. We do our pledge contemplation in bed and then Jasmine brings us eggs and leftover madeleines. She hands Olivia a green juice and gives Mei and me orange and mango ones.

She looks unrested but none of us say anything about her performance last night. Olivia will bring it up if she wants to discuss it. You can give your own parents bad reviews but never someone else's. I haven't told Mei and Olivia about the daily fights I had with mine this summer.

'Cheers,' says Olivia. 'To art.'

'What is that anyway?'

'Kale juice. Tastes like an allotment but it cleans the blood. At least according to my mother.' Olivia holds her nose and downs it, then pops half a madeleine into her mouth.

'And the cake chaser?' asks Mei.

'Yin and yang, my friend. It's all about balance.'

I check my phone for the tenth time since I opened my eyes. My heart gives an embarrassing little squelch; Cal has liked all of our photos.

We get back to Richdeane in time for supper. In the dining hall, everyone shovels down their food without questioning what's in it. What if there's something in the water? A biohack, excitotoxins, or an experiment that's slowly poisoning us. They could feed us the excess insect population from around campus and we'd chew and swallow in blind faith.

By the time the sun dips at around seven p.m., a creative fever spreads among the night Artists, the owls, which will peak in about six hours' time before breaking at around four a.m.

Back in our room, Mei hacks up magazines. There are remnants all over the floor where she's pushed the discarded bits off the side of her bed. She rips out pictures of people on red carpets and at exhibition openings, trims their torn edges and sticks them in her covet book.

There's a pile of cut-out Jade Graces on my bedside table, which Mei has donated me because I've added a few more pictures of her to the one on the wall. She watches as I embalm different-sized Jades with glue and repeatedly lay her to rest between the pages of my hardback notebook. I close the pages and press her to sleep with some of the lyrics from her songs. *They say we're made of stardust, break ourselves to find out, watch it all come pouring down.'* As I hum the song, I see notes on sheet music, stuck in time like deformed tadpoles.

Maybe Olivia's dancing will land her on one of those red carpets one day. Mei could be her agent. I'll be there too, but I don't know what I'll be doing exactly. My mother used to say my problem is that I can't decide whether I'm whisky or camomile. It's actually more like I don't know whether I'm the lamb or the slaughter, but I'm surprised she even knows me that well. I hope Cal will be there too. We'll be so close that when the wind blows our clothes will kiss.

I close my palm around a cut-out of Jade's head, her red hair bleeding down her shoulders.

'How's your head?' Mei asks.

'It's OK, thanks.'

It was such a relief to have a good time at Olivia's. Hopefully, it will get back to the head director that I managed not to have meltdown or a migraine. All I need to do is sit tight until my final test results come back so I can get on the right medication. Then things can get back to normal.

'No looking for corkscrews in your sleep tonight?'

'Can't make any promises.'

I check my messages. Nothing from Jade. Two 'we love you' emails from my mother. A few from my personal adviser. And a reminder from Dr Baystone that we have an appointment tomorrow. I rub the cut on my arm through the dressing until it weeps.

Mei gets into bed as Olivia messages us both goodnight. Although she's the third image in our triptych, her room is actually in Ibsen House.

Once Mei falls asleep, the quiet grows loud and bright. I'm tired but I know I'm not ready for sleep yet.

My father once told me if he complained he couldn't sleep his mother would make him stand under a light looking up until he begged her to go back to bed. Mei is a lark and although she sleeps like a dead person she's unlikely to respond well to this kind of nocturnal experiment. Plus, whatever is in my head is demanding fresh air, so I creep out on to the balcony for the first time since I got back.

Dylan House is the newest building so Mei and I have one of the best rooms on campus with a balcony overlooking the studios and the grounds towards the woods. I always thought the trees were there to keep the baddies out but maybe they're really to keep us in.

Out on the balcony, I stay close to the wall. I'm not scared of heights but something tells me if I get too close to the glass facade it will give way or I'll lose my mind and climb over. Jade's words glow neon in my head as I hold her paper head in my fist. I open my hand and she flies away, a deformed butterfly riding the wind, and then she's gone. As if letting go is that simple.

I drop down onto the stone slabs, sitting cross-legged against the wall, soaking up the cold and looking out through the glass. I am a cold-blooded creature in a glass tank.

No. I'm real. I'm a person with a family and friends.

I run through the pictures in my mental darkroom. My mother. My father. Mei, Olivia, Henry. Olivia's parents. Cal. The head director. They start blurry then reveal themselves like old-school Polaroids.

Georgia. Dr Baystone. Cal again. My boss from the gallery. Jade Grace. A guy from an advert that was on TV every time I turned it on last year. A girl with red hair but no face – probably Jade again. Dr Purves. The side-boob shrink. Other professionals.

The CCTV camera mounted at the base of our balcony clicks and whirs as it adjust its position to track whatever dares approach Dylan House where we precious, or do I mean precocious, Artists sleep. I can't help wondering who is on the other end of the camera lenses and where they are. Are they critics, voyeurs or saviours? How long would it take for an actual human to come and save me if something came out of the woods?

There's a muffled snuffle below me, then a fox reveals itself. Its jaundiced gaze meets mine for a second then it bows its head and trots away, nose to the ground and luxurious tail wagging. I watch it as it zigzags across the grass, gathering pace, disappearing into the thick trees.

Lights are still on in the studios opposite. They're static but they seem to twinkle. One of them might be Cal's. I don't know if he's an owl or a lark, or both.

I lie down and stare up through the open roof of my tank. The cold air clings to me, reaching through my astronaut suit and cooling my thoughts and bones.

Threads of grey cloud streak the sky and across the half-moon. Beyond the clouds, invisible planets tumble round the sun and the smattering of stars seem closer than they are. The more I look, the more of them I see, like an endless chandelier piercing holes through the dark gauze of the sky above my tank.

Maybe I'm lost somewhere out there in that great big terrible sky. Is it even the same one that Mei, Olivia and I slept under when summer began?

I keep staring till I see only stars.

When all the lights in the studios are extinguished, I am numb with cold. Now it's dark enough to sleep.

EIGHT

I sneak back into our room just as the cold dawn breaks over Richdeane.

Later, Dr Baystone finds me on the field under the smoking trees sitting among the fallen conkers, their fuzzy coats making them look like baby hedgehogs. I don't know why we call them the smoking trees – a throwback to when it was the best place to be seen smoking by your peers but not the directors maybe. I ignored his email reminder about meeting him at the talking rooms. I figured I'd just say I hadn't seen it in time.

'Hi, Dr Baystone,' I say.

'Paul will do,' he replies. 'May I sit?'

'We're not allowed to call you by your first names any more,' I say.

'You?'

'You being the tutors.'

'I see. May I?'

'Sure. Sorry.'

'Thanks.' He sits down, not too close, and folds his long legs under him, then he changes his mind and stretches them out in front.

I crack my neck; it's stiff from sleeping on the balcony and I can't seem to get warm again after a night outside.

'So, Lux,' he says, 'or am I supposed to call you Miss Langley?'

He's got to be at least forty; he can call me whatever he wants.

'Lux is fine.'

'Lux is it then. I'm still getting used to the rules here. It seemed like there weren't any at first, but I'm realising there are actually quite a few.'

'Is this the bit where you slag off the man to build trust with me?' I say.

'Just an observation,' he says.

'Sorry, that was rude,' I apologise.

'That's OK.'

'We just have to stick to the pledge, wear black and eat what we're told. That's pretty much it,' I say. 'Oh, and we're encouraged to go to assembly to hear the shares.'

'I see. Sounds simple when you put it like that. I assume drugs and alcohol are no go too.' He looks across the grounds over the still lake into the fields beyond. 'Some people call me Dr B.'

In the distance where he's looking, there's a row of decommissioned power pylons, their towering steel skeletons now cancerous with rust. If you get close to the lake, they reflect in its surface like dying giants. They represent a Richdeane eco triumph – a hard-fought battle by the head director to turn the campus green. Too sick for salvage, their metal bones will eventually be amputated and dismembered but, for now, they rest, monuments to the recent past.

'Sorry I didn't come to our appointment,' I say.

'That's OK, we're both here now,' he says. His notebook lies on the grass in between us. 'So, why don't you tell me a little bit about yourself.'

'No offence, but I don't think we need to do this. I don't know if the head director told you, but I'm just waiting to find out what medication I need to take.'

'That's one of the things I wanted us to talk about, if that's OK?'

My heart gets all twitchy. This is it. 'Do you know what's wrong with me?'

He opens his notebook and reads: 'Full blood count, urea and electrolytes, liver and thyroid function were unremarkable, as were the results of the physical examination. The MRI scan of your brain and cervical spine were normal, as were all the other results.'

'So, I failed the tests?' I ask. I am unremarkable. Damning feedback from the battery of checks. The grass shines greener and ripples around us like a sick sea.

'This all means you're physically OK,' he says. 'You look disappointed.'

'So they can't help me?' My ribcage shrinks and pinches around my lungs and heart.

'They think your headaches are relevant,' he says. 'And the fact that you can't remember what happened before you lost consciousness.'

'No shit,' I say. 'Sorry.'

'They think the underlying cause is psychological. Do you know what that means?'

I shake my head and he says: 'The recommended treatment is pain management in the short term and talking therapy in the longer term.'

'I don't want to talk – I want to get better and be normal.'

'I'm going to level with you,' he says. 'I think it'll take you a lot longer to feel better if you don't commit to helping yourself.'

'Have you treated someone like me before?'

'Not exactly.'

My stomach hurts and I would cry if I could but I think if I did my head would shatter into a million pieces. All the pictures in my darkroom would get mixed up with the grass and the bugs; just the thought of it makes me feel dirty.

'You were hoping you could just take a tablet for all this?' he asks. 'I don't think it's that simple.'

'I talked to other shrinks before I came back to school and it didn't work. There must be a different medicine I can try?'

'I'm afraid talking with me isn't optional if you want to stay here. The head director and your parents are really very worried about you and they're not convinced this is a safe place for you at the moment.'

'Where do they want me to go?' I ask.

'To be with your mum and dad.'

The most unsafe place of all. Panic forces my eyes shut.

'That can't happen.'

I know the answers are here somewhere. In the city. In Jade Grace. The sky.

And proximity to my parents can only amplify my failure. We will fight. They'll lie to me. It will hurt. Worse, if I am close to them, I will be able to feel their love on my skin like sunburn. They will want things from me, like information and to know that I feel their love and reciprocate with some home-grown sentiment of my own. I can't give them what they want at the moment, not without falling apart.

'I can't breathe,' I say.

'Yes, you can,' he says. 'Your body doesn't forget how to breathe; it's automatic.'

'I'll never find out what's wrong with me if I have to leave.' I want to escape him but I can't move and my eyes won't open.

'Lux, I want you to open your eyes and name three things that you can see.'

'I can't. I can't breathe.' I scrunch my eyelids but the colours of the field and the sky force themselves into my brain, flooding it.

'You can. Now, deep breath, open your eyes, then name one thing you can see. Ready? Breathe.'

This must be what it feels like at the top of a mountain where the air is thin or what fish experience when they're pulled from the sea.

'Open your eyes, Lux. And say what you see.'

'Pink flowers.' The words are barely audible.

'Good. Now breathe. Now another thing.'

'Black pylons.'

'And one more,' he says.

His eyes are locked on mine when I manage to hone in on his face. 'You?'

'OK. Are you back?'

'I think so.'

He's the first person to reach me for weeks, but I look away from him and focus on the pylons again. Maybe they won't be scrapped. Maybe they'll be left behind forever so that families of future tourists can visit, imagining the hum of the grid while they picnic. An alternative to Stonehenge.

'I'm scared.' The cut on my arm is bleeding again and there's blood under my fingernails. 'I don't want to fail any more tests and I can't take much more pain.'

'I'm not going to hurt you. I'm going to ask you to do three things and I'm going to help you with all of them. Do you have a pen to write them down?'

'I always have a pen. I'm a writer,' I tell him, even though I've written nothing but messages to Jade Grace since my blackout.

He dictates while I write:

1. *Attend Dr B's Live Performance classes.*

2. *Meet with Dr B when he asks me to and ask him if I feel I need to meet with him outside these times.*

3. *Write down everything my mind tells me, even if I don't think it's the truth or it seems insignificant.*

'I think that's enough for today unless you have any questions,' he says.

I shake my head so he stands up and brushes bits of grass off his trousers. As he walks away, a few stubborn petals cling to the backs of his knees.

He turns back to call: 'Same time, same place, tomorrow?'

He seems to be the only person with a plan for helping me. And the alternative is to be sent away, so I nod.

'And I'm going to let the head director and your parents know we're going to be meeting regularly. OK?'

'OK.'

'Excellent.'

I get the feeling this is the start of a routine that will last for the remainder of my final orbit of the sun at Richdeane; I give him an inch and we both pretend it's a mile.

NINE

The following Friday, Cal and I stand facing each other. Fridays are the texture of wet wood, so I woke up expecting the worst. I skipped my morning pledge and here I am, less than a metre from Cal, steadfastly peeling a mango, letting the skin drop to the floor.

He looks at me for emotional or behavioural clues and finally croaks: 'You can't let go.'

'I can't let go?' I echo. The question mark hangs in the air. I blink it away and refocus on Cal.

'You can't let go,' he says again.

'I can't let go.'

'You can't let go. You want to but you're holding back.'

'I'm holding back.' It's hard to peel a mango while maintaining eye contact and repeating what someone is saying.

'You're holding yourself back and that's holding me back,' he says.

'I'm holding you back,' I say.

'You're holding me back.'

I catch a flash in his eye, a twitch in his cheek, telling me what to say next.

'I'm holding you back and you're getting angry.' A coil of mango skin falls to our feet. The skin is the body's largest organ. Some killers peel their victims and make lampshades or clothes from the skin. They climb inside the fabric of the people they've murdered and wear them like jumpsuits.

'I'm getting angry,' he repeats.

'You're angry,' I say.

'I'm angry.'

'You're angry that I won't talk to you.'

'I'm angry that you're rejecting me.' His shoulders start to sag; it's so easy for him to know how he feels. 'I'm trying to reach you, but all you want to do is peel your sad little mango.'

'I'm rejecting you because I want to peel my sad mango.'

Cal searches my teddy-bear-feelings face for the truthful thing to say to continue our volley when another voice chimes in. 'Enough.' Dr Baystone gets to his feet and steps up on to the raised platform with us. 'Let's remind ourselves of the purpose of this exercise. It's to get you out of your heads and behaving instinctively, responding to the other actor.'

It turns out Dr Baystone trained as an actor under someone who trained under the late, great acting teacher Sanford Meisner himself. (He refers to Sanford as Sandy. Just Sandy, like Moses or Allah or Madonna.) Neither Cal nor Dr Baystone were here last year and I want them to know that I would have nailed this six months ago. I would have contorted my face into shapes of exquisite anguish and elation for the crowd and loved it.

'Cal, good work. How did it feel? How did you feel, I should say,' Dr Baystone asks.

Cal looks at my feet and the mango detritus. This is our first real interaction since the Tate and it's not going well. He says: 'I felt like there was a screen between us. I was trying to reach through it but every time I did she shut down a little more.'

'And how did that make you feel?'

'I wanted to connect with her and I felt like she cared more about making fruit salad.'

'Good, good. You listened, you searched for an authentic connection. You committed to the truth of the moment. Take a seat.'

Cal gives me a little nod, then hops off the stage and goes back to his seat in the front row of the audience where twelve or so critics, aka my fellow Artists, take notes and underline key words emphatically.

'Lux,' says Dr Baystone, 'did you feel how upset Cal was? Why didn't you allow him to connect with you?'

'I was trying to do my activity like you told me,' I say. 'I needed to peel the mango so I could use it for my Culinary Arts coursework. I was on deadline. Those were my imaginary circumstances.'

'You used the mango to avoid connecting with Cal. You were not acting truthfully. The exercise is about truth. Let me ask you something else: what's holding you back?'

These are precisely the kind of psychobabble tangents I was hoping to avoid. I thought acting was about pretending to be someone else; why is it suddenly all about who I am?

I can see Dr Baystone will find it hard to let go himself now he's on this riff so I need to give him something. We learned this in Media & Discretion Coaching. Always avoid a 'no comment' if you can – give them a morsel and tell them you shouldn't be telling them it so they feel like they're getting something bigger. The power of information is all in the way it's framed. We can't control what others say about us, but we can control what we say about ourselves.

'If you could just give me a real script, I could try to act it. I just don't think this is how real people talk.'

'Emotions are real,' he counters. 'Acting is doing. It's tedious for an audience if you just put another mask on top of the one you're already wearing. The goal is to animate the character with your own, uninhibited feelings. And, remember, it's always you.'

I get the feeling he read that in a book but I nod and try to distinguish my face from my mask as he continues, maintaining hypnotic levels of eye contact. Where is that kindness he showed me out on the field? Is he tough-loving me?

'On a positive note, I could see you weren't trying to steal the scene with your activity like some of your fellow Artists have been guilty of. We'll try again next time. Next pair. Georgia, Davy, on stage, please.'

I scoop the mango entrails from the stage while Georgia and Davy throw themselves on to the platform, delighted to follow my failure. We've been doing this exercise all morning so they know the drill. They work for an hour or so, bouncing off each other and crying, shouting, laughing as they freewheel round the sad, mad, glad cycle. It's compelling and makes me feel more distant than ever.

When class is done, I start composing an apology to Cal, but Dr Baystone stops me and does a mini monologue rich in rhetorical questions. As question marks obscure my view, he makes his voice low and quiet so I have to lean in to hear him. Talk about passive aggressive.

'Lux, I need more from you. So does your partner. I'm trying to help you stay here. If you don't engage or connect, the Artist you're paired with can't do the work either. OK? These exercises are absolutely fundamental to the pledge. You're safe here; you can trust me on that. But you're depriving yourself of a basic human experience by keeping those walls up. So, let's see if we can't bring them down. Open you up a bit. OK. OK, Lux?'

'OK.'

But the walls have already come down. The membranes between my senses are flimsy and patched together with soluble sutures that disintegrate at random. And my heart is always open and ready to receive – the wind must have changed the day I blacked out and now it's permanently agape.

'I'm trying to help you get to the truth, Lux,' says Dr Baystone. He's taken a step back but his eyes fix me to my spot.

Make as much eye contact as you like; hit all the empathy buttons and I will absorb your signals. But my porousness only extends one way. Everything pours in, floods me, but nothing leaks out any more.

Back at Dylan House, I add Dr Baystone's definition of acting – *'acting is doing'* – to my notebook full of Jade Graces. Then I write Dr Purves's words to me and my mother: *Trauma reveals us sometimes. Lux just needs more time.'* My hand is unsteady and the pen strokes come out jagged.

Clamping the pen between my teeth, I type another message to Jade.

I think it's the red hair that made me realise we must know each other from somewhere. Maybe from prep school? Email me back. I'm not a stalker, I promise.

The pen slips from my mouth, catching my tender gum. I suck air through my teeth, 'Aaagghh.' My tongue tastes metallic. I press a finger into my mouth and it comes out red. The blood from my gums is different to the blood that comes from the cut on my arm when I claw at it. It's less viscous, not as dark.

I dab at my mouth with a black sleeve.

I'm still smarting about embarrassing myself in front of Cal and at what Dr Baystone said about depriving myself. Sometimes I feel like I've had way too much human experience, but right now I have absolutely no idea what that even means. My head tells my heart not to care; Dr Baystone is just one of the head director's puppets.

I take a shower to wash off the day. My body trembles as the water pelts my skin. I turn the hot water up to scalding, huff in the steam and let the water roll down my face like misery. As I watch my stomach and thighs mottle from the heat, I promise to do better, to give the pledge a chance to save me. But it will be hard to let go. These days, even when I'm by myself, I behave as though an audience or cameras are watching.

I step out of the shower cubicle, a wet performing seal, and enter my dorm room, stage left.

TEN

'I was tough on you in class yesterday,' says Dr Baystone.

I've brought a grey blanket outside and laid it out next to some little flowers. I tickle their little chins, willing them to flourish. An exercise in futility if ever there was one – every year, flowers poke up, breathing through the cracks, before dying and fertilising the ground with their goodness so their offspring can start the cycle again.

We sit while I organise the words in my head and overreact to the occasional bee. That's the problem with living on the most eco-friendly campus in Europe – there are fucking bugs everywhere, in all seasons. Literally, they never stop fucking; it's something to do with the pollen changes or the ozone layer. I sleep with my hair over my ears to protect my brain from amorous insects.

We're pushing it being outside in October. The old smoking trees are sparse so they don't provide much shelter but Dr

Baystone doesn't seem to feel the cold and I welcome the distraction. His faded dad jeans and green jumper look soft.

I tuck my black-clad legs under me and we sit like a couple of wannabe Buddhas while he waits for me to talk. I guess when the weather turns completely against us, we'll have to (not) talk inside in one of the studios or the library instead. Anywhere but the talking rooms.

'Lux, I said I was tough on you,' he says.

'Yes.'

'Why do think that is?' he asks.

'I imagine you think it's for my own good.' It's true; he doesn't seem deliberately evil.

He nods and says, 'So, what would you like to get out of today's session?'

This is my cue to unburden my soul. I've learned not to be silent when a professional sends this signal because they deal in awkward silences and eventually I will crack. In the game of silence chicken, shrink always trumps teenager. So I start jabbering on about the studios and how I don't have one and that I've always just written in bed or in the library. Then I tell him about sharing a room with Mei, about how messy she is and how she says she's lactose intolerant but that she always gets a Frappuccino when we manage to sneak a coffee. I tell him about Olivia's dancing and that I think Isabella doesn't like us any more but it doesn't matter because she wasn't in our inner circle anyway. I talk and talk until I can't think of anything else to say so I shut up.

He nods again and says, 'So, I'll ask you again, what do you want to get out of today's session?'

'I don't know.'

'You're going to have to do better than that. You're here voluntarily so let's talk about what you want.'

'Voluntarily?'

'You made a choice between staying and committing to this or leaving, so I need to know what you want so I can help you.'

There are a lot of things that I want. Mostly, I want things to go back to how they were before I blacked out. I want to stop spending hours in bed each week with a cold press on my head, feeling like my brain and eyes are on fire. I want to stop having crazy dreams and hearing colours. I want my parents to know I love them but I can't stand to be around them because all those stupid fights that I can't even remember properly were excruciating.

'Would you like to tell me about your blackout?' he asks.

I know what's coming. *What happened at the party? How did you get to the hospital? What happened when you woke up?*

'I want to be myself again,' I blurt. 'But maybe a bit nicer.'

He asks me how I think I can get back to being myself and I tell him that question is too big. If I knew that, I wouldn't be sitting in a field with a professional.

'You're right. Let's make it smaller. I know about the headaches and Dr Purves's notes say sometimes you feel you're numb and sometimes you feel like you can feel everything.'

'I don't know, it's just like sometimes …'

'Go on,' he says.

'It's like sometimes I get trapped outside myself.'

'You dissociate?'

I nod. Dr Purves explained this is what it's called when I float away and watch myself from somewhere else. At least it has a name, I suppose.

'Have you noticed any patterns? Does it happen when you're in certain places or with certain people?'

'There isn't any logic to it. Sorry.'

'There's not a right or wrong answer here. What if I tell you that sometimes when we don't want to think about something, our mind plays tricks on us to distract us.'

'Like my mind has a mind of its own?' I ask.

'Exactly. Do you think that could apply to you?'

'What do you mean?'

'Do you think there's something that you might be hiding from yourself?'

This is one of those moments where I'm supposed to have an epiphany. I'm supposed to cry and say, 'Hi, I'm Lux; I pledge allegiance to the arts and I'm an alcoholic or a drug addict or a rageaholic,' like some of the other Artists do in their assembly shares. I don't want to disappoint Dr Baystone but my eyes are bone-dry and the epiphany isn't coming.

'Why did you stop acting? I recognised you, you know; I think my parents used to watch you in something. Did you always want to be a therapist?' I ask. 'I mean, isn't it depressing talking to freaks all the time?'

'Do you think you're a freak, Lux?'

'Sometimes.' I bite the inside of my cheeks to stop myself from asking him to confirm it. Familiar white zigzags appear at the edges of my vision and the space behind my right eye starts to pulse as another headache mutates. Soon the zigzags will obscure my vision. My tongue will grow thick and untrustworthy, prone to slurring out words that are not the ones my brain invited it to say.

'What do your friends think about all this?' he asks.

'I haven't told them. I mean, they know I blacked out and about the headaches and they saw my meltdown at the Tate, but they don't know about the colours or the weird dreams.'

'What do you think they would say if you told them?'

'Does everything have to be a question?'

'How do you feel about being asked questions?'

'They'd want to help me if I told them, but they can't.'

Dr Baystone is more patient than I would be if I were him, but we've gone down enough conversational cul-de-sacs for one day and I need to get to my room before the purer pain takes shape in my head.

'I need to go.'

'OK, but first I need to say something to you,' he says.

I don't know how he keeps a straight face listening to all my poor-little-rich-girl problems. It doesn't always help to know that you are privileged. To know it and fail to feel it means you are even more broken.

'We only have eight weeks left of term so I need to be very clear with you. I think parts of your brain remember what happened when you blacked out and that unlocking that will make you feel a lot better.'

'So you're saying I'm lying to myself.'

My temples grind and panic rises.

'I'm saying there's a reason you feel how you do and you're going to have to work harder to find it. So if you have a thought that doesn't make much sense or you remember a dream or a nightmare, just write it down like I told you. The brain sends us messages.'

I sleep for three dreamless hours when I get back to Dylan House. I only dream in red at night. I guess it's a different kind of sleep when it's dark out. When I wake up, my conversation with Dr Baystone seems hazy and long ago.

I check my messages. Two from my parents and several from my personal adviser, Amy Logan. There are decisions to be made about the future. The last three she sent were marked with red exclamation points to indicate their importance – crimes against punctuation and a total misunderstanding of the concept of urgency. I can't think beyond Christmas yet. My deportation deadline. Anyway, what's she going to do if I don't respond, email me to death?

The personal advisers don't actually work at Richdeane; this branch of pastoral care is outsourced so we have someone independent to talk to. The school likes to give us as many opportunities to communicate as possible. Or maybe it's just cheaper. In my more abstract moments, I suspect Amy Logan isn't even her real name. All the personal advisers could actually be spawned from one automated active-listening system for all we know. An anglicised empathybot that exists only in the ether. I delete all the messages and start a new note to 'Amy Logan' – a quick apology and telling her I'll be in touch soon.

Still nothing from Jade Grace. Maybe my emails never reached her. Maybe the head director created a cybernoose around campus so communications can't get out, or something is stopping her messages getting in. The Richdeane server is very stable but I guess even we aren't immune to cyberattacks. I Instagram and tweet her instead this time.

After talking with Dr Baystone, I'm in one of those moods where excess feels like subsistence. I need more. Passing out drunk and waking up in a hospital two months ago seems an anaemic reason for feeling as lost as I do. I need a justifiable catalyst. I need orphans dying on *Comic Relief.* I need lonely donkeys in charity adverts, and elderly people, especially those who are sad and too proud or scared to ask for help. Legitimate reasons to be upset and confused.

I opt for my guilty pleasure, *El Pueblo* – a soap opera with a high body count. I first came across a clip on YouTube when my parents finally gave me my laptop back. I think it's Argentinean; I can't understand any of the words but sentiment is universal and this show is as addictive as crack.

Today's episode is called '*El Culto de los Recuerdos Perdidos*', not that it matters – every episode is a variation on the following pick 'n' mix of plot points: a deceased person's identical twin that nobody knew about turns up; a bomb is defused two seconds before it was due to detonate; incest is narrowly averted when true identities are revealed just in the nick of time; someone falls/is pushed down a flight of stairs; someone gets brainwashed; a baby of one race is born to parents of a different race; a beautiful but murderous widow moves to town; someone survives a rare genetic disease; and/or a dead body is found somewhere unexpected.

For habitants of a small town, they sure suffer a lot of unlikely misfortune; yet nobody ever moves. Like all the bad things that happen to them aren't real and don't matter.

ELEVEN

The more there seem to be real monsters in the world, the more seriously we take Halloween. As always, most of the school is going to the Watchers' Ball. After two more weeks of Dr Baystone interrogating me about my blackout, how I got home that night, who I was with and what I remember about waking up, I just need to have a night like we used to have.

The old Lux is getting harder and harder to find in the darkroom in my mind. I feel like I'm remembering less not more, but after another supper spent obsessing about whether the food is poisoned I come up with a plan to shock my system into resetting.

I buy Mei, Olivia and myself tickets to the ball to say thanks for looking after me since I got back. My nightmares wake Mei up sometimes even though she's a deep sleeper, and she and Olivia take it in turns to stay close and administer painkillers when my brain is wringing itself inside out. They are tired too.

Dr Baystone got permission from my parents for me to go. I told him that going would help me feel normal. I'm pretty sure I could get away with murder if I told him my inner child wanted to do it. I wish I could have asked them myself but I can't bear the thought of getting into another argument with them. It makes my brain clench just to think of them, so I push them out of my mind as best I can. They continue to email me, and I know Dr Baystone fills them in on the basics of my progress (or lack of).

Anyway, I'm allowed to go on the proviso that I stay with Mei and Olivia at all times. Dr Baystone even had a word with them about not letting me stray.

My growing collage of Jade Grace looks over Mei and me as we get ready. Mei has even tidied up for the occasion, by which I mean she has scooped up the piles of black clothes that usually dot our carpet like overgrown molehills and dropped them into the bottom of her wardrobe. The stacks of covet books, mood boards and decimated magazines have been pushed under her bed.

'Where's Olivia?' I ask.

'She's on her way, allegedly,' says Mei. 'She's been over at Van Sant House with Cal. He needed a dancer for a film project so they're storyboarding or something.'

Mei and I have known each other since we were thirteen so she knows exactly where to poke me to get a rise. I wish she wouldn't pretend storyboarding is an actual word. She believes adding 'ing' to any word makes it a verb and adding 'ed' to any noun can be used to describe inebriation.

'Sorry, sorry,' says Olivia when she finally hurries in, the pink tips of her hair tucked into the neck of her black jumper.

'Fucking finally – where have you been?' asks Mei.

'All right, swear-bear, calm down. I got held up with Cal. We were working on our project.'

The 'our' gives the whole thing away. So communal and unified. So exclusive and excluding. I feel a faint flush creeping across my neck to its hiding place behind my ears.

Olivia is an emotional savant; after years of learning how to open her heart for inspiration, she can read anyone.

'Do you mind that I'm dancing for Cal?' she asks.

'Of course not.' I'm not being truthful but these circumstances aren't imaginary so I don't think I've contravened any rules.

I can't tell her I think I like Cal. I can't even tell myself because, even if he knew and he liked me back, I wouldn't trust myself with him. He and Olivia are much better suited.

'We need to get ready,' I say.

'All right, no need to shout,' says Mei.

Olivia lays her costume out on my bed.

'Remember the last big party we went to?' she says. 'The leavers' thing.'

'Oh god, Lux and Henry – I forgot about that,' says Mei. 'Is he coming tonight?'

'Very funny,' I say. He messaged me a few times while I was doing my gallery internship but we never met up.

'He was too straightforward for our Luxy,' says Olivia.

'Thanks, Olivia.'

'You know what I mean. He liked you too much for you to be interested.'

She pulls out her make-up bag and starts painting her face.

'Red sky at night,' says Mei, nodding towards the window.

It's not just red, it's blood orange and nectarine flesh. Delicious and tempting. To stop my mind from filling with colours that could reappear as nightmares later, I turn to the sea of blackness in my wardrobe and carefully pull out my costume, trying not to disturb the other clothes. I still manage to upset a couple of tops so their shoulders slouch off the hangers. I smooth them back into place then open the other door and refold five of the black jumpers on that side.

'What are you doing in there?' asks Olivia.

'She guards that wardrobe like it's the portal to Narnia,' says Mei. 'Get out of there, stop burrowing, you're not going to find a door. Or anything contraband.'

I don't know about Narnia but she's wrong about the contraband. The red jumper that I was wearing when I woke up in hospital is folded in a bag at the back.

'Back in a sec,' I say.

In the bathroom, I drag the fraying bristles of my toothbrush along my teeth, gums and over my tongue, then blast milky pink spit down the plughole.

'Your mouth is bleeding,' gasps Olivia when I re-enter the bedroom.

'I brushed too hard,' I say. 'Don't worry – it didn't hurt.'

I never feel a thing until afterwards. My pain barometer is out of whack.

I put on my dress and step back to see my reflection in the mirror. The wound on my arm is no longer fresh but the scab is starting to itch and split again where I've been rubbing at it. I press a dressing on to it and put on a cardigan.

I thought about trying to make myself look like Jade Grace but decided to go as a hybrid of the ladies from Lichtenstein's paintings, which means a royal blue dress, faux pearl earrings and necklace, a canary yellow wig, darkened eyebrows and some of Mei's Ruby Woo lipstick. I draw tomato-coloured polka dots on my face, then Olivia paints splashes of aquamarine tears around my eyes. I look like a cartoon character or an avatar and I love it. My outsides almost match my insides for once.

Olivia hasn't deviated from our regulation black, but layered on more. She's blacked out her eyes and painted tombstone teeth across her mouth and cheeks, stretching her face into a skeletal grin that disfigures her well-bred features. Her forehead and cheekbones are painted with spidery swirls of blues, purples and pinks, like Angry Jack's tattoos. Her hair is covered with a matted black wig with dead flowers pinned on one side. The dead bride effect is finished off with a black veil and a floor-sweeping dress.

Mei is dressed in a white fluffy onesie replete with a squidgy tail, enormous wings, little tufty ears and a twenty-centimetre spiralled horn. If she turned without warning, those wings could fell us like trees.

'Flying unicorn?' I ask.

'Pegacorn,' she says.

'Of course.'

I push the little bag of powder that I asked Mei to score for me into my bra before we leave. All part of the plan.

The ball is held in the tunnels under Waterloo Station by *Watchers*, a glossy but gossipy magazine. Underground seems a pretty a safe place to be and the party is in full swing when we get there.

With the little bag of powder tucked inside my costume, I feel more like myself already.

We decide to do the zombie run first. We're furnished with night-vision goggles and sent into a pitch-black maze populated by hired undead. The objective seems to be to get from the entrance to the exit on the other side of the maze without having a nervous breakdown. I cling to Mei's pegacorn tail and Olivia grips my elbow as Mei tries to navigate us through. Zombies brush up against us and leap out as we jump and shriek. They never break character, even when we beg them to point us to the exit. It feels good to have a reason to scream.

'What now?' asks Olivia, when we finally find our way out.

There's an area for making voodoo dolls, a freak show, grotesque burlesque dancers, contortionists and live music.

'Loo, then bar?' I say. It's time to put my reset plan into action.

There's a line of girls at the mirror in the bathroom, adjusting their pom-pom bunny tails and reapplying their kitty whiskers. It all feels so predictable and suddenly I'm proud of Olivia. She is a rare thing: a glorious girl trying to look ugly on Halloween among the clowder of sexy cats and their slutty cop friends.

A ballerina comes out of one of the cubicles and I think of Cal. What will Olivia wear when she dances for him?

I go into the empty cubicle and hover while I pee. I stand up and make a glove out of toilet paper so I don't have to touch the lid directly to close it – another new habit. Then I sit back down, shake the makeshift mitten on to the floor, and take out the bag of fine crystals from my bra. My first pharmaceutical booster since I blacked out – unless you count the painkillers I take for the headaches, which I don't as the professionals encourage me to take them.

My plan is to use some drugs of the recreational variety to reset my head. Little bubbles of something like excitement but more acidic fizz in my stomach. My heart always used to race before I took anything, but that was with anticipation; now I just feel desperation.

I pinch a little of the powder into a tiny piece of loo roll and twist it into a minute cracker. I suck on the inside of my cheeks to generate enough saliva to help me swallow the little bomb and drop it into my mouth. One gulp and it's gone. A trace of sweetness drains down my throat. It should taste like aniseed so I guess I can add my taste buds to the list of things about me that are malfunctioning.

'No paper. Can you pass me some?' Mei's hand appears under the cubicle wall. The last time we used that code was at the Leavers' Ball. I don't know what we'd say if we actually needed loo roll. I drop the bag into her waiting palm.

It comes back to me a minute or two later all but empty. Considering Mei didn't even want to get me the drugs, she's committed rather enthusiastically to taking them. I didn't want to ask her but with Henry gone there wasn't anyone else I could trust not to report me to the head director. 'I thought you were done with all that?' she'd said. 'It's too risky.' But her concerns have clearly dissipated or she wants the old me back as much as I do. I hope the bag found its way down the cubicles to Olivia, otherwise Mei is going to be a mess later.

I'm tempted to scoop out the dregs and rub my powdery

finger into my gums for good measure but I don't want to end up back in hospital or get expelled.

'Just FYI, this is not a particularly loo-friendly costume,' says Mei at the sinks.

'Note to self, do not wear a onesie to public toilets,' says Olivia.

'Seriously, I might have to go nil by mouth.'

'Just stick to shots,' I suggest. 'Less liquid.'

'You, Lux Langley, are a mother-humping genius.'

Drunk girls stagger towards the hand dryers, wet hands held out in front of them like zombies. One of them bashes against me.

'Watch where you're going,' she slurs.

'You watch where you're going,' I say, standing square in front of her so she can't get past. How quickly anger rises to the surface just when I think I've swallowed it all down.

'Calm down,' the girl says. 'I'm just saying you need to watch it.'

'Say that again,' I spit. 'I dare you.'

'Lux!' Olivia is horrified.

'Get out of here,' Mei says to the girl.

'What the hell was that about?' asks Olivia when the girl has wobbled away.

'She started it.'

'So you decided to finish it?' asks Mei. 'You could have got into a fight and then what would have happened?'

'Seriously, Lux, you need to calm down,' says Olivia. 'Here –' she turns the tap on – 'splash some water on your face.'

The water puts out the fire in me.

Whoever was controlling the dial that made me flare up has turned it back down.

'Come on – let's get out of the loos,' says Olivia.

I hold the door open with my elbow so I don't have to touch it.

'So you'll ingest potentially poisonous chemicals but you're scared of toilet germs?' says Mei. Her huge wings swing perilously as she barges out through the queuing girls.

'Yep.'

'You OK?' whispers Olivia. I flash her a grin.

There are some seriously bad-taste costumes about. I clock two dead Bin Ladens in the queue for the fortune teller. What would possess someone to dress so thoughtlessly? I imagine them doing the walk of shame home tomorrow. Or the stride of pride, depending on your outlook on casual sex.

I can't feel the effects of the powder yet but anxiety strobes through me. What if this doesn't work? What if I blackout again in front of everyone?

Olivia grabs my hand.

We hit the bar then check the band list to see who's playing. We've missed the Derivatives, but I've never heard of them so I don't really mind. Stamp Duty are up next and Bond and the Swaps will close. After that, there's a DJ.

A pack of guys dressed as wolves shout hello over the music and disappear to the bar. They'll need straws to drink through their wolf heads. We find some other Richdeane Artists and hang with them a while, doing shots, drifting and dancing through the dusty tunnels and taking in the burlesque dancers. Isabella is there; she waves but doesn't come over. As we go deeper into the night, everyone gets friendlier and more attractive. Is that the chemicals realigning?

An Artist from the year below asks if I'm holding. I say I'm not and it's true; all the chemicals are inside me. I can't feel them like I used to but they're in there.

'Not even pills?' insists the girl. 'Millie told me you've always got something.'

'Well, I don't.'

Hours pass.

The DJ replaces the band. Occasionally, she shouts things she's heard other DJs shout: 'Make some noise!' and, 'Let me see those hands!' and we respond like it's a highly incentivised game of Simon Says.

Someone suggests tequila suicides and we get to work snorting the salt and squeezing the lime in our eyes. The tequila tastes like last summer, of the Leavers' Ball and of Henry. The lime really hurts so we fill the empty glasses with water and wash out each other's eyes. My eyes are streaming and, when I wipe them, black mascara and glitter comes away with my fingers. It must be smeared across my eyes and down my cheeks. I wonder if I look like I'm crying. There is some satisfaction in that, even if they're tears of citrus.

I do more shots and somehow lose Mei and Olivia. The DJ is going through an aggressive speedcore phase and the dance floor starts to look like the inside of a trip so I find a piece of wall to lean against for respite. I think I spot Mei and call out to her but realise it's a guy who has borrowed her wings. The wall is hard and dusty but I let it hold me up as I close my eyes for a bit.

'Your art or your life!' a masked giant shouts in my face. 'Get down, bitch, lick the floor!' He waves a gun at me. It glows like jewels under the pulsing strobe lights. My heart falls through my body on to the floor and I crash to my knees, sending dust all over our shoes and up my legs.

'Oh, shit, I'm sorry – it's just a joke.' The guy drops down next to me, pulling his balaclava off. 'I'm sorry; please calm down; it was just a joke.'

That's when I realise I'm screaming. I stop. Some part of me recognises that I'm not in real danger but I can't stop my body reacting. The blood drains from my hands and my necklace tries to strangle me. How strange we must look – I sweated most of the face dots off hours ago but I'm still wearing the aquamarine tears and yellow wig. People have gathered to watch us, a hysterical Lichtenstein lady and an armed killer crouched on the ground. They probably think it's part of the Watchers' show. Will they applaud? Weapons-grade dread takes over and I push my way through the tunnels and run outside.

Once I'm out in the air, I find another bit of wall to steady myself against. I'm both horribly drunk and startlingly sober. I bite the fleshy base of my thumb and count the orange taxi lights that stream by to calm myself down. When I get to seven, a hoarse voice reaches me, cooling my mind. It's coming from a wolf.

It's Cal, wearing a furry wolf suit and carrying a lupine head under one arm.

I remove my hand from my mouth and manage to say hi.

'Hi,' he replies. 'I saw your disappearing act. You OK?'

'I'm fine. Thanks. Some guy just scared the shit out of me but I overreacted.'

'I saw him. Who comes to a Halloween party as Darth Vader anyway?'

'He wasn't Darth Vader.'

'Trust me, I know a lightsaber when I see one. That guy was the dark lord.'

My mind must have been playing tricks on me like Dr Baystone said it could.

'Either way. It was a pretty douchey of him to ninja attack you like that.'

'He was kind of a douche,' I agree. 'I'm OK now though.'

'You sure? You normally seem so calm,' he says. 'You're shaking. Have you taken something?'

'Hours ago.' Good to know that I appear outwardly normal most of the time.

'You should be careful with that stuff.' I stare at him like I've forgotten English but we don't learn other languages so he has no alternative tongue to try. 'Careful.'

We stand there breathing and metabolising for the longest ten seconds in recorded history.

'I'm sorry about Dr Baystone's class,' I say, finally.

'What do you mean?' he says.

'I'm sorry for holding you back that time.'

'What? Oh. It's just an exercise. We could practise sometime if you like.'

His belief in the pledge shines out of him.

'I should let my friends know I'll find my own way home.' I take out my phone. I already have seven missed calls from Mei and three from Olivia. I send them both a message.

'I'll come back with you if you don't mind. It's getting pretty intense in there. Shall I get us a cab?' he asks.

'Can we sit for a minute?' I'm desperate to leave the city

but I don't think I can get into a moving vehicle right now. My parents' flat is just around the corner and the concierge would let me in no questions asked but the walls might still ring with the arguments we had and I just want to be back in my room at school. Suddenly, I lament my costume choice and my bare back; I wish I had Mei's wings to carry us home to Richdeane.

We walk further round the side of the station and sit cross-legged on the kerb opposite a fish and chips takeaway called Fishcotheque.

'Where were you before you came to Richdeane?' I ask him.

'A normal school.'

I'm close enough to sip his beery voice. That's when I realise he is a little drunk.

'Did something happen?'

'No. Not particularly. I just finally convinced my dad that being a painter is an actual thing that some people do. He said if I got a scholarship to Richdeane, I could come.'

'And you did.'

'Yep.' More taxis pass. 'How about a game?' he suggests.

'Sure.'

'OK. I'll interview you. A quick-fire round.'

'Huh?'

'Just answer the questions. Say the first thing that comes into your head. OK?'

'OK.'

'You have to answer truthfully. That's the only rule.'

'OK.'

'Cool. Best costume from tonight?'

'Not the Bin Ladens.'

'You have to answer positively. Best, not worst.'

'Oh. OK. Um … yours.'

He has the decency to blush, just at the top of his cheeks, right where they meet his temples. 'Ha. Thanks. Davy picked them. Favourite writer?'

'Denis Johnson. John Green. Salinger. Whoever wrote *The Very Hungry Caterpillar*.'

'Writer, singular, not *writers*. I don't think you completely understand the parameters of this game,' he jokes.

'Sorry. In my defence, that was a ridiculous question.'

'OK. Olivia or Mei?'

'For what?'

'Just answer truthfully. Don't overthink it.'

'Olivia.' I choose her because I don't think Mei needs me.

'Interesting. I didn't think you'd answer that one,' he says. 'Write or paint?'

'Write.'

Not that I do either any more.

'Too hot or too cold?'

'Too cold.'

'Owl or lark?'

'Owl.'

'Favourite drink?'

'Wild air.'

'Artist?'

'Jade Grace.'

'She's cool. Best words from a great?'

'Twain. "Write what you know." Although, actually, maybe "write about what you don't know" would be better.'

'Worst?' he asks.

'Um … Meisner and his incessant demand for truthfulness.'

'That was a tough question. I'll throw you an easy one. Colour?'

'I can't even begin to answer that.'

'Just say a colour. I'll even accept rainbow.'

'I take colours very seriously.'

'Remind me, who is the painter in this scenario?' he laughs.

'Night-time blue.'

'You mean midnight blue?'

'Nope. I mean night-time blue.'

'Right. Favourite flavour?'

'Piano.'

'You eat pianos?'

'I mean pistachio.'

'Sexiest animal?'

'Foxes. No, wait. Rabbits! Definitely rabbits.'

'I think so too, but I don't know why.' He continues: 'Most sexually ambiguous animal?'

'Giraffes, obviously.'

'Did you know all giraffes are lesbians?' he asks.

'That makes no sense. That would mean all giraffes were female for a start.'

'Oh. I must have remembered that wrong.'

'Let me interview you now,' I say.

'OK.'

His face is so symmetrical. What a gene pool he must come from.

'Do you look like your mum or your dad?' I ask.

'My mum, I think.'

Funny how boys can look like their mothers.

'Or maybe I just want to look like her.'

I laugh. 'Not many guys would admit to that.'

'She died.'

'Oh. I'm so sorry, I have foot-in-mouth disease.'

'It's OK – it was a long time ago.'

'I'm sorry.'

'Really, it's OK. You remind me of her a little bit. Not her face exactly, but something.'

'Thanks,' I say, even though he's clearly just friend-zoned me.

'Let's smoke,' he says.

His voice is so cracked, I should discourage him, but I don't.

'Cool game,' I say.

'I used to play it with my mum when I was little.'

He pulls out tobacco and skins, rolls two cigarettes, lights them both and hands one to me. I'm surprised he smokes; I'd imagined he was from the 'my body is a temple' school of golden Artists.

'Tastes funny,' I say. It hurts the sore skin in my mouth.

'No chemicals,' he explains though his teeth, holding down the smoke. He breathes out like a dragon and says, 'It's made of daisies or something like that.'

I feel bad about smoking flowers but I'm pretty sure he's joking so we sit there on the kerb, a Lichtenstein lady and a young gentleman-wolf, smoking and flicking ash into the gutter. His fingers are stained from smoking rollies. I haven't smoked since the summer and feel pulmonary pressure build while the flowery smoke fills me. My heart starts banging again and my throat burns so I toss the second half of my cigarette under the back tyres of a passing car. And then I feel so alive and brave, I turn to him and kiss him. He kisses back. It hurts my gums.

Cars pass while we breathe softly into the back of each other's mouths, his hippy cigarette still fuming in his left hand. I wonder if he can taste my secrets through the floral ash of the cigarettes, then I remember he is normal.

I don't know if this is real or imaginary but I'm exhausted from managing to spit out some truth at last. We rest in silence with his wolf head next to us on the pavement as an undead nun wobbles by on a Boris bike.

When I get back to Dylan House, Mei is asleep with the light on. Her pegacorn costume lies tangled on the floor where she's stepped out of it. A discarded mythical chrysalis, its bright white is faded to a grubby cocaine cream. I pick it up, pull the legs back through the right way, fold it and return it to the floor. Too tired for the balcony, I open the window and push it wide, then I turn off the light, undress and slip into bed.

TWELVE

Mei is awake before me in the morning.

A half-moon of make-up is smeared on my pillow when I lift my head. It's stuffy; Mei must have closed the window.

'What happened to you last night?' she asks, reaching up to add something to our Jade Grace collage. It's almost covering a full wall now. 'Sorry we lost you – I was absolutely pancaked but Cal messaged Olivia to say he was with you.'

I didn't know they'd swapped numbers.

'Long story,' I say, getting out of bed. 'It ended well though – I …'

My voice trails off as I move closer to see what she's stuck on the wall. It's a printout of one of the horrible photos Jade took of herself in her bed that had everyone so scandalised.

'Do we have to have that looking down on us?' I ask.

Jade's got her old blonde hair in it too. Suddenly I feel guilty about the little Jade head that I gave to the wind. I hope it carried her away somewhere safe, not into the woods.

'I thought it would be a good reminder not to take things too far. Not to become the tortured Artists everyone seems to think we are,' she explains.

'She's hardly a cautionary tale; she's too successful. You just feel guilty about doing that powder last night,' I say. 'I don't even feel like I took anything. No come down. Not even a hangover really.'

Or rather, hangovers are nothing compared to the skull-grinding head pain I'm used to now.

'Yeah,' says Mei.

'Yeah?' I ask.

'Well, there's a reason you're not coming down,' she says. 'It was just sugar mixed with vitamin powder.'

'What?'

'I'm sorry, I just didn't think you should be taking anything in case you, you know ...' she trails off.

'You can say it. I remember – I was actually there, you know.'

'OK. In case you blacked out again. And, to be honest, I didn't want to do any either.'

'Why didn't you just say that?'

'You know why.' She doesn't raise her voice to match mine.

'No, I don't. Enlighten me.'

'I tried to tell you I didn't want to get it for you, but you were so set on it I thought it would be safer if I just played along.'

'Played along? I'm not a child.'

Her expression reminds me of the child I shouted at in the Tate.

'I'm not a child,' I repeat, 'and there's nothing wrong with me.'

'I'm sorry, I was just trying to look out for you.'

Mei likes apologising as much as I do – that is, not at all – so I just say, 'OK, I'll forgive you if you take that down.'

'Deal.' She slips the bloody picture of Jade inside the pages of one of her covet books, though Art knows why anyone would covet something so gruesome.

'Here, stick these on instead.' I give her some printed pictures from my bedside drawer.

'Snowdrops?' she asks.

'And starfish.'

'I don't get it.'

'From her stories.'

'I still don't get it, but OK,' she says. 'Get dressed.'

She gets out her sharp scissors and tidies up the edges of the paper pictures.

I wonder if Cal will be at assembly. Of course he will; he is one of the golden pledges who always go.

I open the wardrobe and stand close against the shelves inside as I reach my hands in to smooth down any wayward garments. Everything is already folded but my mind is starting to get away from me so I have no choice but to pull out the piles of clothes in great armfuls and drop them on to my bed. Does this mean the drugs plan failed? Mei's eyes sting my back as I shake each black item out, one by one, refold it and set it back inside the wardrobe.

'Anything you want to talk about?' she asks.

'Nope. You?'

'I guess not. Coming to assembly? I'm thinking about sharing today.'

No offence to her but Mei's shares are often quite dull; she's too together to have anything juicy to say.

'I'll catch you up.'

She goes, but then sticks her head back round the door. 'I tested it before I gave it to you. The sugar vitamins. Made my wee bright yellow. So if yours looks radioactive this morning, don't worry about it.'

Assembly is finished by the time I finish folding my clothes and get to the auditorium. Olivia, Mei and Cal are talking by the windows in the foyer when I arrive. Mei sees me first.

'Oh, hi, Lux,' she says, giving all the words extra syllables so they last three times longer than they need to. I probably interrupted them warning Cal I'm damaged goods. No, they wouldn't do that.

'Hi, Mei, Hi, Olivia,' I say, echoing her intonation. 'Hi, Cal.'

Their conversation dries up.

'Secret squirrels?' I ask.

'No,' says Cal. 'We were just talking about how I wanted to invite you to my studio.'

Mei and Olivia give each other 'the look'.

'We'll leave you to it,' says Olivia, dragging Mei away.

'Well, that was subtle,' I say.

Cal laughs. 'What are you doing now?'

'No plans.'

'Come to the studios?'

I haven't been in there since I got back, even though Mei and

I can see them from our balcony. I've never been a visual Artist but I used to hang around there with Henry sometimes. The thought of seeing all the beautiful art inside makes my blood run faster.

'Cool,' I say.

I follow him out.

Outside his block, a girl is slumped against a wall, eating a bag of lettuce as if it's a packet of crisps, her bony fingers like porcelain salad pincers.

'You OK?' Cal asks her.

'Sure,' she says.

I am out of place and clumsy as we walk through the block to his studio. The Artists in here live the pledge with images and icons not words.

One of the studios we pass is open but there's nobody inside. I sneak a peek at the abandoned project they've left. It's pretty crude; featuring explicit depictions of Sylvanian Families doing things family shouldn't do to each other while the cast of *The Wind in the Willows* gets drunk on alcoholic ginger beer. It seems to be some kind of pervert's guide to children's characters. Whatever was being built here must have been deemed non-viable. The Artist will return to this space of conception once the cleaners have aborted and disposed of this failed attempt at creation.

'Wow. This is so cool,' I say when he opens his studio door, quickly instructing myself to stop saying 'cool'.

'Thanks. Come on in.'

'You're so lucky to have a space like this all to yourself. Maybe I should get one to write; I've been kind of blocked recently.'

'You should definitely get one. Next door is empty actually.'

'That was Arlo's, I think.'

'Who's Arlo?'

'Just a guy that went here. He was an actor and a photographer. He didn't come back after the summer. I didn't really know him but he used to keep dead things in there.'

It's true. Fish, birds, stoats. Every now and then, a fox. Nothing domesticated. It makes me wonder if Richdeane has a taxidermist, or if the animals he photographed were just roadkill or birds that had fallen out of their nests and cracked their skulls on Richdeane's perfect grounds.

'You think something happened to him?' Cal asks.

'Like he got sick, you mean?'

'I meant like he did something bad and wasn't allowed back in? Broke the pledge.'

'They let Artists in who have done bad things all the time,' I say. 'Usually it's bad things that have happened to them though.'

'Of course,' he says, as a paintbrush escapes the bundle he's been bunching together and drops on to the stone floor. He picks it up and changes the subject: 'I pretty much live in here, which is why it looks, well, as if I live here.'

Maybe he did something bad himself and he's not ready to say yet.

There are sketches and canvases everywhere, some tacked to the walls, some in piles leaning against the walls, plus stacks on the surfaces and what I assume are current projects on the seven easels. I've be so preoccupied with trying to keep my brain in my head this term that I'd forgotten Artists make amazing things at Richdeane.

Tubes of oil paint and smaller brushes are cluttered on a trestle table alongside pint-sized cans of energy drinks and packets of caffeine pills. Richdeane is not like those places where the school doctor will prescribe what they can to help – Adderall, sleepers and things ending in 'zepam' – or where cocaine binges are unofficially sponsored by generous prop budgets. On campus we get by on clean air, fresh veg and smuggled stimulants. Off campus we make our own choices and usually regret them.

'It's actually not usually quite this full. I'm working on my portfolio to apply to art schools.'

I leaf through a series of line drawings of monsters and clouds. They are childlike in their simplicity.

'Those are old,' he says. 'Check out the date.'

There are misshapen numbers in the bottom corners.

'You did these when you were seven?'

'Eight. I'm already eighteen. I did them for my mum.'

'Did she put them on the fridge?'

'Not exactly.' He restacks them and slides them to the back of the workbench. 'Probably not portfolio material.'

'Sorry, I didn't mean to be nosy.'

'You weren't. I invited you, remember?' Against the far wall is another bench. 'This is where I make my potions.'

'You make your own paint?'

'Sort of – I'm just testing pigments.' There are bowls of metallic dust like milled glitter and a couple of pestle and mortars with various pastes in. I pick up a saucer of murky goo.

'That's coffee granules crushed with dandelion petals. Didn't work well, as you can see.'

'Useful if you were painting a swamp.'

'I have yet to find a compelling story about a swamp.'

'What do you mean?'

He tells me he likes to paint things he hears or reads about rather than just making up images straight from his head. Real things.

'You're a story-stealer,' I tease. I am not good at flirting.

The meal reminder buzzes over the intercom.

He laughs. 'We should get to lunch.'

'Them's the rules.'

I wonder if I should say something about last night. Just when I'm finding the words to tell him it doesn't have to mean anything, he takes my hand and leads me out of the studio towards the dining hall for more of the same: brown rice, protein, greens.

'Come on,' he says. I feel like a bad feminist for letting him boss me, but then I remember it's like Jade Grace's story where she said she was happy to be temporarily absolved of responsibility for her own path. And it's only lunch.

THIRTEEN

When it comes back round to our turn in Dr Baystone's class a couple of days later, I am ready for it.

Cal and I face each other, ready to spar, him in a thin black T-shirt and me in a big hoodie, still cold from sleeping outside on the balcony the night before. He hops from foot to foot, swinging at the air and ducking like a boxer, while I send back exaggerated pretend right hooks.

'Whenever you're ready,' says Dr Baystone.

And then I'm not ready at all.

Things I don't normally let myself think about start looping through my head at light speed. It spins me out until all I can focus on is how unfair it is that Jade Grace won't reply to me, that no one knows what's wrong with me and I'll probably have to leave Richdeane soon.

I look at Cal; he's ready to start, but I know I can't do it properly with people watching. My throat dries up and I shake my hair loose from behind my ears so it hangs in my face.

Cal scans me with his eyes. I do the same to him.

In a flash, the connection is too much. I can't contain myself.

'You're angry,' I say.

He looks confused but stammers back, 'I-I'm angry?'

'I don't think that's it, Lux,' says Dr Baystone. 'Look again, and tell Cal what you see in him. Remember this is about truth.'

I look into Cal, but not too deep.

I'm not cold any more.

How can he feel anything but anger for me when it's the only feeling I seem to have?

'You're angry,' I say again, before Cal can take the lead.

'Maybe we should try later,' Cal says to Dr Baystone.

'You're angry,' I insist.

'I'm not angry, especially not with you. I'm not an angry person.'

'You can be angry without being an angry person. Can't you, Dr Baystone?' I can feel myself losing it. 'Go on, Cal, tell the truth.'

'Cal's right – let's come back to this later,' says Dr Baystone. The other Artists are audibly let down by this.

'It's OK,' I say. 'I can take it. We all want the truth.'

Someone turns my dial round to maximum and everything I've been pushing away explodes.

'He wants to hit me. Hit me.'

'Jesus, Lux.' Cal looks how I feel, as if he wants to throw up.

'Just say it.' I'm burning up so I yank the hoodie off and drop it to the floor. My skin crawls so I scratch, scratch, scratch at it, tearing open the top of the gash on my arm.

He takes a step towards me then stops and says, 'I do not want to hit you.'

'Yes, you do. And I want you to.'

'That escalated quickly,' jokes someone in the little audience, but nobody laughs. I'd forgotten they were there.

'OK, that's enough,' says Dr Baystone.

'Calm down, Lux,' Cal croaks.

'You know what? You want to know how I feel? I feel that I wish everyone would stop telling me to calm down.' Even as I'm yelling I wish someone would stop me because I can't stop myself. 'You have no idea what this is like for me.'

My hands lift to my temples, pushing down in small circles and kneading the skin, while everyone stares at me. No amount of sleeping on the balcony will cool me down tonight.

'We're all the same,' Cal says gently.

I pull my hands down and hold out my bleeding forearm. 'Are we? Are we all the same? Do you have a scar you don't even remember getting?'

He inches towards me with his arms out as if to hug or capture me. I grab one and stab my ragged nails into his skin, dragging them down to his wrist to make us the same. He clamps my hand – not hard enough for it to hurt but hard enough that I know it's not a game.

'Lux, we're not doing this.'

Dr Baystone steps in. 'Lux, I said that's enough – you need to go back to your room now.'

'I'll take her,' says Cal.

'No, Georgia will take her.'

'I'm sorry; I'm sorry; I'm sorry.' I say it all the way along the path back to Dylan House and, when we get there, it already feels like something that happened in the distant past or to another me.

There is blood under my fingernails. Only my thumb is clean.

Georgia leads me into the bathroom. She fills the sink with warm water and lathers soap over my hands. The temperature is perfect.

'Go like this,' she says, rubbing her hands together and kneading her thumbs over her nails. 'Good. Now rinse.'

She takes my hands and lowers them back into the sink. The water tints a pale rusty brown as she washes the soap and the blood away. The gentleness of her touch is unbearable.

'I need to go to the loo,' I tell her.

She arches an eyebrow but says, 'I'll meet you in your room.'

I go into one of the cubicles and sit on the closed toilet lid without locking the door. When the door swings shut behind her, I return to the sink and twist the hot tap all the way round until steaming water rushes out.

I hold the tips of the fingers on the hand that scratched Cal under the scalding torrent and count three long Mississippis to balance out the kindness of the warm water Georgia used.

He will never speak to me again.

Three more Mississippis and it's not my hand any more.

Tucking the red fingers up my sleeve, I turn off the tap with my good hand and go to my room.

Georgia stays with me for a while.

'I don't know what happened,' I tell her. 'Tell Cal I'm sorry.'

As she leaves, Dr Baystone arrives. He perches on Mei's bed across the room from me. 'I'm sure you know why I'm here. I know you didn't mean it, but I can't let you get away with hurting another Artist like that.'

FOURTEEN

I don't want to get away with it.

I barely remember what happened, but I know it was bad. I know I deserve for Cal to be taken away from me or to be sent away myself.

The same people who started the rumour that Cal's voice is cracked because he got shot in the neck make sure that the news I'm a maniac spreads by the end of the day. By supper, people are whispering about me like they did when I first got back and everyone but Mei and Olivia seems scared of me. Isabella blanks me in the dining hall. I've gone from Blackout Girl to Lash-out Girl.

Mei and Olivia flank my sides, but nobody else sits at our table.

I'm awaiting sentencing; this could be my last Richdeane supper.

I force in a few mouthfuls, but it hurts to chew.

'Everybody is talking about me.'

'That's true,' says Mei. Olivia glares at her. 'What?' Mei says, 'I'm not going to lie to her. That stupid little Millie got wind of it and she's telling anyone who will listen.'

'Georgia's Millie?' I ask.

'Yes, but do not say anything to her – you're in enough trouble as it is,' warns Mei.

'Seriously, you've got to keep a low profile,' adds Olivia.

'How can I if she's blabbing about me all over school?'

'She's a moron,' agrees Mei. 'And a shit-stirrer, just like her tabloid-touting father.'

'There's no way Dr Baystone should have made you do that exercise anyway.'

'Yeah,' says Mei. 'He wouldn't get away with pushing you like that at a normal school. He's not even a real doctor, you know.'

'What?' I say.

'I mean, he's got a PhD or whatever, but he's not like an actual medical doctor.'

'I'm not sure that's true, but he's definitely irresponsible,' adds Olivia. 'Anyway, try to forget about it for now. Come to my Culinary Arts thing later? There's going to be a special guest.'

'I have to talk to Cal.' I stand up.

'I don't think that's a good idea,' says Mei.

'I have to try.'

'Dr Baystone told you not to try to see him,' Olivia reminds me.

'You just said he's irresponsible,' I say.

'He is, but that doesn't mean you should make this worse than it already is.'

I shrug. 'I'll see you later.'

They know better than to come after me.

I find Cal in his studio.

'Can we talk?' I ask.

He sets his paintbrush down on the easel shelf and lifts a loose cover over the painting. His arm is protected by a jumper now so I can't see how much damage I did.

I guess I look as terrible as I feel because he takes pity on me and agrees. 'Let's go outside,' he suggests.

We walk out to the field in between the studios and the boarding houses. Artists whisper as we pass.

'Does it hurt?' I ask.

'No.'

'I just want you to know that I'm sorry,' I say. 'I lost my mind in there this morning. That's not an excuse, I know, and I don't expect you to forgive me.'

'I've spoken to the head director,' he says.

'That's OK. If this was the other way around and you'd done it to me, things would probably be much worse and I know that's unfair. Dr Baystone told me I'll probably be kicked out.'

'I told them not to expel you.'

'What?'

'I don't want you to go and I accept your apology, but it can't happen again. Do you understand?'

'Yes.'

We both mean it.

'I just want you to be safe,' he says. 'I know what it's like to be angry and out of control.'

'I thought you said you weren't angry.'

He laughs. 'I'm not any more.'

Of all the Artists, he seems the least likely to lose control even though he lost his mum. He has a real reason.

'I'm sorry,' I say again.

'I know. Just be careful, OK? I don't want anything to happen to you or for you to go anywhere.'

This is my last chance to get better.

Guilt and relief curdle in my stomach, making it ache.

'Cal?'

'Lux.'

'Do you want to come on what promises to be a really weird date with me tonight?'

FIFTEEN

Culinary Arts is in the block behind Cal's studio.

There's a sign on the door when he, Mei and I arrive. It reads: 'Provenance: the Feast of the Snowdrop'.

'Who do you think the special guest is?' asks Cal.

'Maybe it's Henry,' Mei whispers to me.

'Maybe it's Jade Grace,' I say loudly.

'Holy shitballs,' breathes Mei when we enter the studio and see the foodscapes Olivia and the others have created, largely from food grown on campus. The competing smells hit me like a truck. I breathe through my mouth to keep my mind clear.

The first table holds an animal menagerie on two levels. On the upper deck, I take in ladybirds made from Babybels (the one concession to supermarket food), ducks cut from biscuits swimming on a lake of dyed scrambled egg and sheep fashioned from cauliflower florets. In the middle is a huge loaf with the

Richdeane crest – the same one that's replicated in our tattoos – stained into it. Underneath appears to be an animal graveyard created from dried bones, their skulls stuffed with courgetti brains.

Minimalist beats seep from speakers positioned around the studio; almost everything has been taken away from the song, leaving a skeleton, the sound of subtraction. Recorded voices speak over the empty music.

'*The phytonutrients in artichokes inhibit receptors in the mouth, making the next thing that's consumed taste sweet.*'

'What the actual fuck?' mouths Mei.

'*Rhubarb leaves are poisonous.*'

'*The first soup was made in six thousand BC from hippo and sparrow meat.*'

'*Blue cheese contains natural amphetamines.*' Cal catches my eye on this one.

And so they continue, forty or so facts that play on a loop but are spoken by a different member of the collective each time.

Our hosts stand behind a low bar wearing stained butchers' aprons and making virgin cocktails. Olivia beams as she crushes a palmful of berries and muddles them with mint over ice. Her pale eyes are focused and her fingers deliberate. She has fastened her hair in a bun with the pink ends tucked away, the way her mother likes it.

Olivia looks over my head and waves. Kathleen Crown is here.

'Ms Crown,' she calls, skipping over to the minister, 'I'm so glad you could make it. My mum said you'd come, but I know how busy you are. You remember Lux, and this is her friend Cal.'

'Nice to meet you both,' says Ms Crown.

'We've met,' I say. 'At Olivia's house in September.'

'Ah, yes.'

'You remember me, don't you?'

Ms Crown recovers herself. 'Of course – how lovely to see you.'

'You don't remember me. You just said nice to meet me.'

'I'm sorry. I meet a lot of people. I remember you now.'

'Do you really?'

'Lux, please,' says Olivia, her voice tight.

Cal steers me away.

'That was a little rude,' he says.

'I know. I can't believe she didn't remember me.'

'I meant you,' he says gently.

'What? She's the one who should be embarrassed. It's rude to forget people.'

He looks so pityingly at me that I could cry, except I can't.

'I'm just saying she should have just pretended.'

I hold Cal's hand as we try to work out the rules to the cuisine on the various display tables. On the other side of the room, Olivia is cosying up to Angry Jack, who actually looks pretty calm. Some foods lie on a bed of soil, united by the earth, like the sugary woodiness of carrots and the flowerbed taste of nasturtiums.

The facts continue.

'*Orchid vanilla is a by-product of the paper industry.*'

'*Pears, plums and apples belong to the rose family.*'

'*The stamen and stem are the bitterest part of edible flowers.*'

The whole thing is thrilling and different to us.

Some of the combinations don't immediately seem to complement each other but might have, for example, a shared affinity with fromage frais – berries, mushrooms, leeks. Then there are the subversive pairings – vodka and truffles, white bread with gold bullion bouillon, potato and caviar, the food of peasants and kings boldly married in a dish.

'*Coconut water can be used as blood plasma.*' The voices from the speakers get louder.

'Good to know,' says Cal.

'*Food safety guidelines in some countries permit up to twenty whole insects per two hundred and twenty-five grams of raisins.*'

'*Ketchup was used as medicine in the eighteen hundreds.*'

The appalling beauty of the feast coupled with the stereo facts are something of an appetite killer. Plus, we're really not supposed to eat off-menu so we just drink our mocktails and move on to warm plum juice, stirring our liquid rebellion with oversized cinnamon scrolls.

'*Cheese is the most shoplifted food in the world.*'

'That'll be the natural amphetamines,' says Mei.

'*Putting a live frog in milk is thought to keep it fresh in the absence of refrigeration.*'

'I'm sorry about earlier with the minister,' I say to Olivia when I get a chance.

'It's OK.' She squeezes my hand.

'I feel so lost. I don't know how to explain it; I just really need other people to know who I am to keep me in place.'

'I know who you are, Lux.'

I don't deserve her.

After twenty minutes or so, the facts fade to silence and are replaced by the noise of metal chiming against crystal. Olivia and her collective are lined up by the door, clanging spoons against their glasses, an army of toastmasters calling a party to attention.

'To art,' says Olivia, looking directly into the lens of the small CCTV camera above the door. We all raise our glasses. 'Thank you for coming, gastronauts.'

There is no curtain to drop to signal the end so she simply opens the door. She has controlled the food and now she controls us.

As we leave, the collective proffer petit fours. I take one.

Ms Crown stays inside to talk to Olivia.

'Thank Thor that's over,' says Mei. 'Sometimes I forget how absolutely batshit crazy this place is.'

'I thought it was cool,' says Cal. 'Kind of a weird date, as promised. Shame we didn't get to eat any of it.'

'I bet Olivia and those guys are stuffing their faces right now,' I say.

'I highly doubt that,' says Mei.

'Why?' I ask.

'When was the last time you saw Olivia stuff herself,' says Mei. 'She is her mother's daughter after all.'

The petit four is melting in my hand, so I cram it into my mouth whole for lack of a better place to put it and wipe my hand on the inside of my pocket. It's vanilla. Vanilla is an insult to some people, but some days I would give up every flavour in my body to be just vanilla.

SIXTEEN

It's easier to be around Cal than Mei and Olivia. I love them so much but being with them reminds me how much I've changed. I'm unreliable – cancelled plans because of the migraines, waking Mei up with my nightmares, forgetting we've arranged to do things. Cal only knows me as I am now. And he thinks I'm funny.

After our weird date, we're together. It's unceremonious and unspoken. I could easily pull the plug, but something stops me – the will of the muses maybe. His commitment to the pledge runs so deep; I hope some of it will rub off on me, and make me better.

A gentle adrenaline washes through me whenever I see him. He talks more than me but his cracked voice doesn't make my skin prickle like some sounds do.

Dr Baystone apologises to me and Cal for putting us in a volatile situation; he says he should have predicted that the pressure would be too much for me. Cal sets the tone for the other Artists to forgive me, though Millie clearly thinks I should have myself arrested if Cal's not going to. I get a pain in the back of my throat when I think about lashing out at him.

I start to get the pain when I think about my parents too. This is the longest I've ever been without speaking with them. I worry one of them will die in an accident and the last words I'll have said to them will have been: 'I don't want to see you.' But when I think about calling them or seeing them on Skype, the pain in my throat becomes a stab, and a hum of our summer fights starts to build until I'm dizzy and have to push them out of my mind.

In between my migraines and meltdowns, Cal and I hang out with my friends and with his, and sometimes with both. Sometimes we skip class to teach each other things. Sometimes he takes me to the contemplation room to focus on the pledge. He tries to get me to go on his runs with him to blow off steam, but I don't. If this were AA, I guess he would be my sponsor. Except he's the new one and I'm just going through the motions without actually getting any better.

I am out of the Richdeane loop. He's fully plugged in.

'Did you hear about Isabella?' he asks.

'What about Isabella?' I can only imagine. She was my main competitor for the unofficial title of 'Most Fucked-Up Artist With No Actual Problems' last year.

'She's signed on to do a film,' he says.

'Wow. Amazing. What kind of film?'

'Adult.'

'Oh.'

'Yes, oh.'

My first question is what her parents will say.

'Doesn't matter – she's eighteen.'

'What did the directors say?' I ask.

'The usual stuff: sexualisation of children, casting couch, too young to know what we want.'

'Hmmmm.' Trust Isabella to take it further than any of us.

'What do you think?' he asks.

'I don't know really. I was just thinking maybe porn is the purest performance there is.'

'I'm not sure I follow.'

This is getting embarrassing, but I can't stop now or I'll look as immature as I feel. 'Well, they've got to really commit to the moment for it to work. Especially the men.'

He laughs. 'I suppose so, but you know they have people to help with that. They're called fluffers. And they have Viagra.'

'I wish there was a Viagra for the kind of performance we do here. And for life in general,' I say.

'You mean like a truth serum?' he laughs.

'Maybe,' I say. 'I don't know. I'm being stupid.'

'You're not being stupid.'

This is why I should avoid having real conversations; my filter doesn't work properly any more.

He takes pity on me and says, 'Don't get all weird. I can see you sinking. Shake it off.'

'Did you just quote Taylor Swift?'

'You can learn a lot from the teachings of T-Swift,' he says.

'You're a funny boy,' I tell him.

'Don't hate the player, hate the game,' he says, in an accent that I think is supposed to be American.

'You really can't pull that off,' I say, although actually it suits him. Not for the first time, I think he'd make a great American. I thought that about Henry too, so maybe it's me that's different, not them.

'Pipe down, shorty,' he says. 'I'm cooler than you.'

'So? I'm funnier than you,' I say.

He laughs.

'See. Told you.'

'While we're talking truth serum,' he says, 'I have a question for you.'

What happened at the party? How did you get to the hospital? What happened when you woke up?

'Ask me anything. If I know the answer, I'll tell you.'

'How many boyfriends have you had?'

His gentlemanly euphemism allows me not to answer his real question, not to tell him about Henry and the other couple of guys this summer before my blackout. Once I'd broken the seal with Henry, I had some catching up to do so that my experience could keep pace with my reputation. Cal and I never do more than kiss. He's probably trying not to rush me. Or he can tell there's something wrong with me and doesn't want to catch it.

'You can talk to me, you know,' he says.

'Am I that transparent?'

'I can see you're somewhere south of happiness.' He gives me a little nudge with his elbow.

'Sadville. Population: me,' I say. But it doesn't work on him. Usually if you make a joke out of something, you can avoid revealing any more. People will too busy laughing or thinking you're a show-off.

'Don't do that,' he says. 'Just say what you want to say for once.'

'I'm broken. I feel really, really broken and lost. I just want to find myself again.'

'I know. You've got to work at it.'

Why do people keep saying that?

The supper reminder buzzes away overhead.

Well-trained, he says, 'Come on – trough time.'

Time is running out. I dedicate the rest of November to doing as Dr Baystone instructs me, writing down every disconnected thought or dream I have and trying to piece them all together, as if it can drag me back into myself and stop the head director from sending me away. I swallow down pills till I rattle, and fight to stay in my body.

It feels good to write even if it's just decanting things from my own head and sending messages to Jade.

Dear Jade,

I think it's sick that you won't reply to me. You were just like one of us a few years ago. Are you too good for Richdeane now?

The thing about being on a secure campus is that the most dangerous neighbourhoods I can go to are the recesses of my own mind.

I don't hand any of the writing in and nobody asks me to.

When we're alone, Cal and I practise Dr Baystone's acting exercises. He says to think of doing the exercises in the same way as an athlete works out at the gym. So we train in emotional agility in one of the smaller studios most days; the majority of our conversation is improvised dialogue. I make teddy-bear-feelings faces as we talk in sad, mad, glad circles. I'm not sure who is dialling me up and down, but I don't think it's me. I still only seem to have two settings – emotionally comatose or suspended in floating anger.

I have more headaches than ever and hear colours everywhere and in everything. Sometimes when I'm just hanging out with Cal or the girls, flashes of red colour my vision and block my ears. Sometimes red brings her friends orange and yellow. I long for the days when I felt wild and powerful, even though Cal wouldn't have liked that Lux. The further I get from her the more I think she was lost in her own way.

I'm hot inside but winter is cold, cold, cold. The snowdrops appear on campus two months early, as if they know I won't be here to see them in January.

I see myself pulling the sleeping flowers from their soil beds and snapping their drooping heads off to stop them from screaming.

Does Jade Grace think of Richdeane's snowdrops when she's in her lonely hotel rooms or waiting in her trailer to be called to set? She still hasn't replied to me. I write to her again, explaining all the ways that we're the same.

The early snowdrop season passes; I'll have to get through the rest of winter without the balm of the little white flowers, which disappear back into the earth. Were they even here?

On 23 November, I turn eighteen. My friends sing 'Happy Birthday' in complicated harmonies. I float up to the ceiling like a balloon and come back down just in time to blow out the candles. I wish for wellness. My parents leave me a voicemail.

Their voices hurt. I email them to say I love them but I don't want to talk to them yet. I'll be sent to them soon enough.

Becoming an adult doesn't change anything.

I go back to Dr Purves. Dr Baystone, my surrogate parent, goes in to talk to her first, then she asks me all the same questions again about my blackout, paying close attention as if she thinks I was lying the first time and she's trying to catch me out. She tells me I'm taking too many painkillers and that they're probably causing rebound headaches. They give me different pills to take to abort the big ones when I feel them coming.

The doctors suggest I try harder at talking therapies instead, so I keep talking to Dr Baystone and I talk to Cal a little more. Other than that, it's more watch and wait. WAW. I don't have the disposition for it.

'Where do you go when you go away?' Cal asks me one day after a particularly vicious migraine sends me into a trance.

'I just space out, I guess. I sort of go deep into myself and far away at the same time, like I'm an echo,' I say.

'One day I'll paint what's in your head.'

'I wouldn't inflict that on you.' And then I ask him, finally, 'What are you getting out of this?'

'This what?'

'This … us.'

'The same as you, I guess.'

He takes up Mei and Olivia's mantle of supervising me in my room while I try to sleep off my migraines. I wonder if they agreed it between the three of them or if he just wants to. I try to keep still in my sleep but I dream with my whole body, knocking over lamps and books, and wake up aching all over.

I tell Dr Baystone I think it's OK for Cal and me to spend time together as long as neither of us thinks it's permanent.

'What would be so bad about it being permanent?' asks Dr Baystone.

'It can't be permanent. Let's face it – it's been almost four months since I blacked out, I've been back here two and a half months, we've been meeting almost every day and I'm not getting any better. I'll be sent away at Christmas and we both know it.'

'You need to try harder, Lux.'

When I get back to Dylan House, I dye my hair red to match Jade Grace and my raw gums. I recognise myself even less when I look in the mirror. My hair stains my pillow the colour of dreams as I sweat in the night. The ruined sheets remind me of my time on the ceiling in the hospital and that poor girl in the bed below me.

A couple of days later, on 1st December, two weeks before my inevitable exile, Cal meets me in the library.

Etched along one of the shelves, tiny graffiti letters read: '*A pledge inspector is easy to spot. They look just like you.*' There's no tag but I have a sense that Jade Grace did it. I think I hear the whir of a CCTV camera zoom in to get a better shot.

Cal finds me judging all the books by their covers.

'You're really not supposed to do that.' He shakes his head in faux disappointment. 'Old enough to know better, still too young to care. Naughty rabbit.'

'You're philosophical today,' I tell him.

'I love you today,' he says.

Nobody has told me that before. I mean, apart from my parents. I knew they loved me when I was little but I don't remember them actually telling me until this summer. Love: the other side of our fights.

He says it again and something momentous comes to the surface like a whale breaking through the sea into the air.

I say it back, like he really knows me and really loves me. His leather jacket creaks a little as he lifts his hands up to my hair. When we kiss, I move his hands down to my hips so my face is visible in case the cameras are watching.

'Stop it,' I mumble into his mouth.

He pulls away.

'Not you – I was talking to myself.'

'Oh, OK,' he says as if that's the most normal thing in the world.

'I'm sorry. I don't think I can do this. You don't know what you're getting yourself into. I'm leaving soon.'

The memory of Mei and Olivia talking to him outside assembly the night after Halloween spikes. I wish they had been warning him against me. I wish he had listened.

'We're all leaving soon. School finishes in six months,' he says. 'And didn't you read the prospectus before your parents sent you here? We've all got a story.'

One of the laminated posters from the kitchen in my father's old office pops into my mind. Held up by yellow fridge magnets it read: 'You don't have to be mad to work here, but it helps.'

Cal continues: 'This place can help you. It's helping me.'

'What could you possibly need help with?'

'You don't know everything, Lux,' he says. 'Anyway, right now I've got a serious case of basorexia that I'm hoping you can assist me with.'

*   *   *

After I've looked it up, I know I need to write 'basorexia' down, even though it's the cheesiest thing ever. And then something else surfaces, déjà vu, maybe, or a false memory. No, it's real. I have a word collection that I started at my internship.

I find the notebook in a pocket of my suitcase. Did my parents pack it for me?

Word collection:

Saudade (Portuguese, Galician)
– Similar but not equal to nostalgia. A melancholic feeling of incompleteness. Missing people, places and things.

Articulate (English)
– Speaking fluently, clearly.
– Jointed, segmented, hinged for flexibility.

Kummerspeck (German)
– Weight gained by emotional eating.

Koi no yokan (Japanese)
– When two people meet and sense they will fall in love.

Duende (Spanish)
– A heightened state of emotion, attributed to the power of art to move someone. Often associated with flamenco.

Express (English)
– Convey or manifest a thought or feeling.

– Press out liquid or air.

– The appearance in a phenotype of a characteristic or effect attributed to a specific gene.

Communicate (English)
– Share knowledge, make known.
– The passing on of infectious diseases.
– Two rooms with a connecting door.
– Receive Communion.

Gossypiboma (English)
– Surgical complications resulting from foreign materials accidentally left inside a patient's body.

Cavoli riscaldati (Italian)
– The result of trying to revive a failing relationship.

Litost (Czech)
– Torment created by the sudden sight of your own misery.

Nyctophilia (English)
– A preference for darkness or night.

Gezelligheid (Dutch)
– Comfort and cosiness of togetherness.

Lalochezia (English)
– Relieving stress or pain through using vulgar language.

Kenshō (Japanese)
— From Zen tradition, self-realisation.

Confabulation (English)
— The falsification or distortion of memories without the conscious intention to deceive.

Sehnsucht (German)
— A deep emotional state, originating from yearning and addiction.

I add my new word.

Basorexia (English)
— An overwhelming hunger to kiss.

And as I do, the darkroom in my head develops a new picture. A girl. Older than me, maybe twenty-two or twenty-three.

Red hair.

I remember her.

She was a gallery tour guide, I think.

I can't remember her name and when I try to reach for it at the back of my mind a headache starts to creep around it so that I can't quite get to it.

She had a little notebook that she wrote all her favourite words in and I thought it would be cool to do the same. More than cool, it seemed necessary that I be as much like her as I could. She was so together and grown-up.

But her face won't develop in full – just an eye, her silver jewellery, a red jumper.

I breathe deeply like Dr Baystone taught me, and roll my neck back as if it might dislodge more pieces of her from between the grey folds in my brain. I shake my head like a snow globe and once the snow settles I find her painted nails and the tiny infinity of moles on her forearm.

I can't put the pieces together to make a face or attach it to a body, but I remember the feeling I got when I met her. I remember immediately wanting to be her as, before I can stop myself, I always want to be anyone I admire. The same feeling I get with Jade Grace – as if my identity shifts and I'm closer to the truth.

Was she there the night of the party? She might have seen me blackout; maybe she was even the one who called the ambulance. I hope I didn't puke on her; she really didn't deserve that. Did she notice when I didn't turn up to my final day at work?

I'd like to show her my word list, even though I didn't really know her.

The invisible thread between Jade Grace and me twangs, and I send her the list instead.

I get a bounceback straightaway. I must have sent it to the wrong address. Nope, it's saved in my contacts, so it can't be that. I resend it – tapping the address out with my finger just in case there's a glitch in the system. Another bounceback. This time I open it and read: 'Fatal error. User unavailable.' How dramatic. But if she was actually dead it would have been on the news.

A rush of shame fires up from my stomach to my cheeks; she's blocked me, like my mind blocked the gallery girl from my memory.

I don't know how to tell Dr Baystone that remembering these little fragments makes me feel worse. They make me realise I'm not safe. That something is coming for me.

SEVENTEEN

My stomach is chewing on itself when I wake up, as if I've had a fight with someone but can't remember who.

I ask Dr Baystone to meet me in the library after classes because it's too cold and dark outside.

'Before we start, your parents wanted me to pass on a message. They'll pick you up at the end of term.'

'They're coming here?'

'You'll have Christmas in London so you're close to your doctors.'

'So I don't have to go to Singapore?'

'We'll see.'

'I remembered something,' I say.

I tell him about the gallery girl and the word collection.

'That's fantastic, Lux. This is real progress. I'll have to tell your parents about this, OK?'

'Really? But I barely knew her.' I've dredged my memory and checked all my pictures online, but I don't have any of us together – or of her at all.

'How does it feel remembering this and telling me about it?'

I don't trust it. Information that wasn't visible this time yesterday. And what if the girl is at the gallery now telling her new intern what a liability I was and that I didn't even bother turning up for my last day. I thought about looking her up on the website, to remind myself what she was called, but that feels like putting a name to my shame. Or, worse, it'll turn out that I've made her up.

'Sick. Like I want to run away.'

'Where would you go?'

'I don't know. California, maybe.'

'California is a great place to live. If you're an orange.'

Orange is not the only fruit. Orange is the happiest colour. Agent Orange. Nothing rhymes with orange.

'But I don't think they've decriminalised carbs there yet,' he adds. 'That's a joke.'

We sit in quiet. I win silence-chicken for once and he talks first.

'Lux, we need to keep working at this.'

So we go around the questions for the fiftieth time …

'I was at a party with some people from my internship and then I woke up in hospital.'

'Think harder. Who were you with?'

'I can't remember.'

He holds my eyes with his.

'I can't remember. It's like it happened to a different body that got lost, and the one I have now is just full of song lyrics and things other people have said.'

'The way to break down those avoidance mechanisms is to confront what purpose they might be serving you.'

'They're not serving any purpose. I don't want to spend my whole life looking at pictures in my head and not knowing what's real.'

'So we need to find a way for you to let it all go.'

'But what if it won't let me go.'

'You have the power here. You can give it and you can take it away. What is it about red, for example, that preoccupies you?'

'It has the longest wavelength.' I don't even know what that means, I just read it on the internet. 'And it's the colour of Mars. And fire and blood.'

'Are those things significant?' he asks.

'I think so. There's meaning in everything, isn't there? But when I try to think clearly, everything's just colour.'

'And what would happen if the colour went away?'

'I don't know. Everything else would be too loud, I think.'

'So the colour keeps other things quiet?'

'I guess, in a weird way,' I say. 'It's more like a different kind of noise.'

'Red is also the colour of remembrance, you know. Poppies. So, let's try again. How did you get to the hospital?'

Nothing.

'What about when you woke up? What did the doctors say to you? What did your parents say?'

'I don't know. I can't remember,' I say. He thinks I'm lying. I try to swallow down the anger and confusion.

'You can.'

It bursts out of me. 'You don't know what you're talking

about. I don't remember any of it. I was unconscious; I don't know what else you want from me.' I know it's not his fault, but I scream at him anyway. 'You're not helping me. I need a different doctor – a proper one.'

My insides are still boiling when I get back to Dylan. I throw my coat on the bed and grip the edge of my desk, looking out on to the grounds. How do normal people calm themselves down? I wish I could ask Jade Grace what she'd do.

My eyes reach the edge of the fields and land on the trees that hem us in.

'Expose yourself to what you're afraid of.'

Of course. If something is coming for me, it'll come from the woods. I can't stand watching and waiting any more. No more WAW. I must go out and meet it.

Mei will be back any minute, so I leg it downstairs.

I cut straight across the path and on to the lawn. The grass is springy as I pace towards the woods following the whisper that calls me into the trees. I know it's a bad idea. I've seen enough films to know that no good ever comes of a girl running into a forest, but adrenaline thunders through me and powers me forward.

As I push deeper through the woods, it gets dark and dense. Twigs crack under my feet and I slide on dank moss and loose earth. Bark fingers reach for me, dragging across my clothes as I misjudge my path.

The trees and plants vibrate, filling my lungs with their oxygen. I'm running now, leaping over uneven patches of ground as if they're buried mines. I can smell every flower and mushroom, all the earth and all the leaves.

Running, stumbling, running.

Following the whisper.

Breathing it all in.

I don't know where I end and the trees begin until a branch smacks my cheek, slowing me down and forcing me to hold my hands in front of my face to protect it.

I can't hear the call any more. I don't know where I'm going or what I'm looking for.

Immediately as I lose focus, I lose my footing too, and I slip to the ground where the surreal becomes real.

I look around in the twilight. Nothing but trees and dirt, and the sound of my own heavy breathing.

I lie down in the soft dirt and look up. The trees rustle and the ants crawl.

Name three things you can see, Lux.

Trees, trees, trees.

'I'm crazy.'

I sit up and crouch while I pull myself together, collecting my scattered thoughts and steadying my breath.

'What am I doing?'

I wish I had my coat.

My phone buzzes in my pocket. It's Mei.

I send her a message to say I'll be back in ten minutes.

It buzzes again, then again. I switch the vibrate off so I can concentrate, then shine its torch in front of me while I try to pick my way out through the trees back to the school grounds. I stumble around for what feels like forever, mistrusting my sense of direction then looping back on myself. Everything is just shapes now, as if I'm looking at life through a dirty helmet.

The signal goes on my phone and by the time I find my way out back to the grounds I'm shaking. I emerge at the other end of the campus near the driveway and drag myself to Dylan House.

'Where the hell have you been? I've been calling you,' says Mei when I get back to our dorm. 'Dr Baystone said you ran off two hours ago.'

'I needed some air.' I kick off my shoes and lie down on my bed, pulling the blanket up to my chin. 'I'm exhausted.'

My hands are dry with mud. I'm not going to wash them; I need to remember where I've been and that I found nothing there. A trail of dirt runs from the doorway to my bed like filthy breadcrumbs; if anything followed me out of the woods, I won't be hard to find.

'What happened to your face?'

'Nothing. I'm just cold.'

'It's bleeding.'

I'm so tired the truth just tumbles out. 'I got lost in the woods.'

While she works out that I'm speaking literally, not metaphorically, for once, I clarify, 'And a branch hit me in the face.'

'You were in the woods?'

'I was in the woods,' I repeat like we're doing one of Dr B's exercises.

She looks at me like I'm insane. 'Why were you in the woods?'

'I don't know. I think I was looking for something – I can't really remember.'

This is too much for Mei. She bursts into frustrated tears. 'God, you are so selfish. I'm sick of tiptoeing around you. I can't watch you every second of every day, Lux. I'm not your fucking carer.'

EIGHTEEN

Mei apologises first, even though I was clearly in the wrong. Her readiness to let me off the hook is weird, especially given how upset she was last night. She must just feel sorry for me because she can see I'm losing it.

'Please don't run off like that again – promise me.'

She helps me change my muddy sheets and tells me about some changes to assembly. The head director has decided we need to be divided and conquered so the all-school meetings will be cut back to just Fridays and we've each been assigned a smaller group to attend on other days instead. Worst of all, Olivia, Mei, Cal and I are all in separate ones. I'm in Dr Baystone's group. I think this is called 'continuity of care' in professional circles. Either that or he is obsessed with me.

As I walk to the first meeting, I think about sacking it off and pretending I have a migraine because I don't want to see Dr Baystone, but that feels too much like tempting fate.

There are twelve chairs arranged in a circle when I get to the studio. Dr Baystone is seated on one of them. He smiles at me as if I hadn't screamed at him and told him I wanted a different doctor under twenty-four hours ago. Can't he at least be a dick about it so I don't feel so bad?

Georgia and Millie are there, their hands tangled together by the sides of their chairs. Cal is there too, with Luca and Davy. How come Cal is allowed to be in the same group as his friends, but Mei, Olivia and I are all separated?

'Saved you a seat,' says Cal.

'I thought we were supposed to be in different groups,' I say.

'We were. Dr B swapped me in this morning. What happened to your cheek?'

'Dr B?'

'He told us to call him that.'

That stings. I'm annoyed with myself for being possessive over a doctor I don't even want, but I resolve to start calling him Dr B too.

'Your cheek?'

'I scratched it in my sleep.' A lie, but being lost in the woods also feels like a lie now.

I look over to Millie; we haven't been in the same room since she made it her duty to tell everyone I was a maniac.

'Don't,' whispers Cal.

'I know.'

I have to stifle a laugh when I clock an ornate urn on a table by the window. Coffee and feelings, like in one of Jade Grace's rehab songs. No doubt it's full of Richdeane-grown camomile infusion instead of coffee. A weak point in this carefully crafted divulgement ritual.

Dr B starts us in a round robin of 'I feel like saying …'

The twelve of us go round the circle and we take it in turns to say something we feel like saying. That's it.

'I feel like saying I'm proud of you all for coming,' says Dr B.

'I feel like saying I'm tired so don't take offence if I just listen today,' says Millie.

A few of the others admit to their various frames of mind. Feelings snap, crackle and pop in the air.

'I feel like saying I heard from some friends from my old life this week and I'm tempted to go back to the old me,' says Luca.

'I feel like saying I miss my mum,' says Cal.

I'm tempted to say something like 'I feel like a snack' but I find myself saying, 'I feel like saying I think I've been a bad friend lately.'

'I feel like saying I can't wait to start my community outreach project,' says Georgia.

'Thanks, everyone,' says Dr B. 'Anyone care to elaborate?'

'I will,' I say. Everyone looks stunned, which is fair since I haven't volunteered to spill in assembly at all this term. This is me trying harder; sort of an apology to Dr B.

'Great – take your time,' he says.

So I start: 'Mei and Olivia and I used to spend every second together, but this year we're sort of drifting apart. We just don't really talk that deeply any more. I didn't even notice at first, but now I think maybe it's my fault. Something happened to me this summer, and I've been feeling weird ever since, as if I'm one step removed from everyone.'

Then my tongue grinds to a halt and can't seem to manage any more.

'Anything else?' asks Dr B.

I shake my head.

'OK – thanks for sharing,' he says.

'Bullshit,' says Millie. 'How come she gets away with not joining in properly?'

'Shut up, Mills,' says Georgia.

'I thought you were tired,' adds Cal.

'Everyone knows she took too much gak or whatever and passed out. That was months ago. Much worse things happened this summer, so what's the big deal?' Millie's face flushes and she's bouncing around in her seat.

'Stay in your own experience, please, Millie; just sit with it. We never know each other's full story,' says Dr B.

'Fine, but I don't think it's fair she gets special treatment,' says Millie.

She reminds me of myself last year – overconfident and certain – so it's hard to hate her. Besides, her performances in assemblies are always exquisite.

'Let's move on, shall we?' Dr B says. 'And I'd like to remind you all that anything we say in here should stay between us.'

I look towards the window above the urn, where the December murk is closing in against the glass. Millie raises her hand. Georgia whispers, 'Go on, lover.' I've never heard anyone our age use the word 'lover' before. It's so adult and intimate.

Georgia pulls a blank sheet of paper out of her bag and starts folding it in her lap. My fingers stretch out as my hands remember the steadying sensation of folding clothes.

Millie gives a rousing share about how she pities those who do not live by the pledge. The unpledged, she calls them. Her heart breaks for them. She makes no attempt to wipe away the tears as muddy rivers mark her beautiful face. She acts with the kind of reckless self-acceptance that can only indicate one thing: crippling self-doubt.

This is better than sad videos on YouTube. A chance to emote vicariously. My shares have no value but here I can trade silently without the cost, the tax, the shame of outward expression.

'Thank you, Millie,' says Dr B. 'I'm always impressed with the maturity of expression you Artists show. You're not like any other young people I've ever met. Your training coming through, I suppose. That said, try to focus on your own experience next time.'

We all echo his thanks apart from Davy who compliments Georgia on her 'exceptional taste in gash'.

'Don't be vulgar,' Georgia says, but she looks proud.

Dr B pretends not to hear.

'Thank you, Dr B,' says Millie, and then she subtly high-fives Georgia and whispers: 'And that is how you share.'

Luca is up next. His share echoes the style of the head director's assembly speeches: inelegant and full of contradictions, yet somehow compelling. He jabs at our heartstrings, twanging one and then moving on to the next without really putting a tune to the noise. He remembers disjointed, unedited tales of stolen cars and wrong turns. We hold him in our circle while he tries to piece the bits together.

'Richdeane saved me, the pledge saved me,' he concludes. 'Cal saved me.'

'Thank you, Luca, that felt very truthful,' says Dr Baystone. 'Just remember that others can't save us, only help us. And, Cal, you're a born leader but you can't fix everybody.'

Everyone looks first at Cal and then at me, as if I'm the most broken bird of all and he may as well not even bother trying to save me.

These tropes of troubled and rescued teens should embarrass me. I should cringe at the clichés. But words are the most powerful drug, someone famous said that once, I think, and I find myself buzzing.

At the end of the session, I sidle over to Georgia.

'Can I ask you something?'

'Sure.'

'What's with the origami?'

'It helps me make sense of things.'

She starts telling me about her outreach programme. It's to give some Artists the opportunity to pay it forward. Plus, Richdeane has a bit of a PR problem, she confides, and this is a chance to do a good deed and show people we know how fortunate we are.

Georgia isn't as intimidating as I thought and she cares about this stuff. She could be the perfect pledge, like Cal.

She turns to pick up her bag and then turns back to me, holding out an origami bird.

'It's a swan,' she says. 'Serene on the surface but paddling like hell under the water. Like you.'

'What?'

'Takes one to know one.' She gets up to leave.

Once everyone is gone, I ask Dr B if I can speak with him.

'I'm sorry about saying you aren't a real doctor. You are real.'

'Thank you, Lux. Consider it forgotten.'

'I mean it; I'm sorry.'

'I know you are.'

Not much point in him being mad at me, I suppose – I'll be gone in a couple of weeks anyway. Or maybe he just feels sorry for me too. Either way, since I'm on a roll, I need to find Olivia – even though I'm drained from the morning's emotional tourism.

When I get to her room I realise I haven't stepped foot in it this term despite it being only a hundred metres or so from Dylan House. It's the same as always, a single, with a collage of dancers across the walls. Ballerinas, flamenco dancers, old black-and-white pictures of people I don't recognise all join together in a frozen finale, next to pictures of us at the Leavers' Ball. Just like the ones in my head.

She pats the bed and I plonk myself down next to her.

She's on her laptop deleting photos.

'What are you doing?'

'Jack broke up with me, so I'm deleting him,' she says.

'Angry Jack?'

'He's just called Jack, actually, but yes.'

'I'm sorry.' I didn't even know they were properly together.

'Thanks – I'll be OK. I'm just sad today.'

She shows me a picture of her parents' new dog.

'Cute, huh?' she says. 'They weren't going to get another one, but they really missed having Scruffs about.'

'What happened to Scruffs?'

'We had to put her to sleep.'

'Oh god – why didn't you tell me?'

'I thought I did. Francis buried him in the back garden, next to Sprinkles.'

'I'm so sorry.'

It's unconscionable that Scruffs is cold and underground with the worms. My mind chases a terrible idea that she'd been going round drinking up all Olivia's mum's spilt martinis and had died of alcoholism.

'Do you want to see the video Cal and I made?' she asks. 'It's finally finished.'

The least I can do is muster the grace to watch it. Cal's not even in it; he must have been behind the camera. They say the camera adds ten pounds, but it certainly doesn't to Olivia – she dances like a feather in the air. She and the other dancers roll each other in liquid bronze and pewter, and dance a stunning robot dream about the rise of a family of machines. Two miniature ponies also feature. I'm not sure why; maybe they look particularly good on camera or it's something to do with sponsorship.

'It's beautiful,' I say.

'Thanks,' she says, pushing her laptop off her knees on to the bed. 'Can I ask you something? I know you're not speaking to your parents, but do you ever wish you didn't go to boarding school?'

'No. It's not like kids at day school ever talk to their parents – they just go home and go to their rooms. Even if the family are all in the same room, they're either fighting or they've got their headphones in. Besides, we'll be done in under six months.'

'I guess.' Without warning, her eyes spill over. A diamond drops with every heartbeat.

I try to summon my milk of human kindness, but it's sour; I can't find the right thing to say. I want to tell her I love her and that she's my best friend. That I feel like she's on loan to me, and that someday soon her rightful, deserving friends will come for her. Instead, I give her a little headbutt on the shoulder and hope she can translate it.

'I'm sorry – I shouldn't be crying, especially after everything you're going through,' she says.

'I came to see if you're OK, Livvypops?' Mei appears in the doorway.

She joins us on the bed. We sit, three pairs of legs in black skinny jeans sticking out in front of us. Olivia's are the longest, then mine, then Mei's.

'I could kill him,' says Mei. 'That boy has no bastard idea how lucky he was.'

Mei and I each hold one of Olivia's hands.

'This is nice,' she says.

'Careful,' I say.

'Don't ruin it,' says Mei, choking on a giggle.

It feels good to laugh.

I take a deep breath and apologise. 'I'm sorry I've been so distant. I know I've been hard work lately.'

'That's OK, Lux,' says Olivia. 'We know you're going through some stuff. Don't we, Mei?'

That's why she's hard to be around sometimes; she can read me like a book.

'Yes,' says Mei. Their special look passes between them again and I know Mei has told Olivia about me going into the woods last night. 'Anyway,' she continues, 'we're all hard work. All the best people are so don't even worry about it.'

They laugh.

'There's something else,' I say. 'I think I'm leaving at the end of term.'

'We know,' says Mei.

'What? How?'

'Your parents emailed,' says Olivia just as Mei says, 'Cal let it slip.'

'Well, which is it?'

'Both actually,' says Mei. 'Your parents were just checking you were OK.'

'How embarrassing,' I say. 'Please don't talk about me behind my back.'

'They're your parents, Lux,' says Mei. 'And you won't talk to them, so they had to ask us.'

'We hope you don't have to go,' says Olivia.

NINETEEN

That night, I'm scared to sleep and, since I'm probably going to get evicted soon anyway, I decide to sneak into Van Sant House to see Cal.

Inside, the air is thick with sleep and musty with the nocturnal emissions of forty teenagers. I rake my hand through my hair to tidy it, but nobody's awake to see me. I'm halfway up the shiny staircase when an alarm sounds, breaking the opiate calm.

I dig my fingernails into my palms and breathe through the panic. It's just a test, a reminder not to feel too safe. I creep along the upstairs corridor, straining to read the names on the doors. Finally I find Cal's.

'What are you doing here?' he asks. He's wearing checked pyjamas and a grey T-shirt. The first time I've seen him not in black.

'I just wanted to see you.'

'It's three o'clock in the morning.'

'Is it?'

His room is not how I imagined. I'm not sure exactly what I'd envisaged – a shrine to the pledge, perhaps. Or, at the very least, I'd expected the walls to be papered with his sketches and paintings of all the stories he's stolen. But it's just like any other teenage boy's room – not that I've been in loads, but I've watched enough films to recognise the soggy towel on the chair, the hair wax, and so on.

'All my artwork is still in my studio,' he says, reading my mind.

The alarm, though fainter now, is a mood-killer.

'You OK?' he asks. 'Want some water or something?'

I shake my head. We sit down on his bed but, by the time the alarm stops, I'm not sure why I came.

'Can I stay?'

'Of course.'

I tuck a towel round a pillow so my hair dye doesn't rub off on it.

'Why did you dye it anyway?'

'I wanted to be more like Jade Grace.'

'Why?'

'I don't know. I feel like I met her in a past life or something.'

I don't admit that I sent her so many messages that she blocked me. I went back through my sent messages. There were more than I remember sending.

We lie down like spoons, but not touching.

I wonder what he thinks I came here for.

'You ready to sleep?' he asks. So much more tactful than 'Did you come here to have sex with me?'

I nod and try to act like I sleep in boys' beds all the time. No big deal. My breathing is ragged. I hold my breath to slow it down, but that just makes my head pound, so I breathe in and out as Cal does to regulate myself. I'm like one of those premature babies who gets put in an incubator with its stronger twin to keep it alive.

Cal runs a hand down from my shoulder to forearm over and over again. It's the good arm, not the one with the scar. It tickles.

Falling asleep seems too intimate, maybe more so than the alternative – but I don't want to leave. I try to keep my eyes open, but soon enough I'm running from flames and stumbling as dreamers do.

In the morning, xylophone beats of sunlight chime and fracture as they land on the window, forcing my eyes open.

'Did you sleep OK?' Cal asks.

'Did you? I sometimes sleep like a hurricane. I didn't sleep-punch you or anything, did I?'

I don't seem to have done any damage to his room at least.

He hesitates, probably trying to phrase things so as not to embarrass me, and says: 'No – you talked a bit, but no violence.'

'I hope I didn't say anything stupid. I better go and get ready for class.'

'Want me to walk you back to Dylan?' he asks.

'That's OK.'

I clock a few curious glances when I leave Van Sant as people misinterpret my unbrushed hair as a telltale missionary mess. I can hear them thinking. *Blackout Girl. Lash-out Girl. Dirty Stop-out Girl.*

I fumble in my bag for my brush and pull out a memory stick I'd forgotten I had. It has 'CerebroVista' printed on it in bold grape-purple letters alongside a cartoon fist giving an exaggerated thumbs up. Underneath the logo reads the slogan: 'Peace of mind'.

A memory of being inside a machine tumbles back to me. A machine to make visible the unknowable universe in my head.

The MRI scanner is the only place I've been since I blacked out that was louder than my own thoughts. It seems so long ago. My mother waiting outside for me. Dr Purves.

Maybe in another life the fear reversed my bloodstream and I carried on through the tunnel and came out the other side somewhere different. But, in this life, I came out the way I went in.

I thumb the memory stick. A souvenir copy of my brain scans from the good folk at CerebroVista. Better not show them to Dr B – he might want to incorporate them into some kind of elaborate sharing assembly. We're almost out of time together anyway.

All I know is that I never want to go back to hospital.

TWENTY

'This could be one of our last sessions,' I tell Dr B.

I've stopped trying to trick him into confirming I'm broken. I don't need that any more. Confirmation. Diagnosis. Validation. Whatever it's called. Red is red, after all.

'Yes, two weeks to go,' he says.

'My mother always gets her way in the end.'

'The head director fought your corner on that, you know?' he says. 'He convinced your parents you'd be safe here.'

I didn't know that. I assumed he thought I was just a troublemaker. At least the headaches and other stuff have forced me to slow down a bit now. I even look forward to Dr B's Coffee & Feelings meetings.

Cal often shares, relaxed as a cat in sunlight, spilling everything out in that voice that sounds like his vocal chords are inflamed. The bedrock of his confidence is his faith in the pledge. I wonder if he is attracted to the dark in me like I am to the light in him. Maybe I'll ask him before I leave.

'Tell me about the party,' Dr B says, sticking to our usual script. 'Before you blacked out.'

I need to tell him about the toxic tar that lives in me, compacting into a denser and denser sludge. I need his help to get it out because it's metastasising, but it's like dragging rotting hair from a shower drain and showing it to him. I've seen him help the others in Coffee & Feelings; he's an expert at knowing what questions you don't want to answer and at pulling stories out of the human body, slowly freeing orphaned thoughts.

We sit for a bit in our corner of the library. He looks at me while I stare at the books. It's almost like we're tucked between their pages.

'Lux,' he says. 'The party?'

I try to conjure the things I think I know and piece them together. The girl with the red hair, the smell of tequila on my skin when I woke up in hospital, the wound on my arm, the drip, my parents, Eighties music on the hospital radio.

'It was just a normal house party. It went on all night but it wasn't out of control, then the sun came up and I remember thinking that I needed to go home to get ready for my last day at the gallery.'

As soon as I say it I know it's fact.

'That's new. Keep going. What else do you remember?'

I close my eyes and try to see into the past, but my memories are like little silver fish darting behind rocks as soon as I catch a glimpse of them.

'That's it. Then I woke up in hospital, my throat hurt like I'd been throwing up all night and my head was banging. Once I could stay awake properly, my parents took me back to the flat in Waterloo. That was a few days, or maybe a week, later.'

'Go on,' he says.

And then a thought shoots out of my mouth like I'm Jade Grace: 'I think maybe they know more about what happened than I do. Like I did something. It must have been bad for them both to fly in from Singapore.'

'Like what?' he says.

'I don't know, but whatever it was messed up my brain. I want to go back and see them – the people at the gallery – but I feel like I shouldn't, like it wouldn't be the same.'

My eyes hurt and as I breathe the bookshelves close in and my lungs suck down dust. My throat aches and my windpipe starts to burn. I cough and fight to stay in my body. I will not float away this time.

'It's only emotion,' he says.

It feels like war and cancer and terrorism. And necrophilia and death and climate change.

'Just sit with it. This is a breakthrough.'

That's therapist-speak – we're always 'sitting with' things in Coffee & Feelings.

It's so dusty in here; I have to get out.

'It might hurt but it won't kill you. Don't push it away.'

One day I will walk into a Coffee & Feelings assembly and direct whoever's turn it is to share. '*Feel this for me,*' I will say to the surrogate, my host. And when they are done, I will swirl my tongue round the inside of their mouth, scraping out the virus, embracing the emotional contagion.

'Water?' asks Dr B.

I pull a bottle from my bag and dampen down the smoky dust in my throat. 'I need to get out of here.'

He is disappointed but I can't take any more. 'OK – you've done well today.'

'Dr B, I can't handle much more of this. I'm going mad, I know I am.'

'You're not.' His eyes betray him. He knows something I don't.

'What aren't you telling me?'

He doesn't answer.

'If you know something, you have to tell me.'

I feel sick. The room spins – or maybe I do.

'Lux, calm down.'

'What aren't you telling me?'

And then a flash goes off in my head and a picture develops in an instant. The girl in the hospital bed next to me. Oh my god, I put her there. I hurt her. I know I did.

'Did I hurt someone?'

'No, you didn't. I promise you didn't.'

Of course I didn't; I'd remember if I had.

'I have to get out of here. I need to see Cal.'

I sprint to Van Sant to find him; I feel myself disappearing as I go.

Cal's room is unlocked but empty so I run back downstairs, bashing into a fourth former. The collision pulls me back into myself.

'Touch me again,' I call down the hall after him.

He turns round. 'What did you say?'

'Please, come back and touch me.' I push up my sleeves. My arm still hasn't healed because I just can't leave it alone. 'I need you to touch me.'

He makes a complicated face. It shows a mix of many teddy-bear-feelings that's hard for me to read.

'I'll get Cal for you.'

The crazy is already fading. I'm coming back down.

'Don't. I don't need your help.'

I run to Cal's studio, trying to burn off the rest of the crazy before I get there.

Inside his studio block, I stumble down the hall. I know if I can just get to him, I'll be OK.

I slow down when I'm three doors from his and collect myself. Everything dissipates as fast as it formed. Back to numbness.

Cal's door is ajar. He's so absorbed in his work that I wish I could paint or draw just so I had a different way to explain myself.

He jumps when he sees me in the doorway.

'Want company?' I say.

Panic crosses his face.

'Let's go for a walk. These paint fumes are melting my brain.'

'Show me first,' I say.

'It's not finished.'

He starts to cover the easel as I step towards him.

'Why so shy all of a sudden? I share my shitty writing with you all the time.'

'You have literally never showed me any of your writing.'

'Oh yeah. Anyway, gimme.'

Saucers of discarded paint mixes in shades of party icing litter the floor. My organs pinch and flutter as pick my way over them and round to his side of the canvas.

He eases the cover back off the painting.

'I started it in the summer and abandoned it, but I realised I've got to finish it.' He chooses his words deliberately and says them slowly like he's training a dog.

He steps back so I can see the full painting and watches my reaction.

As I take in the canvas, my blood temperature sinks to the cold depths of the ocean while my heart burns and bumps.

The central figure is a snowdrop with proud, fiery petals. Bubble gum and lemon flames lick at a cobalt city, the oily buildings smoulder with Battenberg-tinted smoke which smells like icing sugar and fills the air with fragile piano music. It's a sound so familiar that my fingers long to feel the weight of piano keys under them even though they've never played. Déjà vu of something seen by another me. I wonder how far the scent and sound drift beyond the open windows.

The light intensifies and my lungs grow to the size of cars, impossible to fill without sucking all the oxygen out of the studio. In the yolky studio light, his work is beautiful and frightening.

I sway on the spot and Cal offers me some of his drink. We sip from a warm can in silence and my ears buzz with a woozy hum like fading bees drunk on sticky cola fumes.

'I can't believe this came out of your head,' I tell him. His chin is down but his shoulders are back and his chest puffs up a little.

He takes both my hands in his, zipping our fingers into two rows of scissor sisters. He smells of ambrosia, if ambrosia has a scent, or maybe that's the painting.

As he kisses my forehead, I almost ruin it by telling him I think there's a secret under the brushstrokes, but I don't want the moment to be lost. He looks at me like I am not nothing. Like I'm not a bruised apple that the wind shook from the tree and tossed to the ground before it was ready. And here in his arms I know I didn't hurt anyone.

I imagine that when he leaves the studio the buttery light goes too.

But he doesn't leave the studio. The muses have found him and only allow him snatches of sleep on the studio floor. The next day, I know I need to see the painting again. When I get to the studio, the light in my little sunbeam is fading. He usually smells of sleep and dreams and warmth. Today there are muddy brown crescents under his eyes and he smells ripe. Overripe. A rank bouquet of black-market Nescafé and exhaustion. I catch the dehydration on his breath as he falls into me and whispers: 'Is this real?'

'Of course,' I say as gravity tries to pull us both on to the stone studio floor.

'No, I mean really. You and me.'

The painting is gone and he's nailed a once-white piece of fabric over part of the studio wall like a sail or a shroud.

For once, I'm concrete and present. I'm the one holding us up, and I get this feeling that we're not just playing at it any more.

That we know things about each other that we haven't talked about yet and it breaks my heart that I have to leave soon.

'We're real. You need some sleep,' I tell him, taking his hands in mine by our sides. His fingers are rough with dried paint as he rests his chin on the top of my head.

'I feel like I am asleep,' he mumbles into my hair. 'I'm so tired.'

'School will be done soon. Our orbit is almost over. I have to leave before you. I'm sorry.'

He deflates in my arms.

TWENTY-ONE

Cal's painting reminds me of something that Hitler said – that anyone who sees and paints a sky green and fields blue ought to be sterilised. I have a hot and bloody dream that armies come for him with chemical weapons and fire; for some reason it's all my fault, but I can't protect him because everyone keeps lying to me.

I don't need Dr B to explain this one. A teenage anxiety dream about a boy; I thought I was more complicated than that. Betrayed by my own subconscious.

Dr B isn't in the mood to talk dreams anyway. He looks at me gravely.

'I've spoken with your parents and they've asked me to tell you something.'

A cold yawn spreads across the back of my neck and down the back of my arms. My neck clenches. 'What? What is it?'

They're sending me home early, I know it.

'I need time to say goodbye,' I say.

'What? No, that's not it. I need you to listen to me carefully.'

He draws a long breath and continues: 'Do you remember the other day when you asked if you'd hurt someone?'

'Yes, but I know I didn't. I was just confused. You don't need to tell me that.'

'We think you're starting to remember something.'

'I didn't hurt anyone.'

'We think it's time to try to tell you again.'

Who is this 'we' he's talking about? I know I didn't hurt anyone. I can feel it.

'Concentrate on what I'm saying. There was an attack, Lux.'

'What?'

'There was an attack and you didn't remember.'

I see it now. All this time he's been pretending to be on my side, but he's sicker than I am. 'You're lying.' Spit flies down my chin as I say it. Have we had this conversation before?

'I'm not lying. Sit down.' His voice is even. 'There was an attack and you were involved.'

The feeling I had all summer with my parents is back. Betrayal. Guilt. Confusion. Did they tell me the same lie?

'You're sick,' I say, my throat tearing. 'You should be locked up. I'd remember if I'd hurt someone.'

Cal wouldn't love anyone who could hurt someone. Neither would Mei or Olivia

'Listen to me, Lux. Your parents told you what happened but it didn't stick.'

'I trusted you,' I scream. 'I told you things and all this time it's been you that's crazy, not me.'

'They let Artists in who have done bad things all the time.'
My own words.

New screens have been installed on the walls in the common areas in Dylan House when I get back. Mantras scroll on loop. I pass *'We give it to art and we let go,'* as I crash up the stairs followed by *'A moment not spent creating is a moment wasted'*.

But, inside my room, I feel like wasting myself.

Who will believe me? It's my word against Dr B's. Crazy Blackout Girl versus the celebrity psychologist.

What if it's true?

I dig my nails into my palms and bite my tongue to keep myself in my body.

Where's Mei? I need her emergency stash.

I find the bottle in the back of her wardrobe and twist open the cap.

Mei dunks me in a cold shower and half carries me to bed. She makes me drink some water and double-drop vitamin C tablets so I'm not too hungover in the morning.

'Sip it,' she says. 'Slow down. Drink it slowly or you'll puke again.'

'Again?'

'Again. What happened?'

'I don't remember,' I tell her.

'Did someone say something to upset you?'

'No. I don't think so. I don't remember. I love you, Mei-Mei.'

'Love you too, Luxy,' she tells me.

*   *   *

'Hello, emergency service operator, which service do you need?'
It's a female voice, with a Surrey accent like mine.

'I've done something,' I say.

'Fire, police or ambulance?'

'Police, I think.'

'Police? I'll connect you now.'

Then a new voice, another woman, says, 'Where are you calling from?'

'Come and get me,' I breathe into the phone.

'Miss, where are you calling from?'

'I need you to come and take me away.'

'What is the nature of your emergency?' asks the lady.

'Please.'

'You're doing really well,' says the voice. 'I need to know where you are.'

Mei sits up in bed. 'Who are you talking to? Is that Cal?'

'Come and get me,' I shout into the phone.

Mei swings herself out of bed and takes the phone from me.

'Hello,' she says. 'Who is this?'

She looks at me as she listens, her eyes glistening in the dark, then tells the woman, 'I'm sorry, my friend made a mistake. She's not well.'

More listening.

'Richdeane School. No, we don't need anyone to come. She's just confused.'

Listening.

'Please. You don't need to come. We have a doctor here. Eighteen. She's eighteen. OK. OK. Thank you.' Mei hangs up.

She turns the light on, sits next to me on the bed and swallows hard.

'Did you call them on purpose?'

'I think so,' I say. 'One minute I was asleep, then I was awake and I knew you weren't safe with me. I had to call them.'

'You wouldn't hurt me, Luxy.' I have never seen her look this scared.

'I feel sick.'

I run to the bathroom and make it just in time to throw up more of the tequila I downed before bed. I wash my mouth out at the sink. A girl with faded red hair and dark circles under her eyes bares her raw gums at me in the mirror.

I limp back to the bedroom.

'I'm going back to sleep,' I say.

'You need to stay awake,' Mei tells me. 'The police are coming.'

'But you told them not to.'

'They're coming anyway. They said they had to.'

We see the police car pull up outside the head director's cottage. There's no siren but the blue light slices through the dark. For a second, their arrival is exciting and seems separate to me calling them, but the thrilling taste of emergency quickly fades to shame.

'Stay here,' Mei says.

I go to the window and watch her run to meet the car and the head director as he comes out on to the drive in a dressing gown. An eternity later, the police car sweeps away, this time lit only by its head-and-tail-lights.

Mei and the head director disappear into his cottage.

After a few minutes, my phone flashes in the dark. A withheld number.

'Hello?'

'Lux?' Two voices, one male, one female.

'Yes.'

'Thank god. We're coming to get you.'

'Is this the police?' I ask.

Silence.

'Hello?' I say.

'It's Mum and Dad,' the female voice says. 'Mei just called us. We're coming to get you.'

'I don't want to see you.'

Pain shrieks through my head.

'Please, I don't want you to come.'

'Lux, this has gone on long enough,' she says. 'It's getting out of control. We need to try something else.'

'Don't come, do you hear me? You can't take me – I'm eighteen now.'

'Lux, please,' both voices plead.

The tone of their voices makes me more determined. 'If you come here, I promise that you will never see me again.'

'We love you, Lux,' says the male voice. 'We just want you to feel better.'

'You will never see me again if you come,' I repeat.

I hang up. My head inflates with agony as the echo of their lying voices bounces off the walls.

I try to stay awake for Mei, but I can't.

TWENTY-TWO

The morning brings the kind of blank-sheet-of-paper sky that's so overwhelming I just want to lie there and feel small.

'Do you remember what happened last night?' asks Mei as soon as I sit up.

So it was real.

I nod.

'What happened?' she asks.

'Are you testing me?'

'Yes.' Her eyes meet mine. She looks so, so sad.

'I got drunk and called the police.'

'They'll have to send you away after this. You know that, don't you? The head director is going to speak to your parents again today.'

She doesn't know that I've made sure they won't come, at least not for a couple of days while they figure out how to handle me.

And even once they've made a plan, they still have to fly here. I'll be gone by the weekend though, to be on the safe side. Two days to say goodbye and work out where to go and who I can trust.

'I know,' I say.

'I'm sorry I called them. We didn't know what else to do.'

'It's OK. Can you do me a favour though? Will you stay with Olivia tonight?'

She gives me a list of reasons why it's not a good idea for me to be by myself.

'I won't be by myself. I want to invite Cal over.'

She gets it and agrees.

'You know I'm going to check that you actually invite him, don't you.'

'I know.'

'OK.'

After I've dressed, I down a rehydration sachet and fight the urge to throw it back up.

Mei walks me to Dr B's studio. I think I hear the bees stir in their hives but it's probably just blood rushing around my head.

'You won't tell anyone, will you?'

'People will have seen the police car,' she says.

'Can you just say you don't know anything about it, if anyone asks?'

'I'll try.'

'Thank you,' I say and hug her.

Georgia takes one look at me when I sit down and gives me her bottle of water. Her hair is piled on top of her head, crafted in shambolic topiary. Black feathers hang from each of the six holes in her ears.

'Ugh, star, thanks,' I say.

Dr B stares at me for a second or two then carries on addressing the group.

'We're working towards complete emotion,' he says. 'Use your third eye.'

'I think mine has glaucoma,' I whisper to Georgia.

'Mine's wearing a patch,' she giggles.

I'll miss her.

My hangover has started to stabilise. I've made it through the trauma phase and it's now at the stage where it doesn't hurt but all my reserves are being diverted to the task of cleaning up my blood. I just need to keep sloshing water in to help my organs do their job. With all efforts focused in my kidneys and liver, calm spreads over the rest of me. A good hangover can really take the edge off things sometimes. I'd forgotten that.

We listen to Dr B for a few minutes. When I look back at Georgia she has her forefingers and thumbs inside a paper fortune teller; its four points each with a coloured dot on.

She holds it out towards me and invites me to pick a colour. Being the red-seeking missile that I am, I choose red.

She moves her fingers and quietly sounds out the letters. 'R. E. D. Now pick a number between one and eight.'

'Seven.'

Moving her fingers again, she mouths: 'One. Two. Three. Four. Five. Six. Seven.' She lifts the flap it lands on and shows me what's written inside. It says: *'Time will tell.'*

She bursts out laughing. 'I forgot to tell you to think of a question.'

There was only one question on my mind anyway: should I sleep with Cal before I leave?

Dr B asks me to stay behind after class. His Adam's apple pokes in and out of his throat while he prepares to speak. It's revolting and awkward. 'I just wanted to check you're OK?'

He knows about the police.

'And I wanted to talk to you about our conversation yesterday.'

'Oh god, did I flake on something?' I ask.

For everything I remember, I forget something else. One in, one out.

Then it hits me, the feeling I woke up with almost every day in my parents' flat. 'We had a fight.'

He can't seem to find his words. 'Not exactly.'

'Yes – I told you that you weren't a real doctor.'

'That wasn't yesterday.'

'Wasn't it?'

He changes tack: 'You don't look well, Lux.'

He doesn't look well either. He seems tired, like the conversation is making him want to give up and go to bed.

'Can we skip our session today?' I ask. 'I don't feel good.'

'OK, but we need to talk tomorrow, Lux,' he says. 'You can have today off from all this, but there's something I need to try to tell you.'

One of the explanations for déjà vu is that you know the person you're talking with so well that you can anticipate what they're going to say so when they say it you think you've had the conversation before. Or maybe I just know what's coming: my parents are going to take me away.

TWENTY-THREE

Mei is outside the studio waiting for me when I come out. She walks me back to Dylan and stays in our room pretending not to be watching me.

I have a quick shower to wash the remnants of my hangover away, keeping the water cooler than usual so I don't make my skin all red and ugly, and put on clean blacks. I brush my hair and use my finger to clean my teeth so as not to anger my receding gums, then I move the candles from the windowsill to my bedside table. This could be mine and Cal's first and only proper night together. I want it to be perfect.

He messages me to say he's a few minutes away. It's a warning shot. A chance to give an excuse – Mei is still here, the muses have found me, or not tonight, I've got a headache. I message back with just an 'X'. I need to see him to say my secret goodbye.

'You've got to go now,' I tell Mei. 'He's almost here.'

'My phone is on loud – if you need me, ring me.'

She leaves.

I fumble with clothes in the wardrobe and smooth the pictures of Jade Grace against the wall. She has slipped from my mind since I saw Cal's painting. Something new to obsess about.

Cal seems more like himself when he arrives, as if he's come down off that strange frequency he was vibrating at in his studio. He gives me a wet bear hug, wrapping himself all the way round me, clamping my arms by my sides so I can't hug back. His black hoodie is damp and his hair is stuck to his head.

'Why so sweaty?' I ask.

'Been out inhaling flies by the lake.'

'What?'

'I went for a run,' he says. The lake is a mecca for bugs, all desperate to make a home in the orifices of any passing person. 'You should come next time. It would do you good.'

'Thin ice, Cal. Very. Thin. Ice.'

'Ha! I didn't mean it like that. It might help you run off some stress.' He has a theory about everything so I wait for it. 'Think of sweating as an oil change; getting the pollution out of the body.'

Or use another body to squash it out – concuss it.

'I thought you were going to say something about robots,' I say.

'Why? You're the one who's obsessed with robots, not me.'

'Erm, OK – let's agree to disagree on that one. Anyway, you seem better.'

'Yeah, I think the idea of leaving here caught up with me,' he says. 'I just got stuck in a loop. It used to happen a lot when I was at prep school, but I know how to manage it now.'

We sit on my bed with our backs to the wall. My grey blanket is under us. Its soft wool and muted dots have warmed my bed ever since I arrived at Richdeane. A few bits of dried grass and petals still cling to its fibres from where I took it on to the grounds to meet Dr B. Cal picks them off. I love this blanket, but today the wool feels like a platoon of ants doing battle on my anxious skin. I push it out from under me and adjust my position, pressing the ball of my left foot into the arch of my right and admiring them as they rest; a perfect fit.

Cal and I lean into each other, our heads like two sides of a heart. I kiss him and my actual heart bangs.

He picks up a photo of me, Mei and Olivia from my bedside table. I'm pouting, mugging for the camera.

'You had your head up your arse back then from what I've heard,' he says, nudging me with his shoulder.

'Ha ha, that's true – I was a bit self-absorbed,' I say. 'You wouldn't have liked me then.'

'Who says I like you now? I'm kidding. Knock me a little kiss.' He offers his cheek by way of instruction. I do as I'm told and his cheek doesn't bruise.

'Anyway, I've got a surprise for you.' He gets up to twist the blinds closed and starts singing: '*Boom chica bow-wow, chica bow-wow.*' I assume this is supposed to be striptease music as he's turned to face the wall and is jerking his hips from side to side while he inches his jumper over his head. 'Ready?' he asks. Next he peels his thin T-shirt off to reveal a fresh tattoo of a giant gothic-looking snowdrop inked across his back. Severe black lines of petals rest on his shoulder blades, the fronds creeping up and along his shoulders. It looks wet and I realise it's still covered in Vaseline and cling film to protect it from aggravation while it heals. It can't be more than a few hours old.

'Oh my god, that's enormous.'

'I bet you say that to all the boys.' He turns around to face me. The tips of the snowdrop's fronds crawl down to grip his clavicles.

'Seriously, Cal, what the hell? Why did you do that?'

'Don't you like it? Used-to-be-angry Jack did it. That guy has serious skills.'

'Why did you do it?' I ask again.

'I wanted to do something big, to remind me of the pledge even after we leave here. Do you really not like it?'

'It's amazing, but you're going to have that forever.'

'That's kind of the point.' He sits on the bed, lifts my left hand and rubs his thumb along the snowdrop etched into the underside of my wrist. 'You're going to have this forever.'

'I used to want to have it lasered off,' I say.

'Why?'

'You'll laugh if I tell you.'

'I won't, I promise.'

'For a while, I thought it was Richdeane or art that was giving me the migraines.'

'What do you think now?' he asks.

'I think I blacked out and woke up ill and I probably won't ever know exactly why. And that it was probably humiliating so that's for the best.'

'Can you help me get the cling film off?' he asks.

It's wrapped around his torso like he's a mummy, so he lifts his arms and I peel the film off as gently as I can; it's slick with

Vaseline and faintly Pollock-splattered with dried blood. The dense lines of the snowdrop are raised and angry. I try to ignore the smell of scorched flesh as it coils up my nostrils and spreads out inside my body. Half the taste is in the smell, they say. Am I a cannibal?

'Is it sore?'

'Honestly, it kills. I'll have to go on top.'

A joke, but that's how the decision is made. Without the help of Georgia's origami fortune teller.

'OK.' I nod.

'Are you sure? I can wait; we can wait,' he says. 'I know you're going, but you'll come back. I know you will.'

It's my mind that's rushing right now, not my body. Besides, he doesn't know how soon I have to go.

Cal lights the candles on my bedside table while I push the scratchy blanket all the way on to the floor. He turns off the light so we're lit only by the waxy flesh of churches and terror-site memorials.

He stands in front of me and unknots the cord of his joggers, pulls them down and kicks them to the side.

His body is compact and solid, not wiry like Henry's. He sits back on the bed and his boxers rise up his thighs. Even in the dim candlelight, I can see the scars. A long barcode of lines runs across the top of each leg. The marks are precise, like they were done professionally. I trace a finger over the lines on his right leg, the closest to me. And then because that feels asymmetrical, I lean over and do the other leg.

'I used to hurt myself,' he says.

I nod in the semi-dark. The lines are raised; they must have been deep cuts.

'Are you OK now?' I ask.

'Mostly.'

And because I'm so self-absorbed it makes me think that maybe I'll be able to tell people I'm mostly OK some day.

'I'm glad,' I say.

The candles flicker.

He leans over and baptises me with his breath. I lie on my back. He crawls on top of me and gently pushes my legs apart with a knee. He's in position but not yet inside; layers of black fabric separate us still. Our combined shadow flickers on the wall next to us as we kiss. His tongue seems hot, which I guess must mean mine feels cold to him. The rest of me is boiling.

He lifts up off me for a second, and looks at me. Something like a hunger pain pangs through my body. I nod and pull him back down on top of me. He slides my hands up and holds them either side of my head against the pillow. I'm a kissing starfish. It feels so good that it almost comes back round to feeling bad. And then it feels like nothing at all. The closer he gets, the less I can feel, until I'm not there at all.

I am human. I am real. I am real.

Too late, I leave my body on the bed. Sweaty, supine, broken meat.

On the ceiling, I see starfish rip off their own arms to get away from parts of themselves. I'm a snowdrop, the wintriest of flowers, pressed and wilting between the bed and his body. I'm Jade Grace laid to rest between the pages of my notebook.

'Is this OK?' he asks, running his hands all over me. I spread my fingers over his and push down so his hands knead my flesh.

I'm back in my body, fighting the urge to flip myself over and seek out sand to bury my face in. I try to feel his skin but my hands feel like they're wearing oven mitts. My body is back inside the astronaut suit. We need to be closer, so I grab his back.

'Ahhh,' he winces. 'Careful.'

'Shit, sorry.' I wipe my Vaseline-coated hand on the wall.

'S'OK. Kiss me. Kiss me better.' He pins my hands again, holding them more tightly this time.

The kissing gets greedier, but it's not enough to keep me in place. Our bodies drop away from me and I'm not real again.

From above, we are a snowdrop pinning an upturned starfish. From below, a blackened starfish deflowering a snowdrop. I must let go. Oh god, the pledge. The pledge will never betray him like I will. I can't let him inside; I am still too full of secrets I can't find to make proper room for him. I drop back into my body.

I can feel everything.

Too much. Too much. Too much.

'Wait,' I breathe. That's all it takes to stop us both.

An acrid carwash in my stomach sends saliva to my mouth. I want to vomit but I can't because he needs me to voice what he knows I'm going to say. Like the actual blow couldn't possibly be as bad as the imagined one.

How can I be with him when I can't even be with myself? I can't even keep myself inside my own body. I thought there was hope. That I could hold it in my hands and nurse it and keep it safe. But I need to let it slip through my fingers; spread them apart to hasten the loss.

Breaking up is not a negotiation, it only needs one of us to talk. The words come dancing up my throat, a row of cruel paper dolls holding hands and unfurling across my tongue into the air between us.

'I don't want this any more. I don't want you.'

He leaves, stung by my lies, carrying his jumper. A coil of bloodied cling film the only proof that he was here. I contemplate wrapping myself up in it and taking a selfie, but I toss it in the bin.

I know it will hurt when I miss him, but I choose not contaminating him.

I get up to open the blinds. I need air. There are dead spiders on the windowsill. I pick up their dry carcasses and drop them out of the window. They weigh nothing.

I turn and lean into my mirror so I'm a few centimetres from the glass. Where are my eye drops? I find them and squirt them into my eyes until they spill over. My face grimaces and scrunches as I try to remember what I look like when I cry.

I squirt more drops until they're dripping down my chin and soaking the neck of my jumper. The girl in the reflection looks real but doesn't feel real. Could we swap places? To stop myself trying to climb through into mirrorland, I lay the mirror flat. Then I turn all my photos to face the wall because I don't recognise the me in any of them.

The eye drops are empty.

I bite the cap off an eyeliner and spit it on to the bed. Dragging the kohl across the skin on my knuckles, I write REAL on my left hand and FAKE on my right. It's not enough, so I pull off my black leggings and sit on the floor. Slapping my legs confirms they are still mine.

I make a decision: time to write.

I pick up the eye pencil again and don't stop scribbling until I've run out of skin.

Minutes later, my skin is laced purple with heat and the shower water runs black as my thoughts disappear down the plughole.

What have I done?

I need to write more.

Something is waking up.

Typing. Typing. Typing.

One manic fantasy after another.

I write just to see how it feels to say the words and possibilities, even if it's only with my fingers.

One

Cal arrives with an armful of my favourite flowers, snowdrops, and puts them in the vase that I happen to have by my bed. He throws open the blinds on my windows to let the stars watch. He pretends to touch them, says they're ours. We undress each other, our tenderness causing any reservations to dissipate. I tell him I have been with other boys but that I've only ever loved him, that I was mixed up and crazy because I thought he'd never love me. He tells me he's had lots of opportunities but saved himself for the one. That's me. We make love, we both cry a little and fall asleep holding each other. He is the big spoon, I am the little spoon. I am saved and converted and made whole by his love. Love melts away the red and the headaches in the night. There are no more secrets and no more lies.

Two

I am naked and lying face down on the bed when Cal gets to my room. Maybe my wrists and ankles are tied to the bedposts. An altogether more sexual starfish, but at least I am hairless and face down as a starfish should be. He is wearing overalls with no shirt and has come to fix the broken blinds on my window. Instead, he opens them wide so the critics can look in and watch. I am very aroused by this and tell him so. Then Mei comes in – we argue about her colluding with my parents and decide the best way to deal with it is to have angry make-up sex. Cal provides direction while filming us on his phone and touching himself. We all get rave reviews for our performances.

Three

We are monochrome. Our movements are jerky, comical and a fraction too fast (at least it will be over quicker). My lips are painted in a dark cupid's bow. Cal has grown or pencilled on a moustache for the occasion. When we kiss, it twitches and I sneeze. We have a comical misunderstanding as I peel the cling film from his back and we end up wrapped up in it together, back to back, and dancing around the bedroom like conjoined twins. We knock over a candle; the sprinkler comes on and washes away our tattoos and scars. A vintage clapperboard signals 'The End'.

Four

It's not the future yet so we don't have feelings other than those that we have been programmed to express. Artificial Emotion (AE). We cannot lie. The singularity has not yet come, but our circuits are connected better than those of our human counterparts; our minds are plugged into our bodies. We are soulless soulmates, made of metal and wires and manmade power. An alloy of so many things: materials and expectations. Robotic arachnids shin up the blinds to get a better view; their eight-eyed cameras capture every angle and our automated armour protects us from caring. We are automatons; we were not created in love, we will not die in love and our software doesn't include the code to make it. We are widgets and gadgets and thing-a-me-bots.

Five

I want to comfort her. She is where I was a few years ago, deep in strangled calm. Her heart is a broken fist clamped shut with barnacles of blood. I light candles. 'Careful,' she says, like the matches are the thing in the room that might hurt me. She reminds me of someone I used to love a lot but she's impatient for change and I never want Richdeane to end. Each of us wants the other to contaminate them. So I let her suck the life out of me while song lyrics hang in the air, ready to drop like guillotines. She knows art cannot always protect us, that sometimes it endangers us too.

My real response surfaces at a glacial pace and is, as always, too late. There were so many other ways that Cal and I could have played out and I chose the wrong one.

TWENTY-FOUR

I wake up late, full of holes, and with my stuffing all over the floor.

Out the window, the vegetable beds thrive on Richdeane's rarefied air. Something comes back to me from childhood. I remember my parents finding me in the fruit cage in the garden in the middle of the night, picking blackberries in the dark. And a feeling. That I didn't like being a baby. I didn't like not being able to take care of myself.

I'm remembering all the wrong things. Pushing all the right ones deeper and deeper.

I should pack, ready to sneak out early tomorrow, but the swampy smell of heartbreak clings to the walls. I can't stay in here where I keep bumping into the things I said last night, so I slug my way to Dr B's studio without showering or brushing my teeth.

On the way to class, my resolve to ignore what I've done to Cal, to us, starts to waver, and soon I'm bleeding out on to the path between the vegetables beds and the studios. Red goes everywhere. I will live forever in the earth there; maybe snowdrops will grow red, nourished by my blood. I'm falling apart.

I'm not even sure that it's Cal I'm upset about; it feels like something bigger.

I try some deep breaths, name three things I can see that aren't red – sky, lake, pylons – and, after a while, the walls between my senses sweep up and solidify.

All the heavy breathing means I'm late for class. I sit down next to Georgia and she hands me a little paper robot, which I pocket to add to the snowdrop and the swan on my windowsill. An origami cast of little paper reminders that I'm not alone.

'Cal and I are finished,' I blurt to Dr B afterwards. 'I don't even know why I did it. I feel so cloudy.'

'I know you do. For what it's worth, I thought you two were good together. Sit down a minute.'

We sit on the edge of the little stage. It's peaceful in the studio without an audience or the critics, but I'm having trouble keeping up with which conversation we're having. It's as if there are two of each of us, one pair talking about Cal and one about something my mind can't reach.

I scratch imaginary dirt off the knee of my black jeans until Dr B sticks his head through the invisible wall between us, bringing all the versions of us together, and says: 'It's hard to see you suffer like this.'

Is that a vocational or a human instinct?

I am one of Mei's torn-magazine girls. Get the scissors out. Cut down my rough bits. Keep trimming my untidy edges until there is nothing left of me. Ablate them with a blowtorch if you have to.

'Did you always want to be an Artist?' I ask. I hope it's not too late to get to know him.

'Yes. You know I didn't take the most direct route though,' he says. 'My parents were scientists. Their attention span for anything that wasn't academia or a cure for something had a very short half-life.'

'What do you mean?'

'It didn't live long.'

'Right.'

'So we compromised on psychology. Anyway, I eventually went into acting. And I got here in the end. Anxiety comes from trying to be something you're not and hiding things, you know.'

'Isn't that kind of a cliché?'

'Clichés are clichés for a reason.'

'OK, fortune cookie,' I say.

'If I could give you some of my happiness, I would.'

'Going mouth to mouth, I'm seeking out resuscitation, breathing their air and then saying goodnight.'

He turns to me to continue but, before he kills me with his kindness, I grab his hands and kiss him. He doesn't kiss back but waits for me to finish and then places my hands back in my lap.

'Lux,' he says.

'I know. I'm sorry. That was ... I don't know what that was.' Way off-script. That's what it was. Or maybe goodbye. 'Sorry.'

'It's OK. You're confused.'

'It's not OK.'

'It's fine. But it can't happen again.'

'I know.'

'I vaguely remember what it's like, you know. To feel like this could be your first and only love, and that it's going to get away from you.'

'I made a mistake,' I say.

'Why don't you talk to him?'

Because it's a better story arc if I don't. No, because it will hurt. Because I don't know what to say. Or how to say it. Because I'm going away.

'Go on – we can talk tomorrow,' he says. He doesn't know I'll be leaving in the morning before my parents come for me.

TWENTY-FIVE

Sometimes when I'm awake, life feels like a dream and vice versa. But with this dream, I knew I was asleep – I'd felt wakefulness fall away and the nightmare swell.

Sheets of rain buffet the open window when I wake from it. Mei will miss me, I know, but she won't miss sleeping with the window open.

Georgia's paper presents have blown off the windowsill on to the floor. I must remember to pack them in the morning. I should take the Jade Grace collage down too so Mei doesn't have to feel guilty about doing it. It's hard to remember why I wanted to talk to Jade so much. She doesn't feel like the one I'm looking for any more.

My hands hurt from the rain, but I pull the origami swan gently apart to see how Georgia made it. Several little pills fall out. Did I put them there? I fold them back inside the stomach of the paper bird and lean out of the window. Filthy rainwater gushes along the open gutter. I drop the tainted swan and her pharmaceutical eggs into the pipe and close the blinds as they're washed away.

Mei stirs in her sleep and rolls over.

I take my notebook out from under the mattress to write down what I remember from the dream before it disappears.

As I scribble, the light snaps on in the darkroom in my head.

Of the many pictures in there, it's the image of the city burning that sends me through the deluge to Cal's studio in the middle of the night.

I use my phone to light my path inside the block and into Cal's studio. I tiptoe over to the window and twist down the blinds. In the blackness, more pictures take shape in my mind but I have to risk losing them to see the painting again.

Yellow light floods the studio when I flip the switch, illuminating a sheen of rain where my soaking clothes have dripped across the stone floor.

Part of the wall is still covered with the grubby shroud, secured in place with some bashed-in nails. I jump up and yank the fabric; it falls away from the wall, exposing the violent, vibrant hues of Cal's painting beneath it. A floral arsonist in a sweetshop city that's now bathed in a bright blue wash.

I step back and my mouth fills with heat and ash. A ghost train drives through me and out the other side. I know what I must do.

I'm breathing hard from running through the rain back to Dylan House. My fingers know what to type into the search box on my laptop.

That's when I find the photo montage. A kaleidoscope of Twenty-first century terror and response. Captioned stills of devastation, confusion, gloating kindness.

Anthrax attacks in America. A train detonates an anti-tank mine in Angola. The New York twin towers, the Pentagon, the planes and a lady coated in ash. A party cut short by nightclub bombs in Indonesia. The Moscow theatre crisis. The aftermath of exploding trucks in Istanbul. Train bombings in Madrid, three days before the general elections. Candlelit vigils. The Beslan school siege. A mangled bus and blown-up tubes, London. Bombs in New Delhi, two days before Diwali. Coordinated shootings, bombings and hotel hostages in Mumbai. Deadly car bombs in Iraq. Assassination in Pakistan. A car bomb and island summer camp shootings in Norway. Flowers, teddies and letters for people who will never read them. People climbing flagpoles after Bin Laden was killed. Shootings at a newspaper HQ, hostages and a three-million-strong rally in Paris. Bullets on the beach in Tunisia. The storming of a prison in Afghanistan. A foiled shooter on a train from Amsterdam. Bombs in Beirut. Shootings in cinemas. A truck smashing through celebrating crowds. Bombs in airports. Bombs in cars. Bombs in hospitals.

More and more and more and more. North, south, east and west. Land, sea, air. Everywhere around the world, all born under the same sky, alarms ring in hearts and people bleed.

I don't recognise most of it. Was I too young, was it not reported, was I not paying attention?

There was an attack, Lux. You were involved.

What's missing, who made this?

And then a wide-shot photograph. This one is like déjà vu,

giving me the same impression as Cal's painting, real but not real. A moment captured, like Bin Laden, but preserved forever.

The image shows the sun beaming down on an important London building. The National Museum of Arts, the words engraved in proud lettering. Except the part of the facade that normally holds the 'Arts' is missing and the sun carries on in where it normally meets the resistance of old bricks. The right-hand front of the building has crumbled to rubble to reveal an explosion of colour and flames.

There's something in the foreground. Someone. A small figure of a teenage girl in a red jumper with her back and ponytail to the camera. Caption: '8/8 Ponytail Girl'.

Hot goosebumps spread over my body. My brain folds in on itself, curling itself into the foetal position, like an origami creature left in the rain.

The photo is silent but I know that the song playing through the girl's headphones is John Grant's 'Marz', and that it's turned up so loud she can't hear the sirens. I know that she hears a piano, soaring flutes and a lyrical list of sweetshop memories as her mouth opens and freezes in an O as she breathes down hot ash. That she wears a badge that reads 'Intern'. She wears my clothes. A borrowed jumper. Has my hair. My face. Eyes. Me.

TWENTY-SIX

It hurts. The way only the truth can: completely.

There are spiked stars in my blood again, the same ones that hurtled through me on the trip to the Tate. Stars that are already dead and travelling to my head where they will explode and take me with them as they disappear. But the stars aren't stars but memories of course. And it's remembering, not the carwash of the kidneys, that will cleanse my spiky blood.

As I stare at the back of my ponytailed head in the photo, my memories throw off their manacles and start to fly.

Sweating tequila on my way to work, I'd pushed through a gaggle of language students wearing identical neon backpacks at the crossing and ducked across the busy road. They were Italian, or maybe Spanish. I couldn't hear them over my music.

Men in high-vis jackets manhandled machines to hammer through the pavement on the other side. They loosened great slabs of stone and heaved them to the side to access the pipes below, wiping their faces with their T-shirts.

My phone vibrated with a message.

Don't worry, I'll cover for you since it's your last day.
Joanna x PS You're a Tequila Machine!!

The girl from the gallery.

Joanna.

That was her name.

A kiss. She must not have thought I was a total brat. Maybe we'd keep in touch and I'd dye my hair red like hers. She had her shit together.

I carried on towards the gallery. My jumper was already sticking to my back. It was Joanna's; I'd borrowed it to wear home in the early hours.

One more day at my internship, then a month of summer freedom and day-drinking before starting my final year at Richdeane. Mei would be back from Hong Kong on Sunday and Olivia from her dance camp next weekend.

Instead:

I am twenty paces from the revolving doors of the gallery when a muffled boom reaches deep inside my head, forcing itself through the beautiful song that plays through my headphones. It reverberates through the ground, up into my feet and knees. Birds launch around me as flutes soar in my ears. My heart stops, restarts.

The universe blinks and everything afterwards is wrong.

There's a rupture in the air.

The light hitting the glass panes of the gallery doors changes shape, rippling and shimmering. The glare bounces at an odd angle.

The doors can't be melting. That doesn't make sense.

Tourists and commuters look towards the sky, the gallery, the embassies nearby, and shrug. Nothing to see. Must have been an exhaust backfiring or a traffic crunch further up the road.

To my left, the fountains in the square continue to spill over, their cool water already warming in the morning heat.

Buses roll south on the road behind me.

I keep walking.

The sun beats down, baking chewing gum on to the pavement.

New pigeons arrive and settle on benches.

Everything looks normal but I know it's all wrong.

I can feel it as I step forward. Dizzy, confused, knowing. Cold dread pours down my spine.

Then the crack, fissure and slide of broken glass as the gallery doors shatter and burst from their frame as if from an aftershock.

My guts strangle each other.

Something terrible has happened inside.

I'm going a hundred miles an hour in first gear.

I'm paralysed adrenaline.

My right hand rises and drags my headphones from my ears. My phone slips from my hand. It hits the ground. Slides. Smashes.

Shredded screams echo out from inside the building. Twisted, anguished sounds that are human but not. Getting closer. Louder.

All those people. All that art.

Joanna.

The sweet summer breeze catches dust and throws it in my face, spurring me into action.

I have to do something.

'Call nine-nine-nine!' my scream tears through my throat. 'Nine-nine-nine! Now!'

People are already on their phones making calls, giving panicked descriptions and taking photos.

A man wearing a cap bursts from the mangled doors. No blood, no torn clothing.

Maybe nobody got hurt.

He smashes past me yelling, 'Call nine-nine-nine!'

I lurch forward towards the space where the door should be. Glass everywhere.

Everything clarifies, crystallises.

The ding of a bicycle bell over a relentless jackhammer.

A hungry baby shrieks.

Rivers of sweat run from the nape of my neck down through the valley between my shoulder blades. Strands of hair catch in the delicate chain of my necklace as the smell of last night's alcohol lifts from my skin.

The air a still and swollen vacuum.

Then bodies pour through the doorframe, pushing each other in animal panic. Grey, dusty, terrified. A girl trips on twisted metal and is thrown down into the crunched glass by the surge behind her. She crawls forward. Manages to lift herself. Knees shredded and hanging with broken glass like icicles. Blood trickles down her shins on to the sizzling pavement.

Shaking voices. Some try to stay calm.

'There's been an explosion.'

'It's a bomb.'

'We don't know that.'

'Call nine-nine-nine.'

'The National Museum of Arts. The side entrance.'

More people burst through the torn seams of the building. No familiar faces.

My voice shouts, 'Joanna!'

I try to go forward to find her, but a thick arm around my waist drags me back.

The sun burns.

A voice. Deep.

'You can't go in there.'

'I know people inside.'

Blue lights.

The screech of tyres as ambulances and police pull up.

I am alone in going forward.

A second explosion. A noise like nothing I've heard before.

Thick dust blasts into the air and showers me like filthy fireworks. Broken bricks rain down. My hands fly to my face. Flesh meets something jagged. My arm is ripped open. I am coated in chalk. Breathing it down. Lungs bursting.

Screams. Mine.

Crying. Mine?

The exploding noise again but closer, almost inside me.

A step forward in tandem with the sound, straight into an invisible wall of heat.

Then the corner of the building is gone and I am in the air.

Flying, flying, flying backwards.

Hands grab nothingness. Futile backstroke.

A realisation.

I will die when I land.

Sweat turns cold.

My head will split open.

No more fireworks. No more Peter Pan.

Sirens. Sirens.

Body buckles. Crack. Hot concrete.

Sirens.

The blue lights are the last thing I taste before I slip away.

TWENTY-SEVEN

I feel Mei help me out of my wet nightclothes. The top and vest suck my skin as she peels them off me. My legs buckle. She holds me up while she wraps me in my dressing gown and grey blanket, sits me on the bed and pushes my tangled hair off my face while Dr B instructs the crowd gathered in my doorway to leave.

A light as bright as the sun is on in my darkroom, burning memories on to my cerebral tissue.

I can't breathe. I've been at the bottom of the sea and now I've got the bends.

I know everything. I remember everything.

Three bombs. Homemade, their manufacturers home-grown. Then I was a trace, a shadow.

A hundred fake redheads stare out from the wall. Jade Grace. Something switches and I know she wasn't who I was searching for. She's not Joanna. I throw myself at the wall and dismantle the collage in pieces as big as my arm span.

'Stop it,' says Mei.

I fall to my knees. Everything has gone from my body; I'm just a skin sack full of horror. Mei helps me to my bed again.

She folds Jade's many faces around themselves and tucks them behind the bin.

'Joanna?' Half a question but I already know the answer. I remember my parents telling me. They told me every day for a month. I remember the pain of them hurting me over and over again, and not being able to stand it. Not being able to keep it in my head.

Now it's all there.

I don't have to search to know that the photo was taken on an August Friday over four months ago. The eighth of the eighth. A picture of the day that the inglorious technicolour was turned on in my life. The day the veil between my senses became perforated and slack. The day the migraines came.

I'd made it home from the party, showered, dressed and headed out for the last day of my internship. I'd messaged Joanna to say I was running late and in the time it took me to walk from the flat at Waterloo over the bridge to the gallery, three men came up from the river and spread out across the city before convening at the National Museum of Arts with explosives and good old-fashioned fire. They had attacked its heart with the first bomb and worked their way out to the edges with the second and third.

On the third, I'd tried to run into the building and been blown backwards like a fly cannoned by a hose. Was that the point tiny grains of skin grafted my tear ducts shut?

I was scooped up and driven back over the river to St Thomas' Hospital where I woke up alone and then again with my mother holding my hand. I watched the explosions play and replay on the television in the corner of the ward.

The girl in the bed next to me was not my soul twin or Joanna. She was just a girl. Maybe she was just me as I watched from the ceiling. Joanna was shattered by a bomb. She was dust. Her red hair fizzled to nothing while my body rested and drank from a drip.

I repeat the same questions out loud and in my head, 'Did you know? Why didn't you keep telling me?'

Dr B kneels in front of me. Mei must have gone to get him. His voice makes me tired.

'Your parents tried to tell you; they told you so many times. I tried to tell you myself.' His lie is sending me to sleep like the anaesthetic when I had my tonsils out as a child. A formidable wave that I can't fight but still try to swim against.

'They lied to me,' I say. 'You all did.'

'It was a good lie, Lux,' he says.

Then the lie becomes truth and forces my eyes shut.

'Stay with me, Lux,' he urges. 'Breathe. Open your eyes. Three things you can see. Come on.'

But I'm gone. I fall through a trapdoor and down a well of silence. I see horrible things on the insides of my eyelids. The music that played through my earphones into my head the first time I saw them is gone. Instead there's just a wounded building exposing its burning heart. Red that turns emergency blue then back to red.

*   *   *

I stare at the wall while the hot mug scalds the pads of my fingers and the steam dampens my chin.

'Lux, baby.' An ashen woman and man appear in the doorway. They look like my parents.

'I'm hallucinating,' I tell Dr B.

Someone has injected me with something to keep me calm. I can feel it glittering through my veins like poison.

The woman gentles me into her arms while the man looks on.

'You're in Singapore,' I say to the holograms.

'Your parents have been staying in town,' Dr B says, 'so they could come as soon as you were ready.'

That's the point I break in half. I hear injured, sedated noises coming from me. But I feel no tears.

'I don't understand.' I'm fighting sleep.

'You should rest,' my dad says.

'Why should I rest? Why should I trust you?'

'We need to explain, Marcus,' says my mum.

'Not now, Gillian,' he says.

'Yes, now,' I overpower the glitter.

'We've explained before, honey,' she says in a tone I recognise from when I was five and had night terrors.

My mum sits next to me on the bed, my dad the other side of her. Dr B sits on Mei's bed like a mediator.

Together they tell me what I already know. That every time I woke up in the hospital, I didn't know how I'd got there and they had to explain to me again what had happened. I woke up again and again with bits of my mind missing, and each time I got more hysterical when they tried to piece it back together for me.

I'd lost Joanna who was so kind and grown-up but still so young, and was riddled with guilt like bullet holes. I was saved by being hungover and late – my irresponsibility had been rewarded. The anguish gave me migraines. Then I'd forget. When they told me again, I would hurl hate at them, thinking they were lying and trying to hurt me.

'The arguments,' I say. My parents nod and hold me tighter.

'We didn't know what to do,' Dad says. His sandy eyelashes are wet. I've never seen him cry before, not even in the hospital. 'We seemed to be making you sicker and causing you more and more pain, and all you wanted was for things to go back to normal, so we let you come back to school for a bit.'

'We checked on you every day,' my mum says.

I look over to Dr B who confirms it all with a nod. And then I remember him trying to tell me.

Dr Purves said that trauma reveals us, like a magician had pulled a velvet blanket off me and revealed I was, in fact, a rabbit. Abracadabra.

'Sexiest animal?'

'Foxes. No, wait. Rabbits! Definitely rabbits.'

'I think so too, but I don't know why.'

But the death of twenty-three people, one Joanna, nineteen tourists and three murderers, did not reveal me. I was not materialised or solidified by their act; I was temporarily erased.

TWENTY-EIGHT

I am scared to sleep in case I forget again. My head is full. My scalp and forehead are tingly and heavy, and the space between my eyebrows pulses with the effort of keeping my eyes open. I can see the ends of my eyelashes and parental shapes shifting around the room through the diminishing crack between my eyelids and lower lashes.

When I know I can't stay awake any longer, I force my eyes open wide enough to write myself a note and set an alarm to wake me up after twenty minutes. I sleep without dreaming. My parents must have turned the alarm off, because when I wake up it's morning and I can see them squashed into Mei's single bed. It must have been ten years since we all slept in the same room together.

I sit up and the weight of it all pushes me back down on to the pillow. My remembering wakes my parents up.

I can't speak. My head is too heavy for my neck. I am at the absolute end of myself but anger floats as it has done for months.

Dismantled pieces of Jade Grace watch me from behind the bin. She and I are nothing to each other. Her red hair is fake. Joanna's was so real.

There is a grimy film of grief on my teeth that I don't want to brush away in case I accidentally spit memories into the sink.

Mei and Olivia pack my things. They are solemn and sorry, and we don't know how to be around each other. Without discussion, I am taken to the flat in Waterloo. The journey home is a long white tunnel.

My parents and I sit in the living room where nobody ever sits because the sofas are cream and the carpets are somehow cold. This is the room where formal conversations take place. This is where they told me about the attack again and again. Where I called them liars and hated them until everything hurt.

We all think it: *What do we do now?*

'The doctor said you should rest,' says Mum.

'Which doctor?'

'Dr Baystone.'

'Oh, did he?'

I don't remember that. Am I forgetting again, just more slowly this time?

'I need you to tell me everything.'

I get out my notebook, rip out the pages full of Jade Grace and flip to the blank pages at the back. I fill them with all their explanations for why I couldn't remember.

They explain again that they told me every day all summer.

Something in my brain had shut down. The doctors didn't know exactly what had happened to my memories or how to get them back. A decision was made to stop trying to force-fill the gaps and let me recover them at my own pace so the facts had a better chance of sticking.

They made a plan: they would assemble a WAW team, including Dr B, and we'd wait it out until Christmas while I was in the sheltered safety of Richdeane. If I hadn't remembered by then with Dr B's help, my parents would tell me again and keep me with them until it stuck.

At first, the doctors thought I lost consciousness before the detail of the explosions made it from the short-term holding pen into the long-term memory box in my brain.

Or that my brain made a trade-off – all its efforts were focused on survival and escape, not on laying down new memories.

More likely, my brain made an executive decision to repress the information without consulting me. This can happen with trauma, Mum explains: 'The memories are hidden but still affect the person because the facts and feelings are buried alive, waiting to be dug out.'

Sometimes the tentacles enclosing the secrets grow weaker. A lactic acid build-up from gripping too tightly causes them to loosen their hold. Remembering starts when pieces of memory break away and sneak around the edges of their hiding places, appearing as dreams, slips of the tongue or pain.

I scribble down everything they say, even though I know it all as if the knowledge was there inside me the whole time. I guess it was.

The head director, Dr B and all the directors had known and that feels like cheating. Mei and Olivia knew and had had to tell Cal who put my story in a painting before I've even written it. Though I suppose it is his story too. Terror belongs to all of us, whether we want it or not.

It's sickening to have people know things about you that you don't know yourself, and to look back and see how many clues you missed — their quickness to forgive, the sympathetic looks and reassurances that you took as prejudice, and the halting conversations and coaxing that washed over you because you didn't know what you were looking for. All the conversations that must have taken place behind my back. The briefings, the whisperings, the phone calls, the messages, the desperation. Even my own brain knew things I didn't. It made me lost to protect me.

When I've finished questioning them, we drink tea, pick at food, tiptoe round each other. I have a bath filled with bubbles. The last of the red dye in my hair tints the water pink. Water gets under the edges of the filthy bandage on my arm and inflates it like a child's armband. I scrub myself with soap and the bubbles turn to surface scum, revealing my body beneath the water. It seems a long time since I looked at it, but it's definitely mine — down to the chipped nail polish that's been on my toes for weeks.

Since I show no sign of dissolving in the water, I pick up a razor to shave my legs. The blade glints and I throw it over the side of the bath into the sink.

My mother taps on the door to check on me.

'I'm fine,' I call. 'I'll be out in a minute.'

When the water is too cold to wallow in any more, I lift

myself out of the bath. I lie on my bed in a big towel, humming to the ringing in my ears until I'm dry and the duvet is damp.

My mother comes in, holding a little green bag with a white cross on the front.

She props me up against the headboard like a doll and takes a miniature bottle of Savlon spray and some dressings from the bag. She peels the sopping bandage from my arm and lays it on the bedside table. Its underside is red and yellow with blood and some other stuff that my arm has produced. She picks it up and folds it in half so I can't see the abject fluids, but it's too late.

The water has softened the scab, making the edges white and loose. She sprays the antiseptic along the fifteen centimetres of my open flesh. It smells like hospitals.

'Sorry,' she says. 'Does it hurt?'

'I don't think so.'

She dabs cream from a blue and yellow tube along the wound, then dresses it with an adhesive bandage, making sure the sticky parts are away from the cut. When she looks at me with such tenderness, it seems impossible that I could have thought she ever wanted to hurt me.

'Did you and Dad stay here all the while I was at school?'

'We took it in turns to fly back a few times to sort things out at home but one of us was always here in case you remembered or you changed your mind and wanted us there.'

Singapore is their home now.

She was a person before I was a person. I'll be a person when she's not one any more. Unless I die first.

I wish she would wind the rest of the bandage around my head to keep the memories and this feeling of knowing her inside.

The TV is on when I get back into the living room. My parents are watching a nature programme. Probably the most innocuous thing they could find. No good watching the news or a film; too much war and people blowing each other up, especially now we've launched airstrikes somewhere. I heard that on the radio on the way home before both their hands reached to switch it off. We're dropping bombs on people to encourage them not to bomb any more. It doesn't make much sense to me, but then I've missed four months of the real world.

The programme is old. From the Eighties, I think. It's about fish and other creatures that live in the sea. There are things that live very deep in the ocean where it's totally dark. There are no colours down there, but they are lit up by bioluminescence, where something inside them or on their skin emits light. I am those creatures. There is a light stain on me. A wash of still emergency. Blue and ashy and hot and cold at the same time. Find the right equipment to see me properly and I'd light up like fireworks.

The narrator moves on to talk about herring spawning. The female fish lay sticky eggs and the male fish swim along and come all over them. The narrator uses the term 'curds of sperm'.

'Worse than the Thames,' braves my dad. We snigger together and feel guilty alone.

We give ourselves the rest of the day off from working out how to behave and what action to take next. I am tired and go to bed early.

In the morning, my sheets are as crisp and hospital cornered as when I went to bed. Mum will be pleased. I am used to waking up with them burdened with sweat and twisted off the bed. There's no physical signs of torment but the realisation of everything that's happened blisters like lemon squeezed on to hot oil.

I get dressed without showering and go into the kitchen.

'You don't have to wear that here,' my mum says.

I look down at my all-black outfit.

'Breakfast?'

I shake my head.

'Lux, you have to try.'

I leave the room and we pass another day in polite quiet. Dr B phones to check we're OK. We're waiting for something to happen but we don't know what.

The next day, a dark-green jumper and jeans are on my bed for me when I get out the shower.

'You look nice,' my dad says.

I flip through a book but can't follow it. My brain is full.

I have another bath because it's the only room in the flat with a lock on the door. I stay alone with the water, my body and my thoughts as long as I can stand. When I go to clean my teeth, my gnarled toothbrush has been replaced with a child's one and the toothpaste with a gentler formula.

The next day, an order of board games and jigsaw puzzles arrives. They sit wrapped in their cellophane for two days until one of my parents puts them away. It's almost Christmas so *The Holiday* or *Home Alone* is on every time I turn on the TV.

Each morning and after every nap, the memories come screaming back to me. I'm pinned to the bed or sofa, wherever I fall asleep, until the sweeping waking of those cells passes.

On day six, the crying starts. My tear ducts work after all.

I contain it to the shower at first, turning the water on full blast while I shake, and then judging myself in the steamed mirror through swollen eyes. I didn't die; what do I have to feel so bad about? But my ribs are tight and I feel like a bruise. I wait for nightmares and migraines that don't come. The colours are gone. I almost miss them because now there's nothing. This is my life now.

The hollow days that follow are so blurred into one that I half expect them to stop having names, but they don't. Because, for everybody else, there continue to be Mondays and Tuesdays and so on. I start to call them all Joanna.

To her, I was just a schoolgirl who followed her around at work for a month. Apart from when I'd walked in on her updating her word collection in the staffroom, we only had one conversation that wasn't about me doing photocopying or going on a coffee run. It was at the party the night before the attack. She had invited me to be charitable, I expect. Outside of work, she seemed softer and warmer. She was sociably drunk and told me, in the kindest, sweetest way possible, that I needed to grow up.

What would my parents say if they knew being late and hungover had saved my life?

I gulp with sobs for days. Then the jags get shorter and less frequent, but deeper and more surprising. They come when I'm taking milk out of the fridge or putting things in the bin, and when I'm faced with the overwhelming choice between cereal or toast for breakfast.

I sleep a lot too. After my initial fear of going to sleep

and not remembering things when I wake up, it seems clear I won't forget again. Google tells me sleep is important for laying down certain types of memories, so I clock hour after hour of deathly deep sleep. When I wake up, the lights are blaring in the darkroom in my mind and all the pictures are enlarged and lying out for me to look through before I can start the day.

Mei and Olivia visit on their way home for Christmas. We sit in the kitchen. They hug me like they're trying to cover every part of my surface area. It helps at first, but when it's time for us to hug goodbye, I'm back in my astronaut suit and I can't feel them any more.

I'm not sad. That's too small. A tiny word. Other survivors and the families of the victims of the attack talk about being proud. They have blogged about not being defeated and give tear-streaked, defiant interviews about unity and forgiveness. Am I weak because I'm still scared? Evil if I hate the men who did this? My mum reminds me that they have had four and a half months longer to process the event; half the time it takes to grow a new human.

TWENTY-NINE

My parents don't try to keep the next thing that happens from me. They tell me and I remember.

I shuffle into the kitchen in my pyjamas the morning before Christmas Eve. Dad is looking out of the thick window towards the Thames and the pigeon-grey sky. Mum flicks the kettle on. It's a new one since I stayed in the flat in the summer. It's transparent. The water turns as cloudy as the sky as it bubbles furiously, and the base lights up neon blue. It could shoot into space any second and leave a kettle-shaped hole in the ceiling.

'Disco kettle,' says my dad. 'Morning, honey.'

'Sit down,' my mum says.

Something is coming. Some new information, some new piece to the puzzle when I've just started to make sense of the picture on the front of the box and got some of the pieces laid out ready to start the process of connecting them.

'We have something to tell you,' she continues.

The kettle reaches its climax and its neon lights go out.

Then nobody tells me anything for a few seconds. My mum nods to my dad. They've rehearsed but he's missed his cue.

'One of the papers knows who you are,' he says.

'What do you mean, who I am? Who am I?'

'They called you Ponytail Girl.' My mum sits down next to me and pulls my hand into her cold one. It sounds so stupid that I smile.

'There's a photo of you in front of the gallery as it exploded, but nobody knew it was you apart from us because it was just the back of your head.'

I used to lie in my mum's lap when I was small while she'd stroke my head. When it was time for us to get off the sofa or bed, she'd gather my hair into a ponytail, tie it too tightly with a hairband, and pat me on my way. I'd shake my head to loosen the band but never used my hands, so that when she asked me why it was so messy I could say I hadn't touched it without lying.

'But they know now,' Dad says. 'Do you understand?'

'Yes. My picture was on the news. They didn't know it was me and now they do.'

Will people be jealous of me like I was when the Golf Course Five and the Richdeane 27 Artists were in the papers? This is different. I will be pitied – not famous or even infamous.

'Yes, one of the papers knows. Do you want to see the photo so you're prepared? Dr Baystone said it might be a good idea.'

'I've seen it. The night I remembered.'

I haven't seen the photo since, but I don't need to. I don't have to work to develop pictures in my head any more. I can conjure them in a blink. I can see the back of me, red-jumpered, with big headphones over my ears. I was a few centimetres high on the screen. I could cut myself out and superimpose me into a *Where's Wally?* picture book and nobody would ever find me, but I never want to lose myself again so I won't.

'Your head director says we should get ready for a media storm. He seems to know how these things work.'

Of course. He must have leaked it. All publicity is good publicity, despite what they teach us in Media & Discretion Coaching. This is better than the thwarted suicide-pact story, because this time he can position himself as some kind of miracle memory-healer.

'There's something else,' Dad says. 'Do you know a girl called Millie?'

'She's Georgia's girlfriend.'

'Georgia?'

'A girl in my year; we sort of became friends recently. What's happened to Millie?'

'She's the one who let slip about you. She's terribly upset about it, apparently. Her father owns a newspaper, you see.'

Silly little Millie. She's just like silly little Lux was. Thoughtless. Living for drama.

'The head director said she's desperate for you to know how sorry she is. She's in quite a lot of trouble.'

'Can you call Dr B? Tell him I don't want her to be punished.'

Mum has been quiet so far but now says, 'We'll call him. Whatever you want.'

Dad continues: 'The school have been trying to negotiate with this girl's father. They offered him an exclusive with some ex-pupil called Grace something but it didn't work.'

'Jade Grace?'

'Could be. Do you know her?'

'I threw her in the bin.'

'What?'

'Nothing,' I say. 'She's one of the most famous people on the planet.'

'Not famous enough, evidently.'

Ponytail Girl is more famous than Jade Grace, or she will be when the news hits.

Mum tells me the story will break today and the rest of the media will pick it up. It's a slow news week because of Christmas; we should expect a lot of interest so we'll have to lie low for a few days. Unless I want to make some kind of statement or do an interview. I've done practice interviews in my head and even in class in the hope that one day I would do something interesting enough for people to want to talk to me about, but this isn't it.

'OK, no statement,' says Dad.

My stomach rumbles. 'I'm starving.'

'You slept for fourteen hours.'

I eat three pieces of toast with peanut butter, then grate an apple into a bowl with some cheddar, shake on some cinnamon and eat the mixture with my fingers. I think of Olivia's intense feast and her wiping her hands on her stained apron as Mei laughs and Cal squeezes my hand.

I have a long shower, brushing my teeth before and after. There is no outfit on my bed when I get out so I put on a black jumper with grey leggings. Richdeane from the waist up.

The doorbell buzzes.

'What if it's a journalist?' I say to Mum as she makes for the door.

'It's probably your father. He popped out. And a journalist wouldn't have got past the concierge.'

'My hands are full,' comes Dad's voice from behind the door. 'Let me in.'

He comes through the door back first, dragging something long and heavy enough to force him to stoop to heave it through. A body bag?

'Got us a tree,' he says.

He pulls a netted Christmas tree into the flat.

'I know it's weird but it's Christmas and we should try to celebrate the fact that we're all together.'

His sweetness gives me a lump in my throat.

'Careful, don't bash the paint,' says Mum, bending down to collect the trail of needles Dad leaves behind as he pulls the tree into the lounge.

'Did you get any ornaments?'

'Ah,' he says, 'no.'

'Never mind – it smells wonderful.'

They erect the tree and I busy myself making cut-out snowflakes like we used to in prep school. Mum fastens them to the tree with elastic bands. They look crap but none of us say so, even though they must be really offending Mum's good taste.

I eat some Twiglets and another two cut-up apples. And then the phone rings like we knew it would.

'I'll read what they've written first,' says Dad, picking up his tablet. He reads quickly and slides it across the table to me.

8/8 PONYTAIL GIRL: FOUND

I skim the article. It's just details of the attack rehashed with the picture of me from Instagram and the one of me in front of the gallery. Nothing about the attack that I haven't found from my Google searches over the last week, but they've posted my pictures alongside the image of the lady covered in the dust at the 9/11 site. 'Marcy Borders – Dust Lady' says her caption.

'It's not so bad,' he says. 'A bit hysterical, but I expected worse from a tabloid. It'll be everywhere soon though.'

He's right; the article is OK. I refresh. The comments are rolling in.

BodyOffBaywatch-FaceOffCrimewatch
London, less than a minute ago
They should make a reality show about all the people who survive these attacks. Get that Dust Lady and a bunch of others in a house with this girl and film them. I'd watch that.

Humblebrag98
Richdeane, less than a minute ago
Jade Grace went to the school this Ponytail Girl goes to and look how she turned out – posting pictures of herself covered in blood and dead flowers on the internet. Richdeane is like a cult. They'll both be dead in a year.

JadedGrace
La La Land, one minute ago
@Humblebrag98 Jade Grace is the most successful singer, actor and writer of her generation. You're just jealous. Stop embarrassing yourself.

Lucidwhenconfused

Dublin, one minute ago

This is all just stuff set up by PR people to fool gullible idiots like you lot. Why are they only revealing her identity now? Richdeane is using a tragedy to line up its next big 'star'.

jezzergreen

Earth Sweet Earth, one minute ago

WAKE UP, EVERYONE. There are more important things to think about, like the fact that we'll all soon be underwater. Unless we can figure out how to breed BABIES with GILLS, the human race WILL DIE OUT WITHIN A GENERATION. Check out my blog HERE.

Clickbait_jailbait

West Virginia, one minute ago

This is horrible. Where is your humanity? People died in this attack. May the victims Rest In Peace and may this young woman make a full recovery from this trauma.

Millie

Richdeane, one minute ago

If you're reading this, I am SO SORRY.

I believe she's sorry; even if she told her dad on purpose I know she'll be regretting it now.

Mei, Olivia and Georgia message me. They ask me if I'm coming back to Richdeane after Christmas.

I don't know yet.

Cal doesn't contact me. It would be too much.

Dad tells the concierge again not to let anyone up and takes the phone off the hook.

The stories continue on Christmas Eve. People on TV say 'one more sleep till Christmas', but it's stupid really – it's the waking up that counts. Then Christmas comes. I receive presents but am not present. My parents give me a mindfulness colouring book, scented candles, oils to put in the bath, Disney DVDs. I feel terrible that I didn't think to get them anything. Being together is a gift enough, they say.

As predicted, there is little news between Christmas and New Year so the weekend papers run the story again. Their articles contain the same facts but interpret them differently.

We put the phone back on the hook and Dad fields calls from talk-show producers who want to speak to me, him, my mother, even the concierge. The Richdeane ranks tighten, protecting their own, and nobody says anything other than the head director who tells them all: 'Lux is a gifted Artist and we'd welcome her back any time. There will be no further comment.'

The faceless online comment-makers are let down – they want marrow, guts. They have come here to feel something, the bottom feeders of the trauma triangle. I know, I was one of them.

Watching pictures of myself on the news doesn't feel that different to the feeling of being lost and outside myself that I've had for the past few months. I don't tell my parents that the stories are also strangely comforting. Everything is in black and white now – a safety net to catch me if my memory breaks again.

My parents make a big deal about leaving me in the flat by myself on New Year's Eve while they go for a walk along the river. I have only had two crying fits by three p.m. and they suggest I go with them, but they look in need of space so I tell them to go without me.

'The Ocado delivery is coming, but we were going to ask the concierge to keep the bags downstairs until we get back anyway.'

'It's fine. Tell George it's OK for the delivery person to come up.'

'If you're sure? Check the intercom screen and don't let anyone else in.'

'I know how to answer a door.'

They finally go out.

I feel capable, almost grown-up, waiting in the flat for a family-sized delivery. While I stayed here in the summer, I subsisted on sandwiches and the three recipes I know how to cook (pasta with cheese, pasta with tomato sauce, and pasta with tuna). Other Artists complain about the three-meals-and-two-snacks rigidity of Richdeane, but it never bothered me much apart from when I was in my biohack phase.

My parents message me. I tell them I'm fine.

I sit at the kitchen table reading yesterday's articles about myself and devouring every piece of information I can find about the terrorists, and wait for the doorbell.

'Hello,' I will say, like a completely normal person, 'come in. It's the ninth floor. Take the lift.'

But then the delivery slot passes and the delivery hasn't arrived. When the buzzer finally goes twenty-five long minutes later, I am hot-cheeked and livid.

'Sorry, love, New Year's traffic,' the man says as he wheels the crates into the kitchen. 'Where would you like your shopping?'

'It doesn't matter,' I say, biting down on the consonants. I watch him in icy silence while he unloads the crates, placing the fragile items on the table.

'Nice Christmas?' he tries.

I pretend not to hear.

'These are your freezer bits.' He puts the bag down in front of the fridge-freezer. 'Any bags for recycling?'

I shake my head once.

'Happy New Year – hope it's a good one,' he says just before I slam the door behind him.

A moment of cruelty and control. The thrill of being so unkind is exhilarating for a few seconds, then hot tears spring from my eyes. I open the door and run barefoot down the corridor after him.

'Hey, wait, please – I'm sorry,' I call after him. 'Happy New Year to you too.'

He looks at me like I'm crazy, relief crossing his face as the lift doors open in front of him. 'Have a good one, love.'

'I'm sorry,' I say to the lift doors as the lift descends.

I'm full of shame when I get back inside, but I rub my face dry on a tea towel and force myself to shake it off. I will not unravel over an Ocado delivery.

I open the balcony door to let some air in, then take a couple of apples from the shopping, grab a knife and hack through their waxy skin. Most of the pips fall out and I poke the stubborn ones with the point of the knife. The last thing I need is an apple tree growing in my stomach. I jab at the seeds but the fruit flesh gives way and the blade slices through the base of my little finger. It doesn't hurt but blood ribbons out on to the chopping board. I take a step back and more blood drops in red slashes on to the floor.

'Owwww.'

I rinse the cut under cold water, squirt in some Savlon and wrap it up the best I can with one hand. It looks nothing like the way my mum did it. Soon I will be more bandage than skin.

Gravity and despair want me to slide down the kitchen wall on to the floor and lie down in the blood. I suck in a deep breath through my nose and blast the air back out through my mouth, then do it two more times.

I need to get out of here. I won't be a hostage in my own home just because some loser journalist might get a photo of me if I go out.

It's freezing and bright outside. The world sparkles. I've been in the flat for two weeks and my eyes shrink to slits against the daylight. My ankles and knees make hollow clicks as my legs get used to moving again.

I walk down the side of our building, under the stinking subway, and end up at Waterloo Station. I cross the road under the bridge and keep walking until I find the curb where Cal and I sat exactly two months ago in our Halloween costumes. It's just a dirty pavement though; there's no 'Lux kissed Cal here' plaque.

The Fishcoteque takeaway over the road is open.

At the crossing, a little girl hangs off an arm of each of her parents.

She swings. 'Go, horsies, go.'

'Wait for the green man,' says the dad.

The girl breaks free and hammers the crossing button.

'Don't keep pressing it,' her mum says, 'or it'll stop working.'

Liars.

I push round them and dash over the road into the takeaway.

I order chips. I ask for salt and vinegar, then remembering my shredded gums ask for them plain. They are served in a cardboard funnel, which the man behind the counter wraps in newspaper, a flourish for the tourists. Grease soaks through the paper and I half expect it to reveal my face or the back of my head in print like magic ink.

The chips burn my fingers and the roof of my mouth. I huff out steam into my palm and walk as fast as I can back past our block and down to the brown river in front of the Royal Festival Hall.

Security guards are putting up barriers and a few people are already starting to gather for the midnight fireworks later. Men in high-vis jackets bark into walkie-talkies and shout jokes. They're responsible for keeping people safe during the celebrations and make jovial requests of the tourists: 'Step back, please; mind the barrier; you can't drink here, I'm afraid.'

I eat a few more chips then shake the rest out over the wall for the huge gulls on the riverbank. They laugh at me, beaks wide and mocking. Did any of them see the bombers come up from the Thames?

The cut on my hand starts to sting. Blood is soaking through the bandage. I've been outside for fewer than ten minutes but it's getting dark and that feels like enough.

There are no bins, so I carry the oily paper back to the flat. My face is flushed in the lift mirror.

'Oh my god; thank god, thank god.' My mum pulls me inside when I get to the door to the flat. 'We thought you were gone.' Shaking, she calls, 'She's back.'

My dad runs out to the hallway. 'Thank god.'

'We thought you ...' She doesn't finish her sentence.

'I just went to get some air.' I hold the chip paper out as evidence.

'We were about to call the police. There's blood everywhere. The balcony door was open.'

'Sorry,' I say.

I walk towards the kitchen to put the rubbish in the bin, and they follow. It looks like a crime scene. 'I cut myself slicing an apple and then I just felt really claustrophobic.'

'It's OK; as long as you're OK, but take your phone next time,' Dad says. He takes the chip wrapper, shoves it in the bin under the sink with the bloodied apple and starts wiping away the blood on the floor.

As he erases my accident with kitchen towel, it dawns on me that they thought I'd done something to myself. I wouldn't do that to them or to Joanna.

'It was an accident,' I say.

Mum takes me into the bathroom to wash the cut and put on a clean bandage. She changes the dressing on my arm while we're in there. The feather gash is starting to close over again.

'I don't think you need stitches.'

Guilt starts to creep and I apologise all evening. I even try to help Dad make our New Year's Eve supper.

'We'll keep the balcony door closed. And the blinds too, if you like,' he says.

They are worried about the fireworks. They'll keep me safe indoors like a cat.

The fresh air has made me tired. I go to bed early expecting a display of my own as soon as I shut my eyes, but I fall asleep before any fireworks start.

THIRTY

Once I've decided to go back to Richdeane and we've cleared it with Dr Purves, my parents arrange a meeting with the head director and Dr B. Dad gives them each a bottle of vintage port, which is rather an odd token to me but they seem pleased, so maybe it's a middle-aged thing.

'We'd welcome you back, Lux,' says the head director, 'as long as your doctors say it's OK.'

Dr Purves asked me the same questions as the other times. This time, I answered them with brief facts rather than 'I don't know' or 'I don't remember' and I wondered if all the other times she asked me them she was looking for inconsistencies – to determine whether anything had come back or whether I was faking it.

'Dr Purves is happy for her to try,' says Mum.

I guess the meeting is a replica of the one they must have

had at the start of last term when they agreed how to handle my situation, except this time I'm privy to it, although I don't say much.

The first night back in Dylan House is weird. I haven't had a migraine or a nightmare since the truth burst out of my brain, so at least I don't have to worry about trying to throw up quietly or waking Mei with my loud dreaming.

Lots of things are the same coming back this time. I feel the other Artists looking at me, but I understand why now. The catering staff point me out to each other when they think I can't see them. They don't know I am on high alert.

Mei is the same as always. 'What the front door are you looking at?' she whispers to some poor kid who has turned round to glance at me in assembly.

The significant thing that's different is that we all know the same things about me this time. I know my own mind – what's in its darkrooms and what it's capable of.

'Are you still having the nightmares?' asks Olivia.

'No.' Life is a long white tunnel now, like the one my parents and I drove home through. I just need to stay in my lane.

'Have you seen Cal yet?'

I'm avoiding him. His complicity in the lie hurts the most, though I've known him the least time. I guess because everything I've known about us has been based on a trick. I get it but I can't forgive it.

'Not yet, but we've got Coffee & Feelings on Friday with Dr B.'

'You've got what?'

'The shares meetings with Dr B. That's what I call them in my head.'

'That's funny.' She smiles. 'I've been calling mine "My Feelings Are Louder Than Yours Hour".'

And then she starts to cry and is furious with herself for it, saying, 'I'm sorry, I'm so sorry. It's just been so hard not knowing how to act and being careful not to say the wrong thing.'

I hadn't even thought about how hard it must have been for her and Mei being part of the WAW team and acting as spies for my parents.

That's when the real spring of guilt creeps over me and settles in.

THIRTY-ONE

When we were nine or ten, Olivia cut her foot and it got infected. The side of her foot turned dark and mottled like meat. The infection was slow at first, then she started burning up. By supper, she was delirious with fever. Matron drew a line across the bridge of Olivia's foot so she could monitor it. Within half an hour, the poison had crept over the line and she had to go to hospital.

That's what guilt is like. First it inches, then it takes over. Love too.

Dr B and my parents tell me to take one day at a time; that I can leave whenever I want. A day is a long time, so I break it down – starting with a breath, then a minute, an hour.

Soon after I get back, Millie summons the nerve to talk to me. She's ahead of me; I never apologised for any of my mistakes when I was fifteen. I don't think I even knew they were mistakes.

'Lux, can I talk to you?' She approaches me outside the dining hall with Georgia in tow like a beautiful bodyguard. Neutral territory. Plenty of people around in case I kick off.

'It's OK – I know what you're going to say,' I tell her.

Millie looks square at me but little red circles burn up her cheeks. 'I want to say it. I want you to know how sorry I am.'

I know what guilt feels like so I say again, 'It's OK, really.'

Her arms twitch like she might try to hug me, but she just thanks me, apologises again and bounces off into the dining hall, flipping her hair like she knows all the answers but won't be sharing them.

'That was big of you,' says Georgia.

She doesn't know I'm trying to be kind and grown-up like Joanna. I say, 'There's actually something I wanted to ask you about. Are you still doing that outreach programme?'

'Yep.'

I take a deep breath and ask her if I can join the collective. She says yes and I thank her, even though I'm having visions of us subjecting the children to endurance zentangling and drilling them on the isms – modernism, expressionism, futurism, commercialism and so on.

I'd assumed the beneficiaries would be children, for some reason. Frail ones with thinning hair and brave smiles. But, apparently, Richdeane is viewed as a little extreme for its students to be let loose with sick kids so the project will be with Wood House, a centre for vulnerable adults.

Georgia has chosen me and Millie to go with her for the first official meeting.

This project is an opportunity for us all to do something good. Like Dr B is always saying, I need to get the attention off myself and on to the other actors (I'm guessing the same goes for real life and real people).

That morning, I find a cardigan on the wrong shelf with the neck facing the front instead of the back. I must have put it back carelessly. Taking all the items on the polluted shelf out, refolding them and putting them back correctly makes me late to meet Georgia and Millie. I wash down some painkillers to arrest the headache that's brewing, the first since I got back, and run down to the drive, telling myself it's just a headache and that it doesn't mean the migraines are coming back.

'Ready?' asks Georgia when I find them at the top of the driveway. They're sitting on a low brick wall. Georgia is cross-legged, while Millie swings her legs, dragging her heels against the wall, decapitating the little flowers that grow from the cracks.

'Yep. Sorry I'm late.'

'You sure you're ready for this?' she asks. 'You've only been back a week.'

Millie looks up with sudden interest.

'Definitely,' I say.

Georgia assesses me and then reaches out to ping my blue bra strap and tuck it out of sight. 'Rebel.'

We take the bus as a novelty. A woman gets on who's probably only a handful of years younger than my grandmother was when she died. I go to give her my seat, but she points to the corner seat by the wheelchair space saying: 'I'll be out of the way there.' The back of my throat and tongue begin to ache.

Georgia folds her bus ticket in her lap while she and Millie talk about Georgia's move to Berlin. I wonder if they'll stay together when Georgia leaves, and whether Millie will be allowed to come to the Leavers' Ball. I still haven't thought about what's next for me.

We stop off at the supermarket to buy pastries for the patients. Little sugary bribes. A row of checkout workers sit in pairs, back to back and identical in their manmade-fibre uniforms. They hold plotless conversations over the beeps, seemingly out of the backs of their nodding heads. Each beep makes me jump even though I know it's coming. It's the first time I've been off-campus or somewhere without my parents for a month, apart from the chip-buying incident, so I try to give myself a break for overreacting.

A woman in an apron answers the door when we arrive at Wood House. Under the apron, she wears a bulky jumper, a denim skirt and thick white socks with trainers. 'I'm Jenny – I'm the duty manager,' she says. 'You must be the Richdeane children.'

'Artists,' corrects Georgia with a smile as she hands over the cakes. Jenny takes in Georgia's hair, which is now a grubby orange hue.

'Let me show you our facilities and I'll introduce you to some of our residents.'

I make a mental note not to call them patients. Or inmates.

Inside, it's too warm and smells faintly of mashed potatoes and custard. Everywhere is carpeted. We drop the cakes off at the kitchen, where the smell of easily digestible foodstuffs intensifies.

'Better cheer those outfits up a little – you girls look like you've come from the undertakers,' says Jenny, handing us aprons, each more floral than the previous. It's unsettling to see Georgia and Millie in colour, like they're in costume.

Jenny leads us to what she calls the Leisure Suite. 'Most of our guests and residents have limited mobility and some kind of learning difficulty or other needs,' she explains. 'This is where we do chair yoga and fingerobics.'

There is a small swimming pool, heated so much that a light steam rises from the surface. The last time I saw a pool was at the Leavers' Ball, when I'd dipped my feet and fingers in the cool water. The truth about my blackout has pushed me further away from that me.

Under close supervision, fleshy bodies hang off the poolside, chattering and bobbing like drunk seahorses. My stomach gives an involuntary churn. Is this how normal kids would react if they took a tour of Richdeane?

The alarm must be showing on our faces because Jenny says: 'Don't be afraid – they're exactly like you and me; they just need a little more help.' She leads us to the day room, a space that manages to be all at once depressing, patronising and desperately hopeful. Pictures of chubby babies and watering cans adorn the faded walls. Tatty artificial flowers stand in a smiling Pac-Man mug on the mantelpiece.

A middle-aged man in a green polo shirt sits hunched in one of the armchairs where he sucks his gums and occasionally spits into a soggy handkerchief. The rest of the residents and guests sit on sofas or at the large table, lolling in the direction of the too-loud television or picking at games. I avoid their watery eyes and try not to take in the flappy skin hanging off their slack jaws and sunken cheeks. What happened to the compassion I felt when I visited Grandmother's care home? Does care only apply to people you know and their friends?

'What a bunch of goblins,' whispers Millie.

'Shh,' says Georgia, probably wishing she'd brought people with better social skills – Olivia or Cal, or even Mei.

She pulls up a chair at the table and introduces herself to the women either side of her. They don't seem to register her. Undeterred, Georgia helps herself to some oversized puzzle pieces and starts filling in the sky area of the half-done puzzle on the table in front of her. I take her lead and sit down on the other side near the TV. Millie hovers by the doorway.

The news is on. I never normally watch it, but it's there so I do. There have been riots somewhere, something to do with immigration. Behind the news anchor is a honey-skinned girl with a handmade sign that reads: 'Legalise my mum.' The segment lasts less than two minutes and I find it hard to follow or know whose side I'm supposed to be on; my empathy circuits are in need of repair.

The next package is a preview of a government debate taking place tomorrow about the future of the UK's cultural industries. Then there's an ad break. Adverts full of imperatives for things you didn't know you needed, things to make you feel less, things to make you feel more. Things for when you change your mind.

The ads give way to footage showing different lands where thirsty deserts and pavement cracks soak up blood. Countries that are far away enough to forget but close enough to watch on YouTube. That segment lasts even less time. Watching the horror in distant countries used to make us feel better about the state of our own, but now we're catching them up we're less interested. We feel some countries' pain more than others it seems as the abbreviated dates of terror pile up: 9/11, 7/7, 8/8 and more.

The invisible elastic band is back around my skull and my eyes feel dirty. I shake my head and hear Dr B's voice telling me to get into contact, make a connection. Acting is doing. These people are real. Time to do life.

'Can I help you?' I ask a benign-looking man who is trying to thread plastic fruit beads on to a knitting needle. I notice his nametag.

'Clive? I'm Lux,' I say. 'Do you need any help?'

He ignores me and continues to stab at the fruit with the big needle, hooking them on one at a time and shaking them down to the base. Once he's satisfied with his fruit kebab, he tips them off and begins again. I wonder about his imaginary circumstances.

'Shut your little bumhole mouth,' he says suddenly, apparently to the news anchor on the TV.

A laugh escapes me. I clap my hand over my mouth, but he takes it as encouragement and says it again, louder, 'Fake. Shut your little bumhole mouth.' And then: 'Stop shitting on TV. Stop your filthy shitting. Shut your little face anus.'

'I'll wait for you outside,' says Millie. Georgia tries to kill her with her eyes but she leaves anyway, thanking Jenny for having her as she goes. We've always got those soft skills in our back pockets.

One of the women has clamped Georgia's left wrist to the table and is stroking her hand. Her snowdrop tattoo is pressed against the table. I imagine it staining the Richdeane crest into the tabletop. 'I'm right-handed,' Georgia says with a shrug, as she places the last piece of the puzzle.

I wonder if Millie went with her to get her tattoo done. Mei, Olivia and I smashed half a bottle of tequila before we got ours and, at the time, I thought it hurt like hell. That was two years ago, back when the only headaches I got were hangovers. Before I realised that real pain in your head is unlike pain anywhere else. It can't be pushed away or held at a distance. You are the pain, indivisible, fighting for the same oxygen.

'Get involved, Lux.'

'Clive, let me help you,' I say, with all the conviction I can muster. He turns to me and breathes his mashed potato breath into my face for a few seconds.

'You're not real,' he shouts. 'Counterfeits. You're not real. Fakes. You're fake.' I jump up and he starts jabbing himself in the leg with the knitting needle. 'Fakes!' Jab. 'Fakes!' Jab. Jab, jab, jab. The screaming sets the rest of the residents off shouting and trying to get up from their chairs, apart from the man in the armchair who continues sucking his gums and spitting.

Georgia frees her arm from the woman's grasp and we both stand there uselessly.

An orderly pushes by to wrestle the knitting needle off Clive and then leads him out of the room. Jenny gets to work settling the others with cups of tea, custard creams and little plastic cups of single pills or sweets. She does not extend this hospitality to us.

'I knew this was a mistake,' she says. 'It's not your fault but I think you should go. I can't have my residents being unsettled like this. It's not worth it. I'll call you a taxi.'

'Well, that was a horror show,' says Millie, when we get in the cab. 'What happened?'

We explain and Millie says, 'There's a morning of our lives we'll never get back.'

'What?' says Georgia. 'Are you kidding me? That was incredible.'

'Did we just go to the same place?'

'I just mean those people are so real; they have no inhibitions.'

'You're sick,' says Millie. 'Seriously, you are definitely on the spectrum.'

'Don't say that; you shouldn't say that,' says Georgia. 'I just meant, doesn't it make you realise how sheltered we are? How are we supposed to create real art, something that's authentic, when all we do is go to class and secretly get drunk?'

'And all they do is dribble and fingerobics, whatever the hell that is,' says Millie.

'Those people are real,' says Georgia.

'Oh my god, you're jealous of them,' says Millie.

'I didn't mean that. I'm just saying, imagine if you could collect all those stories and turn them into something.'

'Lux, settle this,' begs Millie.

'They hated us.' My words leave a sulphuric guilty trail that clings to the taxi air long after I've closed my mouth.

'Smell me – I smell like mashed potato,' says Millie after a while.

All I smell is guilt.

THIRTY-TWO

Dr B starts us in a round of 'I feel like saying …' as usual.

I feel like saying I am scared and numb and guilty, but I don't.

Eleven pairs of eyes sting my skin.

I look for a point on the horizon to steady myself and find Cal's face. Our gaze meets for the first time since I got back and he catches the desperation in mine and says, 'I feel like saying I need to tell my story. Can I share today?'

'Of course, Cal, go ahead,' says Dr B.

I think Cal has shared more than any other Artist this year. His stock keeps going up and up.

He starts, 'I think I've been so busy worrying I'll get ill like my mum that I haven't noticed myself turning into my father. He's always trying to fix everything and make everything shiny, like he doesn't exist without helping other people.'

He tells us a story he hasn't shared before: the story of how he lost his voice and found a new one.

When he was small, his mother was sometimes unwell. During these periods, she believed there were neurons in her brain that made her mood mirror the weather. She grew manic in the sunshine and melancholy in the cold. Her love became cloying on close days and she withdrew when the air became frigid. In a depression, when water vapour condensed to form clouds and precipitation, she would cry endlessly until her eyes were dry and raw. When fog descended, she felt the sky sagging and judgement crushing her. The diaphanous skin between this world and the next would give way and she became tormented by faces from the past and possible futures.

One day, when his mum couldn't get out of bed, Cal had crawled under the covers with her and drew her while she slept. 'I was eight,' he said. 'I remember thinking how proud she would be of me when she woke up. I decided to nap to make the time pass quicker. When I woke up, her hands were around my throat, choking me. I'd got the drawing wrong.'

'That's not right!' she was screaming. 'Why haven't you drawn the others?'

'Tell me, Mummy, tell me who else is here,' he'd begged her. She let go of his neck and told him, but not before damaging his young larynx. From then on she would tell him her visions and he would sketch them, translating them into art people could understand. Line drawings of clouds and monsters, like the ones in his studio.

'If my dad knew what happened, he never said anything. It was a good lie.'

There's no such thing as a good lie.

'She was very lost. I think it helped her to know someone else had seen what she saw, if only on paper. I did it for me too though, to make sense of her,' he continues, his strained voice loaded with conviction. 'She died a few years later. Pills.'

Bits of him and us that didn't make sense to me before fall into place. Am I the thing he was trying to make shiny? How did I not know he had lost his mum so violently? On Halloween, he said I reminded him of her. There's ringing and whooshing in my ears. Signals of empathy that are not visible to the naked eye.

'Mother-flipper,' says Georgia. 'That was intense.'

'I'm sorry, Dr B,' says Cal. 'I didn't mean to upset you.'

I turn to Dr B just as he puts a forefinger under each eye to catch the tears as they swell over his lower lashes. He blinks as the water slides down the backs of his hands and soaks into the cuffs of his shirt. 'I'm just moved. That's a heavy thing for you to carry around.'

Cal nods like he feels lighter. Do I look lighter now my secret is out or heavier because I have to carry the truth?

Looking around the room, I see the others are moved too. I want Cal to know I am moved, but my (e)motion is soundless and invisible. The tears are stuck inside me again, but I know they'll come later.

'You've united us, Cal,' says Dr B. 'Even sorrow can unite.'

The head director said that in the first assembly of the year in his address about change.

But there is no collective noun for sorrows, the sad little animals that live under the skin, sometimes writhing, sometimes sedated, but always there. A sting of sorrows. A glacier of sorrows. An attack. A violence. A burial.

There is no official collective noun for any emotions actually, but plenty for animals it seems. A swarm. A brood. A litter. An unkindness. A mob. A colony. A knot. A shoal. A murder. A bloat. A parliament. A tribe. A congregation. Any and all of these could apply to sorrows.

A fleet of sorrows. An armada of sorrows. They sound right too. But there is little comfort in the lights of the other wretched boats bobbing offshore when you know there are submarines and icebergs lurking beneath and that some of the other boats are warships or carry pirates.

Cal must know this too because he slips out of the assembly before anyone has chance to offer him a good lie about how they understand. I want to thank him for telling his story so I didn't have to tell mine yet.

THIRTY-THREE

Cal is in front of me with Luca and Davy. Davy is saying something about music production: 'Multi-band compression is a super-weird thing – it makes the music sound like it's hiccupping into the track. That's that glitch sound you hear on the drop in that mix I sent you last night. It's super-subtle but it makes a difference. Don't you think?'

I have no idea what that means but I can translate Cal's 'Sure, man' as 'I'm going to agree so we can talk about something else.'

Davy doesn't take the hint. 'Actually, it kind of sounds like a baby puking. Like a tiny toddler retch.'

'OK, mate, we get it,' says Cal. 'Let's move on from baby vom, shall we? What are we going to do this summer?'

'Get chlamydia?' suggests Luca.

'Great,' says Cal. 'Aspirational.'

I wish Dr B could hear this proof that we don't always sound older than we are.

'Cal?' I call before I can stop myself.

'I'll find you inside,' he says to the guys and, to me, before I can say anything, 'Mei said not to hassle you.'

I have a mouthful of sour explanations for pushing him away and not finding him to clear the air the second I got back to Richdeane, but instead I just say, 'I'm sorry; I'm really sorry. Everything is just too much.'

'I know,' he says. 'I'm sorry about what happened to you.'

He's the first person to actually say that, although I know they all feel it.

'I'm sorry about your mum.'

'Thanks. It was a long time ago. Listen, I know you've got Mei and Olivia but, if you want to talk, or not talk, I'm here, you know?'

I nod.

'It was terrible for them too. They had to go along with it.'

I feel sick knowing I dragged them into my warped version of reality and ruined their last year at school. Cal too. They had no choice. They must all have felt so powerless. I don't know what to say.

'We did it because we love you, Lux.'

'I know. I'm sorry.'

'Are you writing?' he asks.

'No.'

'You should.'

'I don't feel like it yet.' No more stories about road trips. No more nightmares to transcribe. What would I write?

'We could go for a run together,' he suggests and I laugh properly for the first time this year.

He slings his arm round my shoulder like I'm Davy or Luca. 'Come on – we'll be late.'

Olivia can't conceal her surprise at seeing us together. 'See you later,' he says as his collective waves him over.

We've piled into one of the screening rooms to watch the televised government debate. They're usually about things that don't matter to us, but tonight's is about art – Kathleen Crown versus the Shadow Minister for Arts, James Hake.

Mr Hake kicks off: 'It is very clear to everyone but Ms Crown that this country's cultural integrity has been completely compromised by her party's obsession with commercialising every aspect of our great nation's art. Her marauding gang of conglomerate bullies are hamstringing individual artists and local collectives at every stage of the supply chain and I am here today, on their behalf, to say, "No more".'

When it's Kathleen Crown's time to speak, I cringe thinking about how rude I was to her. She begins, 'Firstly, let me first say that I do hope Mr Hake's doctor is able to find a cure for his amnesia sooner rather than later as he seems to have forgotten the mess my party inherited after years of mismanagement.'

Heads swivel towards me at the mention of amnesia. It's like a trigger word for their curiosity. I fix my eyes on the screen and the heads get bored and swivel back.

Mr Hake goes off tangent, criticising the overcrowding at universities and the skills gaps. 'We urgently need incentives to encourage the study of engineering, medicine and so on

– or we will have another skills shortage of a very grave kind indeed.'

'That's why this government has invested more in robotics than any other before us. Soon we'll have skilled machines that can do anything we can do, except create art of course,' says Kathleen. 'These machines don't get depressed, they don't take sick days for musculoskeletal conditions and they don't go on maternity leave.'

They probably don't miss school because their brains are keeping secrets from them.

'They also don't pay taxes or have ideas or have families to feed,' argues Mr Hake. 'You need to answer to the people who are losing their jobs to machines. This isn't a corporation. We work for the people, not the other way around.'

Ms Crown says our art schools are the envy of their counterparts around the world now, giving our young people and mature students the opportunity to become the best.

'But these schools are elitist,' says Mr Hake.

'Actually, the top schools are selective. Entry is based on talent,' says Ms Crown.

Looking around the screening room, I note this is true, save for a few legacy Artists whose parents' donations fund Richdeane's generous scholarship programme.

'But those fortunate enough to be born with talent also need to be able to pay the colossal fees,' says Mr Hake.

Ms Crown responds: 'Firstly, these children work very hard to hone their talents. Let's not take anything away from them by implying their success is down to fluke or good genes. And, secondly, the schools offer scholarships and bursaries to ensure our most talented children are able to attend.'

'With respect, Ms Crown, that is an utter fiction. These schools make pots of money. They should be giving opportunities to Artists from a wider background instead of spending it on celebrity teachers and golf courses.'

'But where would we hook up?' shouts Davy.

'I'd encourage you to visit one of the schools you're disparaging so you can see for yourself how truly diverse their students are,' says Ms Crown.

'Well, you would certainly know, wouldn't you? Relationships between these schools and your department are embarrassingly close. I wonder what proportion of your team will be made up of representatives from schools like Richdeane and the others in ten to fifteen years' time. We need diversity.'

They talk in circles for forty-five minutes. At times, they seem to be making the same point but refuse to admit it. They both contradict themselves and give answers that belong to different questions or that aren't answers at all.

'The system is not perfect, but what we need is a stable economy for the benefit of everyone; that's how we attract foreign investment and create job security. That's how we keep people safe.' Ms Crown bangs her fist to her chest repeatedly, emphasising her point with corporeal percussion. 'There is more to life than art.'

That's not something we've heard before.

The other Artists buzz and argue as we filter out and I realise it's because this is all real to them. It's now. My friends are hurtling towards their futures and the best I can do is to stay still and try not to slide backwards.

*   *   *

After five years of pure focus on the pledge and telling us that art is everything, Richdeane throws a bit of reality at its final year Artists.

The spreadsheet makes no sense to me. Along the top, the columns read:

Age of Artist
Gender (if known)
No. of years active
Units made per year
Units auctioned per year
Medium (select from drop down)
Digital availability (yes or no)
Education (art or mainstream)
Nature of work (abstract or figurative)
Country of origin
Estimated production cost as % of sale price
% sale price as % of guide price
Average sale price over last ten years.

Then a final column for freehand comments entitled 'Provenance'. Down the side is a list of Artists' names.

'Of course, the software used by art dealers is more sophisticated,' says Director Daniels. She waves her hand at the numbers. 'But this is a simple way of showing whether a piece of art is viable.'

Viable. Like it's a pregnancy. What happens if it's not viable; is it aborted or put up for adoption? Left on a gallery doorstep in a Moses basket.

Mei is rapt – this is just her sort of thing. Olivia has opted out of this class.

'So when dealers start tipping Australian sculpture or Haitian miniatures as the next big thing, it's based on a spreadsheet not unlike this one – not magic, nor intuition,' Director Daniels continues. 'Any questions?'

Cal's hand shoots up. 'What goes in the provenance column?'

'That's for factors like previous owners, celebrity cachet and so on.'

'What about whether it's actually any good or not – whether it makes you feel anything or helps you understand something? Whether it tells someone's story?' rasps Cal.

'Aha,' says Director Daniels. 'Now we're getting to the crux of the matter. Not everyone buys art because it makes them feel something. You need to understand that when you leave Richdeane, the value others place on your work might not be the same as the value you give it.'

'So, a buyer could end up with something on their wall that they feel no connection to that isn't even important to the person who made it? Just because it's so-called "valuable"?' asks Mei.

'Well, that's nothing new,' says Director Daniels. 'Some work never sees a wall or a display case. It will be stored somewhere customs-free until it's sold on.'

'That's sick,' says Luca. 'If the buyer doesn't want to look at it, it should be in a gallery somewhere so people who do care can go and see it.'

I feel myself nodding.

'Well, sometimes when a dealer has bought something, they will lend it for public display, especially if they can't get the price they expected for it. It never hurts to ascribe some academic value to an artwork.'

Is this the gamble that Olivia's parents and their friends were talking about? An endless cycle of productivity and speculation. Casino arts.

'I'm not trying to put you off,' the director says. 'But it would be irresponsible of us to send you into the world without knowing what you're up against. You're taught a lot of different ways to express yourselves, but I sometimes wonder if we shelter you too much. You'd be forgiven for leaving with a very skewed perspective.'

I read about a group called the Cultural Refusalists once. They reject anything they deem superficial. They believe that people shouldn't be focused on aesthetics or self-development while there are others whose most basic needs are not being met. We should all reach the top of the pyramid at the same time, in their eyes.

The director continues: 'Anyway, we're not talking about long-term investment pieces here, we're talking get-in-and-get-out sales.'

The same could be said of us. Five years at Richdeane then off to the markets.

'There will come a tipping point when art, particularly visual art, becomes too accessible, too reproducible. When the market reaches saturation, the lifecycle will end. Or at least the type of products being sold now.'

'So, you're saying art is dead?' asks Luca.

'The bubble will burst, yes – there will be a significant correction in the market – but I believe it will come back stronger,' says Director Daniels. 'More literal affronts on art such as censorship and terrorist attacks have only confirmed this.'

She looks at me, panicked, so I say, 'I was only there. I didn't do it.'

Everyone laughs and I feel brave then cheap, like when I got drunk and threw up in a graveyard a couple of years ago.

'But we can't do anything about all that stuff – those attacks, I mean,' says someone at the back of the classroom. 'So shouldn't we just focus on skill and beauty and creating possibilities?'

'Give me an example of beauty in art and I'll show you how beauty to someone can be ugly to another. This is all subjective; that's what I'm trying to tell you.'

It's cool in the classroom, and the skin on my arm puckers. My stomach is fizzing. I do some deep breaths and name three things in the room like Dr B taught me. Spreadsheet, whiteboard, Cal. OK, so he's not a thing, but looking at him helps me get back in the room.

'In Jade Grace's story, they roll down a bank of snowdrops and end up in a kinder world,' I say.

Director Daniels says: 'In Moscow, if you roll down a bank of snow like that, you will likely find a corpse at the bottom.'

THIRTY-FOUR

Everyone plays their role in my rehabilitation. Mei, Olivia and Georgia keep me in a routine. Even long-lost Isabella messages me to say she's sorry and to tell me about her burgeoning porn career.

I have classes.

Three meals and two snacks a day.

I set my alarm earlier than I used to, to allow for the period of adjustment that comes each morning while my memories fire themselves up. I get more efficient at dampening them down and settling them into guilt.

There's an unspoken agreement between me, the head director and Dr B that I'm unlikely to deliver any new writing or other work; I just have to show up and keep meeting with Dr B.

He is teaching me to feel safe again. He talks about flashbacks and I tell him I don't have them. It's true. Flashbacks imply I ever stop thinking about the attack, when really, apart from the split second before the rush of memories when I wake up, it's with me all the time.

Cal convinces me to go running with him. I am slow but, while I'm concentrating on breathing in and out, and lifting my feet one in front of the other, I'm almost, almost, not thinking about anything else.

My parents visit every weekend. We drive to small towns that don't smell of anything and go for bracing walks along seafronts while the wind slings rain and sea spray at us. I'd like to throw myself into the waves and let them really smash me, then I'd swim back to shore.

Sometimes they take Mei, Olivia and me for lunch near school. Georgia comes occasionally. We keep Millie off the conversation menu. Cal comes once too; my parents find him charming, but I don't invite him again.

At the beginning of summer term, there is a massacre in a beautiful foreign city. In an instant, we know their national anthem and our years of mutual contempt are set aside. I watch it unfold on TV with the sound muted like I watched the replay of 8/8 from my hospital bed. The scrolling ticker updates every time another lost life is confirmed. The newsreaders are animated, excited even. They compare the events to 8/8 but don't show my picture in the bulletin I watch.

Everyone asks me if I'm OK.

For a couple of days afterwards, I resort to old tricks to try to elicit a response. I'm back to scouring the internet for emotional porn in my unsupervised moments. I sit and search 'videos to make you cry' and 'sad videos' on YouTube. Trawling for ones that don't already have the little 'Watched' stamp in the corner. I'm hungry for something that will help me choke up the chunks of grief and guilt that I know are still in there polluting my insides. There are only so many episodes of South American soap operas and heroes' welcomes one person cannot cry at without seriously questioning herself.

Eventually the tears come. A video about a dying dog called 'Last minutes with Oden' breaks me.

Mei catches me staring at myself in the mirror admiring my leaking eyes.

I confess to Dr B that when the tears are away for a while I'm terrified it means I'm forgetting. He tells me it will all come and go.

He's right, except the colours stay away.

Richdeane lays on special sessions to help us cope with the tragedy. Mei tells me they did the same after 8/8 in the fortnight before I came back to school.

In Art Therapy, we sit in a circle and do mindful breathing. Then we must choose three materials to make an artwork with. I start basic: sheets of coloured paper, charcoal pencils and waxy crayons. I draw heads full of fire and lonely stick people, and fold together a book-like structure with secret compartments but no writing. On the cover, I doodle brains with jellyfish tentacles and scribble illegible secrets into the folds. Intestines are over seven metres long. How far would my unfurled brain reach? How far could its secrets travel?

We come back to our circle and talk about 'what came up for us' while we were art-making. Everyone looks at me like I have some kind of exclusive ownership or roadmap for reacting to terrorism. We scatter to corners of the studio again to choose new materials. I take a great lump of orange clay. I sit down and make Joanna. I roll a slender trunk, stick on sausage arms and legs, tease out spaghetti clay hair and stain it with red ink. Since the dye has faded, I dip a chunk of my own hair into the ink. It comes out wet.

We're invited to take our artworks back home at the end of the session. I dismantle clay Joanna and squish her dismembered parts back into a ball. I don't want fake Joanna; I want the real one.

A few days later, we've mostly forgotten about our love for the besieged foreign city and go on a class visit to a performance-party production of *The Great Gatsby*. We can't resist the chance to don pearls and headpieces, and imagine ourselves as glamorous creatures among the decadence and decay of 1920s America, which we learned about in Word Arts. A constellation of bright young things, we delight in pre-show banter and buy moonshine from an illicit vendor. But, ten minutes into the actual performance, the nostalgia party ends. Without the narration of the book, all that remains is beautiful, two-dimensional people doing vile things.

In teddy-bear-feelings terms, I am angry with my friends for enjoying it. I'm angry that those black-tie promises that used to seem so heavy and solid are useless, as light as nests. That I need more in my life than parties now.

'Just because you didn't connect with it, doesn't mean it was bad or your friends are wrong,' suggests Dr B, 'but it doesn't mean you're wrong either.'

The rest of the term is punctuated only by my friends finalising their plans for after Richdeane and meetings with Dr B in the library.

THIRTY-FIVE

The weekend before we leave Richdeane, Olivia's brother invites us to his graduation party. The sun burns off the last of the morning clouds to give us a clear sky for the drive down. Dr B and my parents aren't too thrilled about me going but I managed to persuade them that I'll be safe with my Mei, Olivia and Georgia.

'No one is going to blow up a forest.' A feeble joke but it did the trick.

The countryside speeds by as we play a long game of Shag, Collab or Kill.

When we get to the campsite, about thirty people are already there. They're mostly Lawrence's friends from Richdeane or art school, and they know who I am but are too polite or over it to say anything. Lawrence has booked out the whole place so we have the full facilities at our disposal. There are six yurts and a canvas lodge. Olivia spots him among a group of guys who are assembling spare tents. We wave hello and he comes over. She kisses his bloated moon face; he has waxed while she's waned.

'All right, sis?' he says. 'You look nice. Barbecue starts at seven so you've got about an hour to chill or have a drink. The yurts are all taken but there's space in the lodge or you can help yourself to tents.'

'Lodge,' we all say in unison. None of us are tent people.

'You can take the Artists out of Richdeane ...' says Lawrence. 'And see if you can find something else to wear – you look like you're going to a funeral. Shit, sorry, Lux.'

'That's OK. I didn't have a funeral.'

He gives a little nod, appreciating my effort to let him off the hook. 'Actually I brought Mum's Land Rover; there are always spare coats and woolies in the boot.'

Olivia grabs the car key from her brother and we make our way back through the mud to the car park.

'Why are there more clothes in your parents' car than in my wardrobe?' asks Mei.

'Because you keep your clothes on the floor?' suggests Olivia. 'Kidding. We have my mum's paranoia to thank. She likes to keep the car stocked for a quick getaway. Hence the bottled water and granola bars. Help yourselves.'

We rummage in the boot. It's starting to cool off, so I pull on a thick cream jumper over the top of my black one. It could be Lawrence's or their stepfather's.

'Stop folding, Lux,' says Olivia. 'This stuff lives in the car; the dogs climb all over it.'

I take back control of my hands and place the clothes I'd been working on back into the boot.

'Thanks, Olivia,' says Georgia.

'Yeah, thanks,' say Mei and I.

'Pleasure, treasures. We'd better go and bagsy some beds in the lodge before it fills up.'

We follow the signs back through the woodland – it's not far, but the chalky clay is muddy so we slip about a bit. The bluebells are out in force and the slippery track is edged with dandelions and primroses. They must get thousands of snowdrops here in winter. The sun is dropping lower in the sky and, under the canopy of redwood trees, the light is starting to fade.

Mei catches up to me and walks by my side. I think I feel her telling me not to slip off into the woods and get lost, but maybe I'm just telling myself.

We chuck our overnight bags on the last two free sets of bunk beds when we get to the lodge. The walls are decked with white fairy lights.

'Pretty,' says Olivia and we introduce ourselves to the others staying in the lodge. They're mostly all old Richdeaners, welcoming us with air kisses, and we all head back outside.

There are big logs and some wooden picnic tables to sit at near the cooking station, which includes a fire pit with a large circular grill over it. There are a couple of acoustic guitars propped up against one of the logs.

'Oh god, I am not singing kum-ba-fucking-yak,' says Mei. 'Let's get something to line our stomachs before the apocalash begins.'

We head over to the cooking station where a girl makes us up burgers with tonnes of ketchup. Salad in a roll for Olivia. We grab some beers.

'We should toast the host,' says Mei.

I look around for Lawrence and realise I'm really looking for Cal, even though I know he won't be here.

'Oh shitballs,' says Mei. 'Isn't that Henry?'

'Year-above-us-last-year Henry?' asks Georgia.

'Yep. Henry-whose-heart-Lux-broke-at-the-leavers'-party-last-year Henry.'

'I did not break his heart.'

'Poor guy; he was in love with her for years,' says Olivia.

'He wasn't in love with me,' I say. 'He used to sell me drugs. Which I shared with you, I might add.'

'Heavily discounted, I bet,' says Georgia.

'I love you, Lux, but you treated him like a Kleenex – used once and thrown away,' says Mei.

'Oh my god, I did not do that.'

'Sorry, Lux, but you did kind of ignore him for the rest of the night and made it pretty clear you didn't want to see him again,' adds Olivia.

'I guess you used to be kind of a bitch, huh?' says Georgia. 'So that's why we weren't friends until this year.'

'She was a bitch,' says Mei. 'Still is sometimes, but we love her more now.'

'He's cuter than I remember,' says Olivia, nodding in Henry's direction. 'Shame you had to break his heart.'

'Trust me, it would take much more than me to dampen that guy's ego,' I say.

He is cute though. His blond hair looks almost red in the light of the fire pit. He's taller than I remember; the opposite of Cal, who is much more compact and solid. He stretches his long legs out in front of him, toes perilously close to the edge of the fire. The pit is covered but it still makes me nervous. I watch as he bites into a chicken thigh. He eats with his mouth open, chewing on one side.

'He looks at bit feral,' says Mei.

'Perfect,' says Georgia.

'Please stop staring,' I say.

Fortunately, there are at least fifty people gathered around now, so I don't have to face him.

We find a table and settle in. I sit with my back to the fire pit (and Henry) and we drink. After an hour or so, Lawrence bangs a pair of barbecue tongs on the cooker to get everyone's attention.

'Thanks for coming, everyone,' he says. 'I'm not going to get maudlin now that I'm all old and graduated. I just want to raise a toast. Those of you who went to Richdeane will recognise it. So raise your glasses – or your spliffs, if you're that way inclined – to art and let go.'

'To art and let go,' we toast.

'To art,' Lawrence says again. 'Enjoy the party.'

Nobody needs to tell a Richdeane crowd twice to enjoy a party. Someone puts on some strange ecstatic dance music and we inhabit the spirit of hedonistic camping nymphs.

When we're dripping with sweat from all the dancing, Georgia and Olivia wander off, and Lawrence brings Mei and me more beers. I press the bottle to my forehead; the cool glass feels delicious on my skin. 'I'll be back in a minute,' I say.

'You OK?'

'Just running to the loo.'

'Beware the bears,' says Mei.

I just need a few minutes to myself. I'm drunker than I thought I was. I'd forgotten my resolve to stay sober, my promise to myself that I'd be more like Joanna.

When I get back, Mei and some others are sitting at a table. Henry is there. Seeing him up close is like stepping out of a time machine into the past.

'Hi, Lux. Just keeping your seat warm for you,' he says, shifting along the bench to make space for me. 'It's good to see you.'

'You too.' More air kisses. He smells like summer and tequila.

He offers me a beer; I shake my head and grab a bottle of water.

'Not thirsty?' he asks.

'Just taking a pause for the cause,' I say.

'Pacing the race?' he says.

'Exactly.'

The cool air wicks away my dancing sweat and I'm cold now I'm still. Henry hands me a blanket.

Slowly but surely I sober up a bit until I'm just the right amount of drunk. The party goes on. We talk and talk about things that only matter when you're six beers deep and ready for a whisky. We talk about Richdeane, which we all remember differently. Sometimes nostalgia and memory get lost in translation.

I remember what I liked about Henry; it wasn't just his sculptor hands. I liked his simplicity. What you see is what you get with him.

People sing and dance and tell stories around us. Lips meet and heads are pushed into laps like cafetière plungers and finally people start drifting off to their yurts and tents until there's only a handful of us still up. Olivia has called it a night; Mei and a guy called Sebastian seem to be getting on more than well.

'I'll walk you to the lodge, my lady,' he says to Mei and they stagger off. She shoots me a 'You gonna be OK?' look and I nod. God, I've missed this.

And then it's just Henry and me in the cold night air. We wordlessly agree to clean up and get to work pouring away the dregs of unfinished drinks. He finds some bin bags and holds them open while I drop the empties in along with overcooked meat and paper plates. We wash ketchup and grease off our hands at the cooking station sink.

'That was quite therapeutic,' he says.

He thinks our generation invented pathos. 'Not everything is a metaphor, you know.'

'What?'

'Nothing – sorry, talking to myself.'

I wipe my hands on my jeans and sit on one of the picnic tables with my legs swinging off the end. Henry opens a final beer, takes a couple of swigs and walks over to me, holding the bottle behind his back. I'm still drunk but he is drunker.

I look down at my hands in my lap while he stands in front of me.

'I love nights like this,' he says.

Old Lux loved nights like this too.

And Joanna will never love anything again.

Henry smiles.

I know what a grin like that means and a crackle passes from me to him and back again, connecting us in an electric loop. He pulls me forward to the edge of the table so that he's standing between my legs. He forces my chin up with the knuckle on his forefinger and then splays his fingers out under it around my neck. He looks right into me as he hooks his other hand round into the base of my ponytail. His icy fingers rub at the skin on both sides of my neck, half massaging, half choking.

'Too tight.' My voice comes out hoarse and strangled. I am Cal.

'Shit, sorry; it's so cold I can't feel my fingers.'

'Where are you sleeping?'

'I snagged one of those teepee things.'

'A yurt?'

'I guess so.'

'Lead on,' I say and jump down off the picnic table.

Inside the yurt, there's a mattress with a proper duvet, thick blankets and four pillows.

'No worries about getting a good night's sleep in here,' I say.

'I can sleep anywhere.'

'Ready to finish what we started then?' I say, and then I feel myself flush with the awareness that I sound like something out of a tacky porno. I hope Isabella's film has better dialogue.

We pull off each other's jumpers, kissing and pawing, and drop on to the mattress. I climb on top of him, pushing against him, waiting to feel him get hard. He pushes back and I feel my pulse between my legs. After a few minutes, he makes a whimpering noise that sounds like crying or coming but isn't. Then he whispers: 'I think my cock's broken – too much beer.'

I take that as my cue to roll off him.

'Sorry,' he says, lighting a post-failed-coital cigarette.

'That's OK. Probably wasn't the best idea anyway.'

'Yeah.'

Tiredness wraps itself around me.

He sleeps on his side facing me but with his arms crossed high on his chest, one hand tucked under the bedside ear and the other in his armpit, so I can't steal his heart in the night. The ground is packed solid like ice beneath us, even through the mattress. It creaks under the weight of our bodies, like a frozen lake shifting.

I open my eyes to brightness streaming through a ceiling sunlight. A pungent, smoky smell. Where am I? Please not a hospital. I close my eyes and look for answers on the inside of my eyelids before forcing them open again. I wince and sit up against the makeshift headboard.

I'm sweating and my ears are ringing. I'm dizzy and poisoned. And calm. My favourite kind of hangover. Henry is already awake.

'Breakfast?' he says, offering me a spliff. I draw the line at waking 'n' baking and shake my head. He exhales heavily through his nose and a tiny avalanche of cocaine sprays from his left nostril.

'Heavy night,' he says, rubbing the snotty drug dust into the duvet cover.

We get dressed and go outside. The ground has thawed during the few hours we were asleep.

We make small talk and look out on to the chilly campsite.

'I better go and find my friends,' I say.

'OK,' he says. 'Sorry I didn't ask about what happened to you. It sounded heavy.'

'That's OK. I needed a night off from it.'

'It was good to see you again.'

'You too,' I say as we hug. And I mean it. 'Careful.'

'Huh?'

'Take care.'

'See you around,' he says.

I turn back once as I walk away and catch him shaking his head and smiling.

The others offer nothing but smirks and hangover comparisons when I get back to the lodge. We decide not to stick around for more barbecued food and say our goodbyes to Lawrence and the others.

'Sure you're OK to drive?' he asks Georgia.

'I didn't drink,' she says. 'I'm officially back on the wagon.'

'Wish I could say the same,' he says, hugging us all goodbye.

As Georgia points the car towards Richdeane I wonder at what point these times will become the good old days – a year from now, five years, ten?

We debrief on the party until something furry runs out from the hedgerow and dives between the front tyres before Georgia has time to swerve.

There's no bump.

'What the fuck?' says Georgia. 'Did I hit it?'

'It ran straight down the middle under the car – I saw it shoot back off into the bushes,' says Olivia.

'Was it a fox?'

'Rabbit, I think.'

Georgia turns on the radio.

I stare out of the window at the passing trees. What do they look like to someone who was not born or moulded early into an Artist? Poor Dr B, child of chemists. Does he see fibrous structural tissue perfectly packaged for fuel and construction? Compounds of things I can't name? Or the twisted features of black skeletons held up by light like I do? Perhaps he has a hybrid perspective I could never understand.

I don't feel good about Henry. Really it's as if I've cheated on Cal, even though we aren't together. The only way I can rationalise it is that I needed a dip into the past, to visit someone who only knew me before all this. Someone who has never lied to me.

As we sweep past green and yellow fields, it hits me that I didn't remember this morning. Or rather, I didn't wake and feel it all come roaring back. I knew when I went to bed, I knew in my sleep and I still knew when I woke up. I did not feel the act of remembering, of one cell of information firing up and igniting the next until the whole of my body was ringing with it. I just woke up and I knew, and I don't feel good about that either. It's a different kind of guilt.

Back at school, Georgia tells me she is leaving tonight. Ahead of the curve, as always. She gives me a paper marionette with no strings, and a hug.

THIRTY-SIX

School ends. There is a Leavers' Ball. Nobody expects me to bring the party favours or light fireworks this time.

On the final day of term, no one wants to be the last person to go. We all prefer the idea of burning short and bright to fading away so we leave quickly with an uncharacteristic lack of ceremony. An extended summer rolls out before us.

Cal goes early. We hold on to each other as if we're surviving the collapse of our sun. His ribcage inflates with each heavy breath, a life vest for us both. My knees go dizzy and my heart hiccups but, when we let go, I don't fall apart and my pieces are not whipped away by the wind.

'Careful,' we say.

I feel it all, the good and the bad. And then, it doesn't feel like goodbye.

Olivia and Mei wait for me in the taxi. We're leaving our black clothes behind; travelling light, taking only our imaginations with us. It helps to know that ours is now a bone-deep, load-bearing friendship. The best kind of ship.

I have one last person to say goodbye to. I'm not sure of the appropriate protocol but before either of us knows it I'm clinging to Dr B like a starfish. Eventually I peel myself off him, still feeling the crackle of connection.

As I walk away, I feel Richdeane and I begin to move in different directions. The view starts to pixelate and I notice damp dew on my cheeks. Must be raining, I think, as I look up to the bright, dry sky.

PART TWO

THIRTY-SEVEN

Metal tinkles against china as he stirs a few drops of milk into his coffee. It will be muddy, so thick you could stand a spoon up in it. He tries to tread lightly between the kettle, the fridge and the sink even though he will pad back into the bedroom to wake me with tea in a minute. It's been the same every morning for two months since we found each other again.

The blinds are still closed but I can make out a feline shape in the bedroom doorway nudging the door further open and testing the threshold with a paw. I kiss the air a few times, and the cat trots in and joins me on the double mattress. He follows in behind wearing just his boxers.

'Teapot?' I ask as he sets a tray down on the grey blanket in between me and the cat. We don't know her name yet but I know she's a she from the way she acts with him. 'Why so fancy?'

'I found it in the cupboard,' he says. 'Thought it might be civilised to use it.'

My mum must have retired it to the cupboard when she and Dad went back to Singapore a few months back. The disco kettle with its neon lights and violent boil is long-since dead.

I take a bottle of sparkling water off the tray, loosen the cap to let some of the fizz out, and put it on my bedside table for later.

I sip scalding camomile tea while he flattens the cat's ears, dragging his thick fingers over the top of her neck and down the sides of her cheekbones. She makes noises as if she likes it. Is that how we'd look to an outsider if they could see him touching me when the lights are off? Stupid; we are nine stories up and the blinds in the bedroom are almost always closed.

We sip in sweet silence until my cup is empty. He swills and chugs the rest of his coffee and lies back down before I can. He never lets my head hit the bed without his arm behind it. I make noises as if I like it. The cat purrs too.

He nuzzles my shoulder. Coffee stings the centimetre of air between us. Two years, four months since Richdeane, and I still think of coffee as contraband.

I wake up twice most mornings. Before and after tea. Camomile has tryptophan in it, which doesn't act on everyone but makes me dozy. It gives me a little extra sleep. The gentle, cosy kind you can have when the sun has come up.

Sleep is harder to come by these days. I'm so used to not falling asleep now that if I feel myself starting to fall quickly after shutting my eyes, I get up again because I think it means

I'm dying and I don't want to die in my pyjamas with robots on them. When Morpheus finally visits, he usually finds me surfing the endless waves of the internet, reading books by white men, drinking decaffeinated, coffee-flavoured water – pretending not to be waiting for him.

I don't often have nightmares any more, but I wake some nights with a gasp without knowing why. Maybe the dreams have just gone deeper so I can't remember them when I wake.

I lie and listen to the water fizzing in the bottle next to the bed.

When my eyes open, I'm alone. The tray and the cat are gone from the bed too, and there's scratching in the hallway.

'Let the cat out, would you? She needs to go home,' I call, then glug some of the water. It's still too bubbly and traps my breath in my lungs for a second or two.

Scratch, scratch, scratch. 'Hen.' Scratch, scratch. 'Henry?'

THIRTY-EIGHT

In the bathroom, our toothbrushes stand on opposite sides of the sink. Mine is electric. A little robot inside it protects me from myself by stopping the buzzing if I press too hard. It's wet. Henry must have used it instead of his plastic blue one.

I lift a thick black jumper off one of the shelves in my wardrobe, taking care not to muddle the rest of them. I don't have time to refold them all.

After throwing on my coat and backpack, and winding a scarf around my neck, I walk the thirty minutes to the gallery as I do most days. Lately, Henry walks with me, but not today. He has an interview.

The Thames is coffee-brown with a milky froth bubbling where it hits the banks and the pillars of the bridges. I don't want to think about the reasons the river might be fizzing, so I pull my eyes back to my boots and watch myself walk. The city is just feet and lost or unwanted things if you don't look up.

The colours from before are gone and hard to remember, like baby teeth. I find new colours where I can but it's not the same. This time of year, the trees give up parts of themselves for soggy boots to stir into a leaf stew the hue of old pears and goldfish corpses.

The backpack bangs against my spine as I walk. I tuck my thumbs under the straps at my shoulders to ease the weight. I am already used to Henry carrying it for me and resolve to do it myself from now on.

I take the same route as always. Along the south bank of the Thames for twenty minutes, then drop away from the riverside deeper into the south of the city. Eyes up long enough to press the button and wait for the green man at the crossing. Look left and right as the traffic slows at the lights; doing as the machines tell them. Take in a bin full of umbrellas stuffed beak first like mechanical crows, their dislocated wings splaying over the sides.

I used to write letters to Cal and post them into bins around the city; he never wrote back. By the time I'd realised we were the same just like he said, it was too late or maybe it was still too soon.

I wrote to Joanna's parents too, anonymously, to say I was sorry for their loss.

Cross road. Eyes back down, striding through more leaves, bits of dirty string, orphan socks, sawdust. Takeaway packaging. Earring butterflies and a broken bracelet. A puddle of sick. A jagged glass bottle neck with no body. A needle (I see a lot of those these days, but not generally on the ground). More busted umbrellas, dead in their gutter graveyard.

The gallery neighbourhood is both two miles and a million miles from my parents' flat in Waterloo. Here, as many people sleep on cardboard and filthy sleeping bags as slumber in our apartment building, which is named, without irony, Whitehouse.

'It's called class tourism what you're doing, you know?' a friend of Henry's said to me in the pub one night. 'Slumming it there during the day, then going home to your palace.'

I decided not to debate it with him. He's one of those people who protests gentrification even though he's a symptom of it. He helped vandalise a small, trendy business in an area he'd lived for six months because he thinks it represents 'the man'. He doesn't understand if the guys that run that business move out, a Starbucks will move in.

When I get to the gallery, an old local authority building at the end of a crumbling terrace, Doris is blocking the buzzer. She told me to call her Doris the first time I came here, but I don't know if that's her real name.

People sometimes use fake names or get given a moniker.

When I was trying to get the hang of living in the city after Richdeane, I sometimes introduced myself as Emily. I couldn't seem to get the balance right between concealing and revealing my past. I was either Emily or a wildly declarative Lux, announcing my 8/8 experience early in a relationship then never mentioning it again so the person I'd told might think they'd dreamed it. Others intuit substance in my shadow or read something in the way I run my fingers along the faded feather scar on my forearm. 'Did something happen?' they'll ask, with time. 'Yes, something happened,' I'll reply, and they'll nod, drawing their own conclusions. Those conversations are fewer and further between now that I've got a tighter grip on myself.

There were incidents at first.

Hyper-vigilance, the professionals call it.

An early-morning outburst at a bus stop because I thought there was a cockroach burrowing into my carotid artery. It was the cord from my earphones brushing against my neck. Even now the number of times I've fled from a supermarket because I've seen someone carrying a backpack continues to escalate.

Then there's the stubborn avoidance of the tube because, down there, escape is far less likely. I've already had one free pass; I don't expect to be granted another. I have been down there three or four times, and it was bearable until the train was held in a tunnel because a passenger on the tube in front had been taken ill. In the minute or two it took for our train to start moving again, I had tied up my hair, held my breath and prepared to die.

For months I wondered if all my progress at the end of Richdeane was inverted. If I'd been dragging myself up walls but the whole time the earth had been upside down and I'd just been crawling deeper and deeper into the hole.

I ordered myself to remember that, of the thirty thousand days I can hope to live, 8/8 was only one. Of the seven-point-three billion people on earth, those who wanted to destroy life and beauty were only three. And in the eighty-six terabytes of room in my head, those memories are dwarfed by others and by empty space.

I told myself it is possible to be more than one thing – sequentially, in parallel and/or in alternating phases. I am not just an Artist; not just my memories.

Now, I meditate. I run. I sleep. I work. The routine helps. It keeps things manageable. People say the three little words I hate most: 'You look well,' but unless you've had surgery to replace your occipital lobe with an MRI machine or you have telepathic abilities, you have no idea whether I am well or unwell or both. It's clear my body and my mind respond to this repeatable life proposition, but it's boring. I am colourless and bleached inside; I miss the rainbow. Life seems less than I wanted.

Now I am stable, I am ungrateful and long to deviate.

So I don't mind if Doris's name isn't really Doris; that's her prerogative.

'Coming in, Doris?' I ask.

She beats the sides of her enormous Puffa jacket as if trying to deflate it, then slowly shakes her head.

'OK,' I say and she swings her bulk aside so I can push the tattered buzzer.

In the doorway, if you don't look up, if you're avoiding seeing things explode or planes flying into buildings, you won't see that half the letters have fallen off the sign. There's no money left for the service so they'll probably close us soon and take the rest of the letters away. The articles have already started: *'Closure "likely" for controversial shooting gallery'* and *'Residents protest legal drugs consumption site'*.

I don't know where I'll go if it closes. I really was going to go to Singapore with my parents. I quit my job at the salad-packing factory. (Monotonous. Iceberg lettuce. If it fell on the floor, I just picked it up and packed it.) I told people I was going. I took clothes off hangers, rolled them into cases, and then I thought about Joanna's family and whether they'd given her things away.

I changed my mind about going because I realised I'd still be me when I got there, and then I had to repopulate my wardrobe and un-tell everyone. I still look in charity shops in case I find things that look as if they might belong to her.

Before I found this place, my attention was spraying around everywhere, looking for something to absorb it.

I press the buzzer again and this time the door creaks with electricity so I can push it open and step inside. To think I used to be scared of needles.

THIRTY-NINE

It's called 'harm reduction' what they do here.

But the gallery has its critics. The locals don't mind needle exchanges, but they prefer addicts to take their clean needles away and shoot up somewhere hidden, not in a government-funded room with alcohol wipes and squares of foil laid out on metal-topped tables.

'Morning, Lux,' a voice calls down from the top of the stairs.

'Hi, Thomas,' I call back and climb the steep stairs to the office.

'Thank god you're here,' he says, before I've had a chance to sit down and turn my computer on. 'Any chance you can do the update by eleven?'

'Sure.' I don't need to ask what update because I only have one job here: numbers. Unless Justin needs help typing up reports for the incident database, which just means transcribing interviews with service users and security.

'I've said it before and I'll say it again, Lux Langley, you are a godsend.' Thomas's back is turned and he's already striding away to his office.

I shrug my backpack off and set it down next to my desk then check I remembered to put my trainers in. The sole is starting to peel off one of them. I run home every evening after work and they have seen better days.

Sarah smiles good morning at me, head tilted with her phone tucked under her chin. Justin holds out his hand for a high five and I tap his palm with mine.

'That was rubbish,' he says.

It's just the four of us who work up here in the office, plus the nurses and security downstairs in the consumption room and coffee area. Sarah handles medical liaison and Justin manages funding and reporting. Thomas is the centre manager, which means he looks after everything else. Lately, this means dealing with the press and finding spaces elsewhere for the service users we can't accommodate. I do spreadsheets.

I hang my coat up and get to work. Music plays softly from Justin's computer as he occasionally mumbles 'Tune,' and hums along.

After an hour, I finish the update. It tells us what we already know: we have more service users than we have supplies to keep them safe. Safer. We'll run out of clean needles before we run out of drug users.

'Thanks, Lux,' says Thomas. 'Don't look so crushed. You're not responsible for what the numbers say.'

'I know,' I say. 'I just wish I could fix them.'

The buzzer creaks.

'That'll be the *Evening Standard* guy,' he says. 'Why don't you help me show him around?'

'That's OK,' I say. I'm not really into journalists.

'Come on.' He smiles. 'They're sick of hearing from me and you've got quite a way with words – when you actually bother to talk.'

I follow him downstairs, watching his bald patch bob as we descend. The journalist introduces himself as Rob Frayn. He's younger than I thought he'd be, maybe twenty-five or twenty-six, and skinny. His handshake is dry and brittle. Thomas turns on the charm and starts parroting statistics about how the centre has helped reduce hepatitis C and contributed to bringing down theft and overdose rates in the area.

'It's slow progress but we're connecting high-risk users with social and health services,' explains Thomas. 'We've even got some people into treatment.'

'So, can I see the consumption room? Is that what you call it?' asks Rob. 'I know the picture desk already asked about photos, but I'd like to see it.'

'"Consumption room" is fine – we prefer that over "shooting gallery" or "fixing room",' says Thomas.

I call it 'the gallery' in my head, but never out loud.

'OK,' says Rob. 'The woman outside said I was in for a shock.'

He means Doris. I wonder if he thinks she works here.

'Oh,' he breathes when we step into the main room and he surveys the quiet booths. Eight on each side, each with a desk lamp, chair and plastic trays of needles, saline solution, alcohol wipes and foil squares. Three men sit with their backs to us, uncurious as to our arrival.

'You were expecting something a bit more *Trainspotting* perhaps?' says Thomas. He gets a real kick out of proving the press wrong.

'No, no,' says Rob, meaning yes.

'Good morning, gentlemen,' says Thomas to the men. 'Just showing a guest our facilities. He's a journalist but he doesn't bite.'

The men are used to this parade of voyeurs lately as we fight to keep the centre open. Rob starts to wave at them, then thinks better of it.

'It's almost like a library,' he says.

'People who inject cocaine can become very sensitive to noise,' says Thomas.

'People inject cocaine?' asks Rob. Poor, innocent Rob.

'Yes, that's more of a problem locally than heroin, actually.' I find my voice. 'Though heroin users do use the service too.'

Keeping a wide berth of the sharps disposal bins, Rob wanders over to the wall where a large anatomical print illustrating the body's main veins and arteries hangs. He makes a few notes in his book – maybe a sketch.

'Don't they give you iPads for that these days?' goads Thomas.

'Papers don't have any more money than this place does, mate.'

At the nurses' station, Rob points to a white device which looks like a large remote control. 'What's that for?'

'Accu-vein,' says a nurse.

Another pipes up, 'Lights up veins like a Christmas tree – helps the users find a healthy one to stick.'

Rob starts to look a bit green.

'All mod cons, eh,' says Thomas. 'We've lined up an ex-service user for you to talk to if you're interested?'

'Oh, yeah, great. Thanks.'

'Not in here,' Thomas reassures him. 'Grab Rob some literature and meet us in reception, would you, Lux?'

As I pick up a *How to Inject Safely* booklet from next to the nurses' station, the man in the end booth flicks the top of a needle and then holds it between his little yellow teeth while he clenches and unclenches his fist and taps his arm below the elbow. A navy pea coat hangs off the back of his chair, a worn leather satchel at his feet. He looks like an intellectual or a professor. I wonder who gave him his first hit. Did this all start for him with some party favours at a school disco? In a toilet cubicle at a costume party? I should know better than to watch, but my eyes follow the needle as he pushes it into a swollen tagliatelle vein. My throat grows watery and I remind myself I chose to be here. I promised Joanna, even though she'll never know it.

I drop the leaflets off to Rob and Thomas. They're talking to Miles – he used to be one of the regulars, and now he's training to be a drugs counsellor. Miles says he has dead taste buds and claims that's what led him to heroin.

'Ask yourself, Rob,' he says, 'if you couldn't taste anything, would you eat more or would you eat less? And, if you ate less, what would you do instead?'

I've heard this before – he tells the same stories every time he's wheeled out for one of these interviews. I've also seen him, Thomas and Justin do a doughnut challenge and watched him lose because he couldn't resist licking the sugar off his lips. When I asked Thomas how come Miles could taste sweet things but not everything else, he said, 'He an addict, Lux. Addicts lie.'

'We're all hungry for something, you see, mate,' continues Miles, as Rob jots down a few quotes.

'I'll leave you to it,' I say. 'Nice to meet you, Rob. See ya, Miles.'

Back upstairs, I cram extra strong mints into my mouth to remind myself that my taste buds are very much alive. My eyes water as I crunch. If I kissed Miles with this mouthful of mints, he'd have to pretend it was like pushing lumps of chalk around my mouth and that he didn't understand why his tongue was numb and tingling afterwards. Don't be weird, I tell myself.

I open the stock spreadsheet and a familiar song plays quietly from Justin's speakers. 'Tune,' he says to himself.

'Who's this by again?' I ask.

'Jade Grace,' he says. 'Remember her? She was going to be the next big thing.'

I nod as Jade sings:

'Found you at a meeting, full of coffee, loss and shame,
The kind where people wait to speak to reapportion blame.
I loved you in my sleep but now that's dust and scars.
We thought we were the only ones to love a love like ours.

'Home sick and so sick of home.
Five days and want to go.
Preferred us from a distance,
Where I thought I missed us.
The closer we get,
The sicker it seems to try to fix it.'

She's wrong though. I am going to try to fix things.

FORTY

Forgetting about Jade Grace was probably a different kind of memory lapse, since I recalled her as soon as Justin mentioned her and I remember how her stories and songs had filled me up at Richdeane for a while. But it doesn't stop me toying with the idea of resurrecting my memory-training programme just in case my brain has forced another glitch in the matrix.

After Mei and Olivia went to uni and dance school, and Georgia moved to Berlin, I implemented a self-prescribed regime of activities to keep my memory healthy. Eating six Brazil nuts a day, spaced out in halves at two-hourly intervals for maximum impact. Placing twenty random objects on a tray – a tomato, a leaf, a tampon, a Euro, an eyelash and so on – then covering them with a tea towel and writing down the ones I could remember. Not stopping until I could remember them all within ninety seconds and ignoring the cramp in my hand as I scribbled the list. Then finding twenty new objects and repeating the process.

After I found an old *London A–Z* map in a charity shop while looking for Joanna-esque things, I spent days and days memorising street names, tube stops and overground stations. If I could drive, I would pass the London taxi Knowledge test without breaking a sweat.

I learned everything I could about the men who blew up the gallery. Where they went to school, their siblings' names, what they were wearing, their last known words, their routes to the gallery, anything I could find out about them. I didn't write any of it down. I stored it all in a mental dossier and practised remembering it every day. Some scientists think each time a memory is recalled, it's strengthened.

In the phase when I was memorising the names of other survivors of terrorist attacks and wondering whether to reach out to them somehow, Marcy Borders, the 'Dust Lady', died. She succumbed to stomach cancer, fourteen years after she escaped death on 9/11.

I was offered big money for a memoir. They wanted to call it *Ponytail Girl: A Survivor's Tale* or some shit. Too many tails/ tales; Mei had laughed. I told the publishers I didn't write any more. They were stunned that I'd thought I would be required or allowed to write it, and said, 'We'd get you a ghostwriter – you'd just have to talk to them.' I should have done it and given the sickening advance they'd promised to charity. But I just couldn't. I couldn't talk about it like that.

The memorising went on for more than a year. One obsession faded and was replaced with another in a whack-amole of anxieties. It didn't leave much time for anything else and it was lonely, but I was Memory Girl for a while and I preferred that to Blackout Girl or Ponytail Girl.

It also took up space in my head. My 8/8 experience got squashed until it became just a set of uneven steps for my mind to walk down.

Loud.

    Explosion.

        Lies.

            Lost.

                Truth.

                    Found.

                        Quiet.

I could make a mnemonic for it, I suppose, but there's no need because the facts are calcified between the soft folds inside my skull.

The more I crammed in my head, the more I could remember, as if memory were a muscle. I worked hard to keep mine fit so it could remember anything I needed it to since they don't sell human hard drives on the internet yet.

I even worked on improving the amount of numbers I could hold in my head and recount to my bedroom walls, taking pride in my growing mental digit span. I had to whisper because it freaked out my parents to hear me reciting strings of numbers to myself.

I stayed close to them until they had to go back to Singapore. They put their lives there on hold for over two years. After I'd decided to leave, then decided to stay, I found the shooting gallery.

And then Henry found me again.

A few days after the *Evening Standard* guy's visit, Henry starts doing chin-ups with a metal bar he's brought over from his flat and fixed in my bedroom doorway.

I tell him about the book I'm reading while his face turns pink from the exertion of lifting his long legs from the floor and crunching them to his chest. I'm up to a bit in the book about the Golden Record, a cosmic mixtape/slide show of earth sounds and pictures which was sent into space in the Seventies.

When he's finished hoisting himself up and down, Henry pulls off his boxers, wipes the sweat off his chest with them and bounds naked on to the bed. He tries to make me laugh by kneeling and toppling sideways without using his arms to break his fall. It makes me think of handcuffed hostages with bags over their heads falling over with exhaustion and humiliation. I don't laugh so he does it again and again until I ask him what he would send into space if we ever got the opportunity to do a sonic remix.

We list all the sounds and images we'd send to aliens or just preserve if we ever got the chance. Neither of us suggests the 8/8 photo though I guess it is part of history now. We don't agree on many options. Henry wants a loud life.

Henry is not Cal. But he cares. And when Henry found me, I wasn't ready for Cal.

In the morning, Henry walks me to work with his hand in my pocket and I feel like we're doing the three-legged race.

'That little fucker,' says Thomas. 'That grade-A piece of shit.'

'Who's a grade-A piece of shit?' asks Justin.

'Rob fucking Frayn,' says Thomas.

'Who is Rob fucking Frayn?'

'*Evening Standard.* Have you seen this?' Thomas slaps an open paper down on my desk as Sarah and Justin gather round.

We are used to Thomas's outbursts; they're never directed at us, just the vultures, as he calls them. He gets dialled up and down easily like I used to.

Justin lets out a low whistle then reads, '"Our reporter goes through the back door to drugs legalisation and finds ..."'

'That's not even the back fucking door,' says Thomas, pointing to the picture of the front door guarded by Doris. 'What the fuck has that picture got to do with anything anyway?'

'Hold the bus,' says Sarah, 'have you actually read this?'

'I don't need to. Look at that picture. That's what people will remember.'

'But it's a good piece, Tom,' says Sarah. She always calls him that even though he prefers Thomas; I think it's her way of flirting with him. 'Really good.'

Thomas takes the paper from her and sits in one of the worn office chairs.

'Well, I never,' he says once he's finished reading, 'I take it back.' He folds the paper and rests it in his lap. 'This might just do it, you know; this might just save us.'

'Looks like you owe Rob fucking Frayn a pint,' says Justin.

Thomas looks so relieved I wonder if he might cry, but he takes the paper back to his office and starts making phone calls.

'I love his passion,' Sarah whispers to me. She reminds me of Georgia sometimes, and Mei a bit.

'What was the problem with the picture anyway?' I ask.

'Not WASP enough to get sympathy,' says Justin.

'WASP?'

'White Anglo Saxon Protestant.'

'Oh god. Really?' I say.

'Yup. Sick, isn't it? Poor old Doris.'

'But she never even comes inside.'

'Doesn't matter. Can't tell that from the picture,' says Justin.

'Images are sticky, you know?' says Sarah.

'Oh,' I say because it would be weird to say nothing and I can't think of anything other than how naive I am and how unfair everything is.

Justin turns his music up a fraction, and he and Sarah settle back down to work.

Images are sticky, she's right.

We hear Thomas crow into the phone the other side of his office door, 'This could save us, do you understand? Let's not waste this.'

I understand.

No more wasting my life like rain.

FORTY-ONE

I change my mind three times and call my mum twice on the way which means I get to the park almost fifteen minutes late. It's not quite seven-fifteen p.m. but the sky is already black and the air night-time cold when I enter the south-east side.

This is the park where we keep things some people want to remember and some people want to forget: the Holocaust memorial, the Animals in War memorial, the fifty-two stainless steel pillars that make up the 7/7 memorial, and more. I pass the pillars on my way up Lovers Walk and stop for a second to nod to them. My fingers twitch inside my gloves as if they want to mark the four Stations of the Cross on my chest, even though I don't think I believe in that.

The trees will be just a few minutes further up ahead. At the edge of the park and opposite the Dorchester hotel, the map said.

Light wetness falls across my nose and cheeks like cold

freckles. It's something between rain and snow. The park gets even darker as the street lamps become fewer and further between. The trees grow menacing. They remind me of that lost Lux who ran into the woods at Richdeane. But this time I know what I'm looking for.

I'm reaching for my phone to light my way when the twinkling lights seem to come out of nowhere, even though I was expecting them. The scatter of brightness bouncing through the dark propels me back to that day outside the gallery. A sickly coldness spreads over my chest and pours through my arms into my hands. And I live it all over again: I watch the sun shatter and refract as it hits the glass of the gallery doors, blown outwards by the force of the first blast. The snow that dusts my coat as it patters towards the ground becomes the smash of flying bricks, tearing a slit in my forearm. In the peaceful quiet of the park, I hear the fractured screams of people trapped among burning art.

An echo of terror.

The back of my ponytailed head.

The crack of hot concrete.

The taste of blue light.

My lungs are inside out and I'm breathing backwards.

I let the flashback pass; I've learned not to fight them too hard.

'You're fine,' I tell myself once the fear has lifted. 'It's just a park.'

I could still turn back but I promised myself I wouldn't. I focus on turning my lungs the right way around while my legs keep walking towards the little lights until I see them: twenty saplings still inside their mesh tree guards and lit by white lights. I could walk right in between them if I wanted, but I don't. On the grass in front of the trees is a raised slab of marble. I don't need to get closer to know it will be the commemoration plaque with the names of twenty dead chipped into it. Joanna will be one of them.

Twenty trees for twenty victims. Nineteen tourists and one Joanna.

Twenty trees. One for each of the years I've been alive, though I'll be twenty-one next month. A year younger than Joanna was when she was killed.

The ghost train that drove through me when I saw Cal's painting slams into me again, whistling through my heart and out the other side. I could have been a tree. I would have been if it hadn't been for Joanna letting me be late.

'Lux?' A voice comes out of the darkness behind me and I spin round.

'Mr Burton?' I say it like it's a question, but I know it's him. He has Joanna's mouth and chin. Her red hair. Or rather Joanna had his. Her dad. Words tumble out of me: 'Thank you so much for coming to meet me. I couldn't come by myself. I should have got in touch properly ages ago. I'm so sorry. I'm sorry about Joanna.'

'Shall we sit down?' He takes me by the elbow and leads me though the dusty snow to a bench. I hover, not sure if it's a memorial bench and just for show, but Mr Burton sits so I follow his lead.

'There,' he says.

I'd hoped he would look happy and healed but there's no light in his eyes. It's sort of awkward sitting side by side without looking at each other, so I shift to face him but he stays facing forward, like we're at a bus stop, not quite looking at the tree memorial.

'Thank you for meeting me, Mr Burton,' I say again.

'It's Mike. Call me Mike.'

'Mike.'

'Lux,' he says, like it's not a real name, not even a real word.

It is real. I am real. Too real some days.

'How are you?' I ask.

'We're doing OK,' he says.

'We?'

'Joanna's mother and her brother and me. Well, her brother isn't doing so well, to tell you the truth, but he had his problems before all this.' He nods towards the saplings.

'I didn't know she had a brother.' I didn't know her very well at all.

'Yes. Patrick.'

'She saved my life, you know?' It doesn't come out like I practised it in my head, but he turns to me and looks at me properly for the first time. Suddenly I am a bit more real to him.

'I wasn't in the building because of her. She saved me.'

Specks of snow as light as paper circle around us. Most of them disappear before they land. If I wasn't sitting next to my dead colleague's dad and swallowing down grief, it could be romantic.

'I just wanted you to know that, even though I know it doesn't help.'

His eyes are small and watery but his face is resolute as I explain about the party and my hangover and what came next.

'I wanted you to know how good she was,' I say.

'It's kind of you to say that,' he says. 'She always had a way about her. She knew how to talk to people. Very direct, you know? She didn't talk round things. She knew how to talk to her brother when her mum and I didn't.'

'Patrick,' I say, uselessly.

'She was the only one who could get through to him. He came back from over there with the sickness,' he says. 'They call it PTSD now – Post Traumatic Stress Disorder. The lads he served with call it Paid Till Suicide or Death.'

'Is he …'

'Neither,' Mike says. 'He's hanging on.'

'I wrote to you. It was a card with snowdrops on it.'

'We got lots of letters after it happened.'

'It was later.' Because I forgot for a while.

'I'm sorry I don't remember it, but we kept them all.'

I nod and ask, 'Have you been here before?'

'Not since the unveiling service,' he says. 'I was on TV.'

'I didn't watch it.'

'They call it a living monument,' he says. 'Run out of ideas for concrete memorials, I guess. Or they've run out of concrete.'

'Are the trees labelled?' I ask.

'No. There's one for each person, but I don't know which one is supposed to be Joanna.'

'That makes sense. I suppose one of the trees might die, so it's better not to know which one is … oh my god, I can't believe I just said that.'

Mike makes a wheezing noise and I don't look because I don't want to see him crying, then he does it again and I realise he's laughing.

'What was she like?' I ask. 'I only knew her a month and she was always kind, but I didn't get to know her properly.'

'Joanna was like all girls her age. Excited to be living with friends and making a go of it.' He seems to enjoy saying her name out loud and tells me about how naughty she was as a child. 'They say there's no such thing as a bad baby but, my god, she was a horror.'

'Me too,' I say, even though I don't know if that's true. Maybe I was a good baby; I should ask my parents.

Snowflakes flutter and slowly swirl. Their flight paths are unpredictable but they're gentle, respectful of each other. Each flake keeps its distance from the next; connecting would make them disappear. They need to get stronger before they can withstand the impact, like Mr Burton and me.

His phone beeps in his pocket.

'My wife,' he says, 'checking you're not an axe murderer. Listen, love, I'd better get going. We'll catch our death out here in the snow.'

The snow isn't settling, but I know he means he's ready to go home. I want it to carpet the pavement so we can both leave footprints as proof to Joanna that we were here.

'Thank you for meeting me,' I say. 'I'd like to meet your wife and Patrick one day – I mean, if they want to.'

He nods and asks, 'Which way are you going?'

'I'm going to stay here for a bit.'

I see him balance the wisdom of leaving a twenty-year-old girl alone in a park at night versus the understanding that I need some time here by myself.

'Just for a few minutes,' I add. 'It's not even eight yet; I'll be fine.'

After some convincing, he leaves, looking back just before disappearing out of the reach of the memorial light.

FORTY-TWO

'And then what did you do?' asks Henry.

I sat on the bench and cried until I felt better. Built myself up from a snowflake to a snowball and rolled home.

'I put my trainers on and ran home.'

'It was brave of you to go. Do you feel different?'

'A little. More as if I might feel different in a while.'

Having his head so close to mine on the pillow makes the room feel smaller. It's how he likes to lie. I liked it too, at first. Now I sometimes think that if his hair were longer, he would plait our strands together while I slept. We'd wake up woven together like conjoined twins. I'd have to cry from the claustrophobia, and eventually he'd loosen the braid and free me for a while.

He wriggles down the bed like a worm and rests his head on my chest. Between my ears, I hear my brain exhale as if it had been holding its thoughts inside while our heads were so close together.

'Your heart is beating so slowly,' he says.

'It's shy,' I tell him.

He moves his head further down until it's between my legs.

The sex is good. And while it's happening, it means something. But he outstays his welcome afterwards, as he's started to do lately. He breathes into my neck until I'm forced to reach down and slip him out of me.

Henry flings himself through the stages of grief when I tell him a few weeks later that we shouldn't see each other any more. It doesn't feel good to make him act like this, but I'm suffocating and he deserves more. Now that I've realised I am using him, I have to let him go.

'You don't mean that. You'll want me back,' he says. 'You shouldn't make decisions when you're in this kind of state. You're still reacting to meeting Joanna's dad and seeing the trees.' *Denial.*

'I'm sorry, Henry,' I say. 'I shouldn't have let this turn into something.'

'I guarantee you, you'll change your mind when you realise you've lost all your friends and you don't have anybody.'

He's wounded and cruel like I expected. Like he should be. He makes teddy-bear-feelings faces. *Anger.*

But he's right, I have pushed a lot of people away and now I don't know where they are, but I'm going to try to fix that. I will unpick the dark threads that hold me inside this sick pillow. I will repair old ships with old friends.

'I'm sorry. I didn't mean that. Let's try again,' he pleads. 'We can both try harder. Nobody understands you like I do. Don't throw us away.' *Bargaining.*

'It's not fair on you,' I say. 'And it's not fair on me.'

'I knew this would happen,' he says. *Depression and detachment.*

'This is the right thing for us both, Hen. I promise you.'

Soon we're using grown-up words like lover and goodbye and sorry, throwing them around like we know what they mean. He was born in the summer, in the middle of the night, so he's not a wintry man – but he's giving it a try. Someone needs to say 'when', so we can go our separate ways and try again.

'I'm taking the cat.' *Acceptance.*

'It's not our cat, Henry. It belongs to next door.'

FORTY-THREE

I enjoy the weight of my backpack as I walk to the gallery the next day. Doris stands on the doorstep clutching a copy of the *Evening Standard* with her photo in it.

'I'll sign you a copy.' She lets out a peal of laughter and rings the buzzer for me.

Upstairs, I tell Thomas about a few small ideas I've had for the campaign to keep the centre open and he is pleased with me. I wonder if we could get Jade Grace and some of the other Richdeaners down for a fundraiser.

Sarah is happy I've broken up with Henry. Justin keeps out of it and mouths along to his music.

'He wasn't The One for you,' she says, though she only met him on a few occasions when he walked me to work and she arrived at the same time.

I don't believe in The One. I believe in many possible ones, but Henry isn't one of them any more.

The day speeds by. The phones ring with promising news and Thomas ducks in and out of his office at the end of the room, clapping his hands and occasionally punching the air. I draw mind maps and do research into how similar centres are run in Canada, Germany, Spain and Australia, compiling a spreadsheet of success stories.

At six p.m., I wonder whether I could run to my appointment, but I don't want to arrive sweaty.

I take ten deep breaths and name three things I can see when I get there before ringing the doorbell.

'So, let's start by introducing ourselves properly, shall we?' the woman says, once I have nervously used her bathroom and we've shaken hands and settled ourselves, her in an armchair and me on the small sofa. The room is reminiscent of the talking rooms at Richdeane. Soft lighting, pot plants, tissues.

She is younger than the other professionals. Bohemian. Her office is on the top floor of an inconspicuous building at the back of Oxford Circus towards Harley Street. Discreet plaques by the front door are the only indication of what happens inside. She shares the building with an acupuncturist, a celebrity nutritionist and some kind of training facility. There are two other doors in her space and a shower in the bathroom. Is one of the rooms her bedroom?

'You can call me Carla, if you're comfortable with that?'

'Carla,' I say, testing it with my tongue. It causes me no discomfort.

'And what do you prefer to be called?'

Party Girl. Blackout Girl. Lash-out Girl. Ponytail Girl. Memory Girl.

Emily.

Starfish, snowdrop, astronaut, robot.

'Lux,' I say.

'Great. It's very nice to meet you, Lux. Any friend of Paul's, I mean Dr B's, is a friend of mine. I'm pleased you got in touch.'

We get straight into it. I tell her a bit about my history. She knows all about it from the extensive folder of medical records that my mum helped arrange to be sent to her in advance, but, Carla explains, she needs to hear it in my own words. To gauge how grave a case I am, I imagine. The dossier contains an alphabet soup of posited diagnoses: type 2 this, retrograde that, PTSD, OCD, ABC, 123.

'So, is it terminal?' I joke.

Carla smiles. She is fresh-looking, like the kids at Richdeane who kept their emotions close to the surface. Her hair is long and wavy, pushed back behind her ears, and a gold stud is pressed into her left nostril. People who don't know her probably think she is frivolous.

'You're a good candidate for the trial, Lux.'

She explains the aim would be to help me talk about the attack with the help of medication and then, gradually, without it.

'You'd come for a series of appointments with me and I'd give you a tablet, which, among other things, mediates the body's response to adrenaline. In other words, your heart wouldn't know how scared you are and, without those physical symptoms of panic, it should make it easier to talk about things and to go deeper than would normally be possible for you.'

She says this method is being experimented with more and more but that I should read up on it before committing. I'd have to go through the truth all over again. But it won't be like before when my brain was like a patient awake in surgery but unable to communicate. She might even go with me to the attack site.

'We'd be deliberately reactivating the frightening memories so they're in a more fluid state,' she explains. 'We think the way it works is that the medication can help us block them before they reconsolidate. But there have been similar trials before and the results have been mixed. We don't really know exactly where memories live in the brain. Do you understand?'

'I think so. We have to wake the memories up so we can neutralise them, but it won't hurt as much because I'd be on drugs. And it might not work.'

'Couldn't have put it better myself,' she says, and my inner praise whore takes a little bow. 'The results of this trial could help a lot of people, but I want you to go away and think about it. Think about how intrusive these memories are for you; whether this is the right next step for you. You can contact me with any questions.'

'OK, I will. Thank you.'

'And Dr B says to tell you to go and visit him at Richdeane.'

While I'm still riding the wave of momentum I got from setting Henry and me free from each other (though judging from the messages he's sent me he doesn't yet see it that way) and the possibility of joining the treatment trial, I decide on one last confrontation.

Shooting gallery aside, I haven't set foot in a gallery since I went to the Tate with Richdeane and it feels like it's now or never. I can't go back to the National Museum of Arts, though it has been rebuilt. I'm just not ready for that yet. But as it turns out, my search engine does know me better than I know myself and presents me with the perfect alternative.

FORTY-FOUR

On an October Friday – a colourless, odourless Friday – I pace around the flat, tidying things that are already tidy and boiling the kettle but not making the tea.

I leave an hour earlier than I need to.

In a practice act of bravery, I take the tube from Waterloo to Piccadilly Circus. It's only three stops. I will be underground for fewer than ten minutes if I time it well.

The escalator down to the Bakerloo Line is long and the air quality drops off as we descend. A scrunched-up McDonald's bag rolls down the middle aisle. I name three things I can see and decide that if I still can't breathe when I get to the bottom, I will huff into the bag and then run back up the other side.

I make it to the platform.

On the tube, men and women in sharp suits fill the carriages.

There are cautionary signs about reporting suspicious people, places and things, which read '*See Something, Say Something*'. What if you see something that's not really there – should you still say something?

A woman a few seats down rips something from a free paper and holds it in her mouth while she flips through the rest of the pages.

An alarm starts to sound, like the ones I used to hear at Richdeane. I hold my nose and pop my ears until it stops.

There are no orange taxi lights to count to keep calm, so I replay old conversations and games in my mind.

The newspaper lady gets off at my stop and darts away like she lives down here.

Security is high when I get to the Royal Academy of Arts. The coffee cart and patio furniture that used to be outside have been replaced with three uniformed guards and a sniffer dog. The doors look different too, as if they've been reinforced somehow.

'That's good,' I tell myself under my breath. 'It means we're safe.'

The queue trails out of the doors and my heart bangs against its ribcage as we snake our way up the steps.

Another security guard asks me to empty out then repack my bag before passing it through an X-ray machine as I step through the metal detector. They're not X-raying people yet, but I know what I'd look like if they did: monochrome, just like normal people.

I'm even earlier than I planned to be, having caught the tube instead of walking, but I buy my tickets and walk up the ornate staircase into the first exhibition, an Anselm Kiefer retrospective.

An Artist who works with horror and history, mythology and memory, he has thematic appeal. It's impossible to look at his work without being confronted with your past, present and future. 'Big art with big themes', the reviews call it.

I have an hour, so I make my way around the exhibition at my own pace, telling myself I can leave any time but that I should work my hardest not to.

I stand in front of *Winter Landscape* and steady myself. Made from watercolour, gouache and graphic pencil on paper. A head suspended in the sky, pink blood misting from its carotid artery, spoiling the snow below. Its sister painting is *Ice and Blood*. Sparse trees, a small figure in a military coat, right arm raised. More bloodied snow. Art with conscience.

Next, overgrown sunflowers, their sunny faces deadened with black seeds. They tower over the body of a man, leaves pulled down by gravity. I don't know if the plants are weeping, grieving for the man or the end of summer, or if they killed him.

I stride from room to room. I don't recognise all the colours. Cousins of pink, grey, blue and brown. A pale charcoal.

A couple read a sign on the wall.

'Oh, mixed media,' she says.

'That old chestnut,' he replies and they laugh.

It is comforting to think that every material has potential – physical or otherwise. Hyper-materialism in a dematerialised world; it reminds me I am real.

I am captivated by a giant book. Twelve pages of lead. It stands without support, the pages fanned and buckling under the weight of the leaden memories they hold. Its title is *The Secret Life of Plants*. A work depicting flowers, stars and numbers that will never decay. Leaden letters that can kill nerve cells and cause paralysis.

In the next room, there are more giant books, their illustrated pages caked and stiff with paint. Full of blood and hurt. They make me remember things I have never seen.

Looking at all the pain hanging on the walls, it hits me that mine will be in a gallery some day too.

At some point, someone will decide enough time has passed since 8/8 and the photo of Ponytail Girl will be exhibited in some sort of terror retrospective. I will be art to some people. Will I be more valuable than the art that was obliterated in the attack?

There will be postcards of me for sale in a gift shop.

I don't need to see that photo again, but someone else might.

Finally, I find the *Book with Wings* sculpture. A winged tome supported by a steel lectern. Art on steroids. One of the reasons I came. I read the synopsis.

Kiefer consistently returns to the book as a subject, as a symbol of learning and as a repository and transmitter of knowledge. Book with Wings *is a three-dimensional manifestation of the Artist's exploration of world knowledge. The book's majestic wings are poised for flight but, being made of lead, are unable to fly. Herein lies the paradox: it is both transcendent and tragic. The grey colour of the work reflects a world where absolutes are impossible; where history can be forgiven but not forgotten. As Kiefer himself said: 'The truth is always grey.'*

What a longwinded way of saying he makes books to find his way through history and stories.

There's no writing on the book but I'm lost in someone else's memories when an alarm rings out and paralyses me.

It's a real one, not like the ones I used to hear at Richdeane.

'Please, no,' I hear myself say. My feet are welded to the floor, leaden and stuck like the book's wings.

Galleries are supposed to be safe now. I came here to be saved.

'Careful.' A cracked voice breaks all over me, slowly, like an egg, the yolk dripping into my ears and diluting the adrenaline. I'd recognise that voice in the dark.

Cal.

I can see into his sketchbook. I've never known him to draw botanical pictures before. The page is full of green shoots and petals, delicate and veined like the skin on a young wrist.

Cal.

Still just a sapling but sturdy as an oak. He tells me he would give me all his energy, all his light, anything I need to keep me on my feet. He tells me about Pando, a forest in Utah made up of one big super-tree that lives off a network of roots. We will be one, like Pando, he says. He will become a scientist and discover a new renewable energy source to sustain us. He will mine for iron ore and build the world's biggest furnace to keep us warm.

That's a lie; he doesn't say any of that.

He says: 'The machines again.'

'What?'

'You're too close to the book. There's a sensor in the floor. Step back.'

I step back. The alarm stops.

'There you go,' he says. 'Much better.'

'Thank you.'

'I'm glad you came. I saw you from the window,' he says,

stepping closer to me. 'My exhibition is upstairs in the little space. Mei and Olivia aren't here yet. You're early.'

'I couldn't wait any longer.'

We reach out across three years and are right back where we started. In a gallery, in silence.

Heavy drips slide down my cheeks. His eyes fill.

'I missed you,' I say. It doesn't change anything between us, not really, not yet. But a few little pieces of me, some of the bits that hurt the most, fall away, like tiny lead feathers. Just a few, but enough to lighten the load.

FORTY-FIVE

There is one more story to write. I can't sleep, but I'm too scared to turn the light on in case I wake myself up properly, so I feel for my notebook, and lie writing by the light of the banana moon and custardy stars.

At first, I think it's blood all over the sheets. Then I realise it's blue. Ink. I've shared my bed with a leaky pen. I was up until the moon went out, writing myself back into existence. In a journal, you can make your story up, line by line. Like they say, if you're feeling blue, paint yourself a different colour. You can curate your own life, pack a notebook with superlatives and action, set it in the future because you're failing at now. But I haven't done that.

I've written about finding salvation in unlikely places – in a mango, a conversation had while wearing a yellow wig, sharing a can of warm Coke, origami gifts, a spreadsheet full of needles, in a pledge.

I've written of hunting love and friendship, stalking them but trying not to kill them.

About a painting of a lie that's the truth.

Learning that light fades and bleeds too, but the sun always comes up.

About being heroic in love in a place that holds the most fear – a place where they frame thoughts and feelings, and hang them on walls.

A snowdrop, a starfish, an astronaut, a robot.

When I read it back, it seems like hormonal ferment, a soup of coming-of-age narratives. I could debride it, fill in the connective tissue, but then it wouldn't be true.

The story is full of me, gifts and shrapnel, smudges and shadows, starting to reveal themselves.

Word by word, stitch by stitch, I am found.

ACKNOWLEDGEMENTS

Very special thanks to my incomparable agent Clare Conville who saw something in my writing and knew exactly how to help me dig out the right story. And to Richard Skinner, master of clarity and the first person to believe (months before I did) that this book could actually happen.

I'm so proud and lucky to be represented by C+W literary agency – thank you to the warm and talented team led by Clare, especially Emma Finn, Allison DeFrees, and Dorcas Rogers.

Polly Lyall Grant and Anne McNeil at Hodder – I'm so happy Lux and I found a home with you. I sometimes think you understand this book even better than I do and it's such a joy to work with you. Thank you to Lucy Upton – hand-holder, interviewer, and mastermind behind all things marketing. Extended thanks to everyone doing amazing things across Hachette, especially Katy Cattell, Rachel Graves, Hilary Murray Hill, Rebecca Logan, Alison Padley, Chloe Parkinson, Laure

Pernette, Emily Thomas and Natasha Whearity. Thanks also to Fritha Lindqvist.

Maura Brickell – publicist and all-round bon oeuf – thank you I'm in awe of your creativity and drive.

Thank you to all my classmates at Faber Academy for your encouragement and feedback on early chapters. Further heartfelt thanks to Michael Dias, Sarah Edghill, Chloé Esposito, Ilana Lindsey, Kate Vick, and Felicia Yap for reading the full manuscript and for all your constructive criticism and generous ideas. Thanks to Omar Al-Khayatt for helping me nail the first line. It's wonderful to feel the support of other alumni - I'm rooting for you all.

Thanks also to other early readers – Martyn Beardsley, CJ Flood, Andrew Smith, and especially Dayna 'Bear' Brackley.

The first draft of this book was written between migraines and MRIs – sincere thanks to my neurologists and all the medical professionals who helped me get my brain well enough to finish it.

Thank you to Tazeen Ahmad for reminding me of the power of writing. For inspiration – thank you to Actors' Temple, the Royal Academy of Arts, and Tate Modern, and to John Grant, Anselm Kiefer, Jenny Offill, Mark Rothko, and Owen Sheers.

Big thanks and hellos to my friends – you're all so bright and brilliant.

Finally, thank you and all my love to my family.

READING GROUP QUESTIONS

1. How is colour used in the book – does it help tell the story and develop Lux's character?

2. Creativity is an important theme. Part of the school's pledge is, "We give it to art and we let go." Do you think creating things can help people understand themselves and each other?

3. What clues does the author give regarding the truth about Lux's blackout? Did you pick up on any of them before the truth was revealed?

4. Did you find the book funny? Why is humour important to the story?

5. How vital is setting to the story? Did the writer give a strong or weak sense of what Richdeane Arts School is like?

6. Do you like Lux and does that matter? Do you consider her a heroine?

7. Is the ending satisfying? Do you feel hopeful for the characters' futures?

8. What will you remember most about *The Taste of Blue Light*? This might be a particular image from the book, a feeling you got while reading it, a character or an idea.